David Lyman Phillips, Freeman E. Huddle

Biographies of the State Officers and Thirty-Third General Assembly

of Illinois

David Lyman Phillips, Freeman E. Huddle

Biographies of the State Officers and Thirty-Third General Assembly of Illinois

ISBN/EAN: 9783337014452

Printed in Europe, USA, Canada, Australia, Japan

Cover: Foto ©Raphael Reischuk / pixelio.de

More available books at **www.hansebooks.com**

BIOGRAPHIES

OF THE

STATE OFFICERS

AND

Thirty-Third General Assembly

OF

ILLINOIS.

ILLUSTRATED.

CONTAINING BIOGRAPHICAL SKETCHES OF THE GOVERNOR AND OTHER STATE
OFFICERS, AND EACH SENATOR AND REPRESENTATIVE IN THE
THIRTY-THIRD GENERAL ASSEMBLY.

Springfield, Illinois:
THE BIOGRAPHICAL PUBLISHING COMPANY.
1883.

Springfield, Illinois.
STATE JOURNAL, PRINTERS.

PREFACE.

In the preparation of this work, much difficulty has been experienced on account of its novelty and the erroneous impression that whatever might be said in praise of the subjects presented, would be construed as having been written by themselves. Such is not the case, and, after many trials and tribulations, resulting from our own inexperience in soliciting, and from the diffidence and discourtesy of a few members of both branches of the Assembly, we now have the pleasure of submitting our work. We should have been pleased to embody within this volume the biographies of the Judicial Department of our State Government and the various boards and commissions in charge of the charitable, agricultural and reformatory institutions of the State; but limited time prevents the consummation of our desire. We hope to see our initial volume meet with approbation; but it is human to err, and, although no time or pains has been spared in the preparation of our work, we shall be most agreeably disappointed, if it proves to be absolutely correct in every part. We have endeavored to make this album of sketches a valuable, handsome and interesting volume. How well we have succeeded, is left to the judgment of its readers. To the daily papers of Springfield, we extend our thanks for numerous favors. We are under special obligations to the STATE JOURNAL and ODD FELLOWS' HERALD for the privileges of access to their files, for valuable information, and kindly notices of the progress of our labors. Hoping that our days of hardship and nights of waking have not been in vain, and that this book will be accepted as the honest work of honest men, who have employed no misrepresentations to attain success, we leave it to its office, with kind regards for our liberal and numerous patrons.

SPRINGFIELD, ILL., MARCH 10, 1883.

THE BIOGRAPHICAL PUBLISHING CO.

STATE CAPITOL BUILDING.

THE CAPITOL BUILDING.

After a spirited contest over the location of the State Capital, the erection of the State House was begun in 1867, in the city of Springfield. The site is a gentle elevation, located between Second and Spring streets and South of Monroe, its northern boundary.

The ground plan of the structure is in the form of a Greek cross, 366 feet in length, exclusive of porticos, and 296 feet wide, from point to point on the cross. The style of architecture is a mixture, in which the Corinthian predominates. The material, of which the outer walls are constructed, is smoothly dressed, drab-colored stone. The building proper is three stories high, including the basement, which is twenty-one feet in height, from the ground to the water-table. The first story above the basement, which is termed the Executive floor, is thirty-three feet high. At the extremities of the main wings, are lateral wings, or extensions, in the form of a "T." At these extreme points another story is superadded, having a mansard roof and dormer windows. The cornices are massive and ornate. The height of the building, from base to cornice, is ninety-eight feet; and, from the cornice to the apex of the dome, two hundred and sixty-six feet. The total height is three hundred and sixty-four feet. The Capitol of the State of Illinois is said to be higher than any other building on the continent, except Trinity Church, in New York City. Our engraving shows three porticos, projecting from the main entrances on the North, East and South, a distance of twenty-two feet each. These are, as yet, unfinished, and the symmetrical appearance of the building is very much impaired by their non-existence. The cornices and capitals of the columns for these porticos are finished and ready for mounting. It is to be hoped that the next general election will provide means for the completion of these necessary appendages to the structure. Not only are these grand porticos necessary to the harmonious appearance of the building; but they are demanded for the protection of the entrances and gables. The entrances, being very spacious, are much exposed.

The building contains no less than two hundred and thirty-six windows, of heavy, plate glass; the inner doors at each of the three main entrances are also of heavy plate, and these, together with the sky lights, make a total area of 2,284 square feet of lighting surface. The building is said to be the best lighted of its size in the whole world. The total area of roofing is 59,800 square feet. The structure contains 2,000,000 feet of stone and 22,000,000 brick.

The great dome consists of three sections or stories; the first forming the base; the second, the main stem, and the third constitutes the arched crown, which is surmounted by a smaller dome, termed the "lantern," from the popular supposition that it is intended for an electric light. Between the windows and constituting a portion of the massive walls, are immense columns or pillars, resting upon heavy bases and surmounted by ornate capitals. The cornices and friezes, at the gables, are of richly carved stone, the design of which materially relieves the structure from an appearance of over massiveness. The east approach to the building, (the only one now completed), consists of terraces, each of which contains a flight of steps seventy-six feet and ten inches in length. The whole is flanked, at either side, by a panneled wall of stone, capped with a heavily moulded rail. The general appearance of the structure, upon its exterior, is striking owing to its magnitude. Although impressed with its colossal proportions, the beholder is deceived so much by the harmony of its various features, that he does not realize its great extent, in all its fullness, until he is within its walls. The hallway, leading from its main entrance, is thirty-one feet wide; its floor consists of mosaic work in white and colored tiling. As you enter, you are confronted by a life-size statue of Lincoln on the left, and one of Douglas on the right. Both are mounted upon appropriate pedestals. The wainscotting of the hall and corridors is of highly polished marble, in long panels, which are alternately arranged according to color. At intervals of about twenty feet, along the hall, are tall pilasters of dark red marble, panneled and ornamented in the center with green marble discs, and, at the ceiling, with foliated capitals. The ceilings are decorated with cornices and foliated center pieces in plaster of paris.

Upon the right, as one enters the main hall, are the Governor's rooms and Executive Chamber, the walls of which are frescoed in the highest style of the art, the work about the casings being painted in soft tints, which lend to these apartments an air of rare elegance. Upon the opposite side of the hall are the offices of the Secretary of State. These rooms are finished in white-oak, cherry and walnut, so arranged that they produce a rich contrast. At the west end of the main hall is the grand stair way, consisting of five easy flights of granite steps, and guarded by marble balustrades. The wainscotting of the walls about the stairway is paneled in white, grey and black marble. The corridors above and on either side are flanked by tall columns of mottled granite, which support the roof and an arched sky-light of ground and stained glass. The corridor, running through the building from North to South, is in finish similar to the main hall, and is probably the longest passage-way in any building in the United States.

Commencing at the North end of the corridor, the first office on the right is that of the State Auditor. The main room of this office is the most spacious of any of the office rooms upon the executive floor. The ceiling is lofty and decorated with a deep cornice and foliated center pieces in plaster of paris, and supported in the center by two fluted columns. The wood-work is of walnut and ash. The offices on this floor are similar in decoration and finish, and the above description will suffice for all. Opposite the Auditor's office is the Department of Agriculture, divided into four compartments. Some of the plaster-work represents the cereals grown in this State, and heads of native animals, and is very appropriate. The museum in this department is very complete and excellently arranged. The office, next the Auditor, is that of the State Treasurer. It is finished in keeping with its character. Opposite the treasury is the office of the State Board of Charities. South of the main hall, on the right, is the Department of Justice, embracing the Supreme and Appellate court rooms. The former is the most richly finished and artistically frescoed room in the building. The figures, employed by the artist, are emblematic of the uses to which the

room is put, and are executed in the finest style of the art. It is
said that no other court-room in the United States is equal to it
in its appointments. Opposite these rooms are the State Library
and the Index Department of the office of the Secretary of
State, and, at the extreme south end of the corridor, on the left,
is the office of the State Superintendent of Public Instruction.
The second story contains the Senate Chamber and Hall of the
House of Representatives and their corridors, galleries, stair-
ways and committee-rooms, cloak-rooms, closets, etc. The Senate Chamber occupies the north wing, the Hall of the House
being located in the south wing. Both are flanked by inner corridors, separated from the halls by ground glass partitions, some
eight feet in height. The chambers are lighted by sky-lights of
stained glass, surrounded by beautiful bas-relief work in white
plaster. From their high ceilings depend beautiful chandeliers,
hung with prisms and clusters of crystals which give a rich effect by gas-light.

The interior of the great dome towers in naked, raw and unfinished glory above the head of the beholder, and, to the dis-
grace of the voters of Illinois, proclaims that the elegant finish
and polished beauty of the corridors and stairway, below, are
but roseate paths to a cupola resembling a ventilator in a first-
class barn, in its labyrinth of scaffolding and walls of naked
brick. The bas-relief work and statuary for its decoration are
completed, and only need an appropriation to put them in place
and surround them with a finish of plaster and paint, which
would render the dome a thing of beauty to endure forever.
No one, who has ever visited this most substantial and elegant
structure will ever again vote against an appropriation for its
completion.

It is now provided with the electric light, with which its corridors and dome are brilliantly illuminated each evening.

An elevator runs from the basement to the legislative floor.

JOHN M. HAMILTON.

STATE OFFICERS.

HON. JOHN M. HAMILTON,

GOVERNOR OF ILLINOIS.

John M. Hamilton was born in Union County, Ohio, on May 28th, 1847. In 1854, he came, with his parents, to Illinois, where he worked upon his father's farm until sixteen years of age, when the promptings of patriotism caused him to enlist in the army. Young as he was, it is said of him that he was a brave and capable soldier—one who neither shrank from danger or faltered in the hour of peril. After the war, in 1865, he entered the Wesleyan University, at Delaware, Ohio, where he was graduated with honor in 1868. In 1869, he located at Bloomington, Illinois, where he began reading law. During one year of his course, he was Professor of Languages in the Illinois Wesleyan University. He completed the necessary course of study in 1870, and was admitted to the bar. He soon afterward formed a partnership with Captain J. H. Rowell, the firm continuing in business until his accession to the office of Governor, in 1883. The firm is well known to the Illinois bar, and its extensive and lucrative practice is the best possible testimonial of its ability and energy. Mr. Hamilton has always been a close student, and is one of the most brilliant lawyers of his age, in the West. His knowledge of the statutes of Illinois is said to be almost phenomenal. In addition to his legal accomplishments, he possesses a very fine vocabulary, an excellent voice, and a most laudable fund of general information. He is truly a scholar, as well as a lawyer and statesman. He has always been an ardent Republican in political belief and practice, and entered the arena of State affairs as a Senator from the Bloomington District, in 1876, defeating his opponent by a majority of 1,640 votes. His triumph in the election was but the foundation for one of the most substantial testimonials of public regard, ever bestowed upon a young man by the State

Senate of Illinois.   His energy, knowledge of parliamentary practice, and dignified bearing won for him the unqualified esteem of the party of which he was one of the most active representatives, and the good will and personal regard of the opposition, during the session.   He assiduously addressed himself to the responsible duties of his position, and was instrumental in securing the passage of some of the most important measures of the session.   He introduced and procured the adoption of the bill creating Appellate Courts, and was the author of the bill, which created and defined the duties of the State Board of Health. Both of these measures have proven to be very beneficial to the people and the State.   The act establishing the State Militia and providing for its government, owes its existence, in a great measure, to his skill as a parliamentarian, during the celebrated struggle over its passage in the Senate.   In the organization of the Thirty-first General Assembly, he received such a testimonial of the regard of his party, as seldom falls to the lot of one of his age—a unanimous nomination for President *pro tempore* of the Senate.   He was elected by the full party vote and that of Senator Artley, an independent member.   He discharged the duties of his high office so well, that he received the commendation of the members of the Senate, without regard to party lines.   He made a brilliant and successful canvass for the office of Lieutenant-Governor, in 1880, and served as such until the resignation of Governor Cullom, in February, 1883, when he became Governor of the great State of Illinois, by virtue of the provisions of the constitution, at an earlier age than any of his predecessors.   Mr. Hamilton retired from his presidency of the Senate amid the universal regret of his peers, who testified their sorrow at losing his valued services, and, at the same time, their joy over his promotion to the chief executive office, by appropriate resolutions introduced by the Hon. Thomas E. Merritt, the recognized leader on the Democratic side of the Senate, and adopted by a unanimous, rising vote.   The writer occupied a position in the gallery of the Senate Chamber, during the transaction of the business pertaining to the resignation of the gavel by Governor Hamilton, and the silent attention and profound solemnity of the occasion will not soon be forgotten.   During the delivery of his address, the Lieutenant Governor's usually oratund voice was modified by the solemn circumstance of parting, so far as former relations were concerned, and, at times, there was a faltering, suggestive of the deep emotions of his great heart, wrought by the change in official station, which was so soon to be consummated. His inaugural address was brief and simple, and showed conclusively that he had an adequate sense of the weight of the duties, which he was then about to assume, as Governor. He retired from the Chamber, and, ere we could reach the Executive Office, had taken the oath and received the congratulations of his numerous friends. There was no pomp or tinsel connected with the great event, and, a few hours later, Governor Hamilton's attention was engrossed with the business of his new and exalted station. He is not addicted to ambition for empty fame, nor does he fret beneath the honors of his position. His highest aim is the honest discharge of duty, and no man can labor more diligently to attain the goal of his desires, than he has done, and is now doing.

HARRY F. DORWIN,
GOVERNOR'S PRIVATE SECRETARY.

Mr. Dorwin, eldest son living, of Phares A. and Caroline Dorwin, was born in Springfield, Illinois, August 4th, 1855, and has always resided at the Capital. His education was acquired in the public schools of his native city, and his attainments are an endorsement of their excellence. After leaving school he entered the employ of the State National Bank, of Springfield, but, in July, 1876, after a service of five years, he was obliged to leave that institution on account of failing health. When Governor Cullom took possession of his office, he tendered Mr. Dorwin a position, which he accepted and continued to fill during Governor Cullom's entire term of six years. When Governor Hamilton succeeded to the office of Chief Executor, on February 5th, 1883, he appointed the subject of this sketch, as his Private Secretary, which position he now holds.

LOUIS C. FERRELL,
ASSISTANT SECRETARY AND STENOGRAPHER.

Mr. Ferrell was born in Marion, Williamson County, Illinois, in 1855, his father being a farmer. His father enlisted in 1861, in the 31st Illinois Regiment, and was killed at Atlanta, Ga.,

July 21st, 1864. Louis was educated in the public schools of his county until he was ten years of age, and attended college at Carbondale for six months, in 1869. He worked on a farm until 1872, when he learned telegraphy at St. Louis, and was employed by the Illinois Central Railroad in 1882, the last four years as Ticket Agent and Manager of the W. U. Telegraph Office at Carbondale. In 1882, he was appointed to his present position by Governor Cullom, being re-appointed by Governor Hamilton, upon his accession to the office in February, 1883. Mr. Ferrell is an Odd Fellow, and has secured a position in the War Department at Washington, where he will have entered upon the performance of his duties, ere this book is published.

FRANK Y. HAMILTON,
GOVERNOR'S ASSISTANT SECRETARY.

Mr. Hamilton was born December 27th, 1862, at Richmond, Ohio, and removed, with his parents, to Illinois in 1854, where he worked upon a farm until 1866, when his mother died, and the family became scattered, but was re-united by the second marriage of his father, in 1869. Mr. Hamilton's education was acquired at the Wesleyan University, at Bloomington, Ill., and by a three years collegiate course at Adrian, Michigan, where he was graduated. From that time until 1881, he taught school. He then began reading law in the office of Rowell and Hamilton, at Bloomington. He is a Presbyterian and Mason. As may have been inferred by the reader, Mr. Hamilton is a brother of the Governor.

HON. HENRY D. DEMENT,
SECRETARY OF STATE.

Mr. Dement was born at Galena, Illinois, October 10th, 1840, his father and mother being natives of Tennessee and Missouri, respectively. The subject of our sketch began his course of study in the common schools of Dixon, Illinois, and afterward pursued it in Rock River Seminary, Mt. Morris, Ill., a Catholic School at Sinsinawa Mound, Wisconsin, and a Presbyterian College at Dixon, Illinois. At the commencement of the war, he had not yet completed his course in the latter institution, but he enlisted in the Union Army, and was commissioned as Second Lieutenant of Company "A," Thirteenth Illinois Volunteer Infantry. On the succeeding day, he received his commission as First Lieutenant of his company. He was actively engaged in the battles at Arkansaw Post and Vicksburg, and, for gallantry, was brevetted Captain, retaining that honor until the close of the war. He served with Generals Fremont and Curtis, throughout their campaigns west of the Mississippi River; was with Sherman, at the time of his defeat at Chickasaw Bayou; accompanied Grant on his march to the rear of Vicksburg, and was engaged in the principal assault made upon that Confederate strong-hold, throughout the siege. He also assisted in the capture of Jackson, Mississippi. After the war, he became a member of the firm of Todd and Dement, plow manufacturers, at Dixon, where he was engaged in the manufacture of flag bagging, for the protection of cotton bales, at the time of his election to his present office, in 1880—in fact, is now largely interested in the same industry. He was married to Miss Mary F. Williams, of Castine, Maine, October 20th, 1864, and five children were born to them, three of whom, all daughters, are now living. Mr. Dement is an Odd Fellow. In political faith he has ever been a Stalwart Republican, and was honored by his party by being elected to the lower house of the Twenty-eighth and Twenty-ninth, and to the Senate of the Thirtieth and Thirty-first General Assemblies. In 1880, he was elected Secretary of State, and has ever since performed his duties with a remarkable degree of accuracy and dispatch. He is a man of great force of character, and is generally admired and esteemed.

JAMES H. PADDOCK,
CHIEF CLERK, OFFICE OF SECRETARY OF STATE.

Mr. Paddock was born at Lockport, Will County, Illinois, May 29th, 1850. He was educated in the public schools of Kankakee, and became a Page in the State Senate of Illinois in 1865. In 1867, he was Assistant Postmaster of the Senate. In 1869-71-73-75, he was Assistant Secretary of the Senate, and Secretary in 1877, 1879 and 1881, being employed in the office of the Grain Inspector at Chicago, in the intervals between sessions. June 1st, 1881, he was appointed Chief Clerk in the office of the

Secretary of State, by Mr. Dement. He was married at Kankakee to Miss Mary L. Crawford, October 9th, 1873. His father was a member of the Constitutional Convention of 1862, and Lieutenant Colonel of the One Hundred and Thirteenth Illinois Regiment of Infantry, and died at the hospital in Memphis, Tennessee, in 1863, from disease contracted during the siege of Vicksburg. The subject of this sketch and his wife are both members of the Episcopal Church. Mr. Paddock was Secretary of the Railroad and Warehouse Commission from July, 1876, to January 1st, 1877, and a clerk in the United States Marshal's office from January 1st, 1877, until January 1st, 1879. He is accurate and swift in the performance of clerical work, and is much esteemed by those with whom he is and has been associated.

CAPTAIN JOHN M. ADAIR,

CHIEF CLERK IN THE DEPARTMENT OF INDICES AND ARCHIVES.

Mr. Adair was born in Franklin County, Pennsylvania, May 11th, 1840, his father being a farmer. When eight years of age he came, with his family, to Carroll County, Illinois. His education was acquired in the common schools of Pennsylvania and Illinois. At the age of seventeen, he began clerking in a store, following that occupation until 1861, when he enlisted as a private in Company "E," of the Forty-fifth Regiment of Illinois Volunteers. He was promoted to First Sergeant in November, 1861. In December of the same year, he was promoted to the Second Lieutenancy. He assisted in the reduction of Fort Donelson and the battle of Pittsburg Landing. He was also at the siege of Corinth. During General Grant's Mississippi campaign, his command lived on ear corn for two weeks, three ears being a ration. He was also at Vicksburg. He became First Lieutenant during this campaign, and, the Captain having been promoted to Major during the siege, Mr. Adair succeeded him and became Captain of his company. In 1865 he resigned on account of ill health, and soon afterward became Deputy Circuit Clerk of Carroll County. In 1867, he was Assistant Secretary of the State Senate, and was one of the editors and proprietors of the *Gazette*, Lanark, Ill., from 1868 to 1871. In 1869 he was Enrolling and Engrossing Clerk of the State Senate.

After leaving the *Gazette*, he became sole proprietor and publisher of the Mt. Carroll *Mirror*, conducting it until 1874, in July of which year, he was appointed to take charge of the Department of Indices and Archives in the office of the Secretary of State. It is said that the index and reference system of Records in Illinois is one of the best in the Union, and Captain Adair is entitled to the honor of raising it to that standard.

JOHN C. HUGHES,

STATE PRINTER EXPERT.

Mr. Hughes is probably the hardest worked employe in the service of the State. Upon him rests the responsibility of reading the proofs and overseeing the entire work of the State Printer. He is busy at all hours of the day, and, frequently, until late at night. He is necessarily an experienced printer and a finely educated man, in the practical fields of literature. When the Legislature is in session, he has no time to rest or answer questions, and could not give us the information upon which to base a sketch. We append his remarks:

"My life has been passed in Springfield, and has been utterly uneventful. There is nothing in it from which to weave a biography, as I am neither a statesman, politician or chronic office-seeker. I therefore respectfully decline the honor of a historical sketch."

He is a very agreeable man and a perfect gentleman. He is a member of the Order of Odd Fellows.

PALMER ATKINS,

STATE PROOF READER.

Mr. Atkins was born at Rome, New York, August 28th, 1841, his father being a manufacturer of stoves. He came to Chicago in 1856. He was educated in the ward schools of New York City. In 1858, he located at Dixon, Illinois, his present home. He followed the printing business at Dixon until his enlistment in the army in 1861. He served at Military Headquarters of General Curtis for some time, and was detailed to publish a Union newspaper known as the *Shield*, at Helena, Arkansas, which he did from August to December, 1862. He then served at Gen. Grant's headquarters until the latter was transferred to the East, when he went to the headquarters of Gen. Thomas, at Chattanooga, by Gen. Grant's recommendation. He served the remainder of his term at Gen. McPherson's headquarters, where he was in the Postoffice Department. He then resumed the printing business, at Dixon, until 1876. In 1881, he was appointed State Proof Reader, by Secretary of State Dement. He is an Odd Fellow and Republican.

D. EDITH WALLBRIDGE,
ASSISTANT STATE LIBRARIAN.

Miss Wallbridge was born in Erie County, Pennsylvania, October 2d, 1854, her father, Wing K. Wallbridge, being a farmer. In 1857, Mr. Wallbridge removed to Iowa, with his family, where he died in 1869. Edith was educated at Hillsdale College, Michigan, where she was graduated in 1878. She then removed to Hoopestan, Illinois, where she resided until appointed to her present position by Secretary of State Dement, in 1881. She is a member of the Free Will Baptist Church. Miss Wallbridge is a well educated, accomplished and estimable young lady, who is thoroughly conversant with the magnificent State Library.

WILLIAM E. SAVAGE,
CHIEF JANITOR OF THE STATE HOUSE.

Mr. Savage was born in Whitesboro, Oneida County, New York, in 1845. His father was a merchant. The family came to Knox County, Illinois, in 1855. The subject was educated at Champlain Academy, in Clinton County, New York. He removed to Whiteside County, Illinois, in 1861, where he resided until appointed Chief Janitor of the State House, in 1881, a position which carries with it a greater weight of responsibility than one might at first suppose. He has been an ardent Republican ever since he became a voter. He is a member of the Congregational Church, and the Ancient Order of United Workmen. He is trustworthy and faithful in every respect, and fully worthy of the confidence reposed in him.

ANDREW WALKER,

STATE HOUSE ENGINEER.

Mr. Walker was born on the Isle of Man, in 1840, his father being a manufacturer. He came to this country when Andrew was but a year and a half old, locating at Elmira, New York. His literary education was acquired prior to attaining his tenth year, in the common schools of New York State. He went to New Orleans when quite young and served as a striker and engineer on a steamboat until the war began, when he came North and enlisted in the 39th Illinois Regiment, serving for three years. He then served as a locomotive engineer until appointed State House engineer—nine years ago. He is thoroughly familiar with his business, and is a very reliable man. He is a member of the Independent Order of Odd Fellows and Ancient Order of United Workmen, and has always been a Republican.

JOSEPH E. WOODS,

STATE HOUSE CARPENTER.

Mr. Woods was born at Knoxville, Frederick County, Maryland, in 1834, his father being a blacksmith by trade. Mr. Woods received his education in a private school and learned his trade in his native State. In 1855, he removed to Ohio, and came to Springfield, Ill., during the next year. He was married to Miss Sarah E. Morse, of Springfield, in 1857. His wife died in 1860. He served three years as a private in Co. "C," 124th Illinois Volunteer Infantry, being mustered out of the service at Chicago in 1865. Most of his service was in the Mississippi campaigns, under Generals Logan and McPherson. In 1867 he was again married, linking his fortunes with those of Miss Esther Thompson, of Morris County, New Jersey. He removed to New Jersey in 1870, returning to Springfield in 1873. He worked upon the State House under the commissioners, and was appointed to his present position by the Secretary of State in 1877, and re-appointed by Mr. Dement in 1881. He has charge of all repairs and improvements, and is a very superior workman. He is a Republican and Odd Fellow, being a Past Grand and Past Chief Patriarch in that order.

HON. JOHN CORSON SMITH,

STATE TREASURER.

Mr. Smith was born in Philadelphia, Pennsylvania, February 13th, 1832, to parents of Scotch and English extraction. He received a very good English education and served an apprenticeship to a carpenter and builder. Upon attaining his majority, he left home and spent a year in New York City and Cape May, when he came West, locating at Galena, Illinois, where he pursued his trade and erected some of the most valuable and substantial buildings in the city. In 1859 he entered the employ of the government, as Assistant Superintendent of the erection of the Custom House Building at Dubuque, Iowa. In 1862, impelled solely by patriotic motives, he entered the army as private in Company "I," Ninety-sixth Illinois Infantry Volunteers, was elected Captain and subsequently elected Major by a vote of the rank and file of his regiment. His regiment was ordered to Ciuciunati, in October of the same year, to defend that city against an attack of the Confederates, which was then imminent. He participated in the second battle at Fort Donelson, at Franklin, etc. He was soon afterward assigned to duty upon the staff of Brigadier General Beard, of the Regular Army, where he served with distinguished ability and bravery, until transferred to the staff of Major General Steedman, under whom he participated in the battles at Chicamauga, Lookout Mountain and Mission Ridge, where he was commissioned Lieutenant Colonel in recognition of his heroism and eminent services, being highly complimented by Generals Steedman and Granger. After the army had fallen back to Chattanooga, he was assigned to the duty of planting batteries upon Moccasin Point, immediately under the guns of Longstreet, on the mountain, which task he accomplished so successfully that when morning dawned and these batteries opened fire, the Confederate guns were soon silenced and those who manned them, driven from their position. At his own request, Colonel Smith was now relieved from staff duty and placed in command of his regiment, participating in the action at Buzzards' Roost. He was subsequently placed in command of the post and made president of a board of claims at Cleveland, Tennessee. He participated in all of the important battles of the Atlanta campaign, until that of Kenesaw Moun-

tain, where he was severely wounded while commanding a brigade in repelling a night assault. Though suffering from his wound, he returned to the field in October of the same year, and participated in the Battle of Nashville, after which he was assigned to duty as the president of a court-martial, and, afterward, of a military commission at Nashville, where he remained until the close of the war. He was brevetted Colonel for gallantry, by President Lincoln, afterward promoted to the full rank of Colonel, and, in June, 1865, brevetted Brigadier General by President Johnson, for "meritorious services." After the war, General Smith was appointed Chief Grain Inspector for the city of Chicago, where he now resides. He was one of the Centennial Commissioners of Illinois, and was elected State Treasurer on the Republican ticket in 1878, and again in 1882. He is a man of strong character and great popularity. In person, he is tall and finely formed; dignified, yet courteous and polite in bearing, and obliging, generous and noble in natural impulse. He is a man of unsullied reputation and unquestioned integrity, firm and accurate in judgment, and deliberate in speech and execution. He is a Past Grand Master, Past Grand Patriarch, Past Grand Representative, and at present Grand Scribe of the Independent Order of Odd Fellows, and a Thirty-third Degree Free Mason, in which order he is also a Past Grand Commander of the Knights Templar.

JOHN T. PETERS,

CHIEF CLERK IN THE STATE TREASURY.

Mr. Peters was born in Greene County, Illinois, June 20th, 1844, his father being a farmer. The family came to Springfield in 1848, and Mr. Peters received his education in the public schools of the Capital city and the old Mechanic's College. He was a dry goods clerk five years, connected with the Wabash Ticket Office a year, Cashier of the United States Mustering Office during the war, and Teller of the Marine Bank in 1864, several years. While in the bank he was elected City Treasurer of Springfield, being one of the first Republicans ever elected to office in Sangamon County. He was Chief Clerk of the Auditor's Office under General Lippincott, eight years, came into the Treasury under Rutz, having been Chief Clerk, and was retained by General Smith; again became Rutz's Chief Clerk, and is now occupying the same position under Smith for the second time. He has always voted the straight Republican ticket, and is excellently qualified for the onerous and responsible duties of his office.

HON. CHARLES P. SWIGERT,
STATE AUDITOR.

Mr. Swigert was born in Baden, Germany, in November, 1843, and came with his parents to the United States when but nine years of age. In 1854 the family located upon a farm in Kankakee County, Illinois, where Charles worked in summer and attended school in winter, until seventeen years old. He had begun supporting himself by driving oxen at four dollars per month, when but twelve years of age, receiving an advance of two dollars per month the second year, and another two dollars advance the third year. During these three years he is said to have assisted in plowing over four hundred acres of raw prairie lands. In 1861 he volunteered as a private in Company "II," of the Forty-second Illinois Infantry. He was one of Captain Hottenstein's twenty picked sharp-shooters who rendered such efficient service by running the gauntlet at Island No. 10, on board the "Carondalet," thus opening the river to Memphis, previous to the Battle of Pittsburg Landing. During the siege of Corinth, Mississippi, May 9th, 1882, his right arm was struck by a solid, six-pound shot, which carried away all of that part of the limb between the shoulder and elbow, except a shred of skin by which the hand remained suspended from the shoulder. Seizing the stump of his arm firmly with the remaining hand, he saved his life by compressing the arteries sufficiently to prevent rapid hemorrhage. No one was near him, and he was compelled to walk three-quarters of a mile, when he was placed in an ambulance, and, after the team had run away, during which time he was obliged to continue the compression upon the wound, was at last cared for in the hospital. After three weeks treatment of the remains of that amputated member, he was sent to the Jefferson Barracks, Missouri, and afterward to Quincy, Illinois, where he was discharged in December, 1862. After his discharge he pursued a course of study in the Bryant and Stratton

Chas. P. Swigert.

Business College, then taught two terms of school in Kankakee County, after which he became a letter carrier in the postoffice at Chicago, following that business until 1866, when he became Deputy County Clerk of Kankakee County. He passed the school years of 1867-8 and 1868-9 in the Soldier's College at Fulton, Illinois. He was a Stalwart Republican, and was elected County Treasurer of Kankakee County in 1869. He was re-elected five times in succession. In November, 1880, he was elected to the office which he now occupies, for a term of four years, from January 10th, 1881. In 1869 Mr. Swigert was married to Lavina L. Bigelow, who was born in Vermont. They have a family of four sons. Mr. Swigert is a very generous, obliging and popular gentleman, and an efficient and honest officer.

WILLIAM H. HENKLE,
CHIEF CLERK, AUDITOR'S OFFICE.

Mr. Henkle is a native born capitalist—that is to say, he was born at the State Capital, May 15th, 1853, his father being a Carriage Manufacturer. He resided in Decatur, Illinois, from the time he was two years old until he became fourteen, being educated in the public schools of that city. Upon his return to Springfield, he worked in his father's paper mill, at Riverton, two years, when he became a clerk in the store of Woods & Henkle, one of the oldest clothing firms in Central Illinois, serving four years, when he was appointed to a clerkship in the State Auditor's Office by General Lippincott, in 1873. He has been Chief Clerk since Mr. Swigert's accession to the office. He was elected Secretary of the State Board of Equalization in 1881, and still holds that office, also. He says that his ancestors have very strong symptoms of Republicanism from the organization of the party, and they are not modified in him by any means.

JOHN J. BRINKERHOFF,
CHIEF CLERK, INSURANCE DEPARTMENT, AUDITOR'S OFFICE.

This gentleman was born at Gettysburg, Pennsylvania, his father being a farmer. The subject of our sketch received his education at a college at his birth-place, graduating in 1869, in the fall of which year he came to Springfield, and, with the exception of a portion of two years, passed in law school at Albany, New York, has resided in that city ever since. He was a clerk in the Auditor's Office from 1869 until 1872, and after the completion of his legal studies, he resumed his station. He was appointed to his present position by Auditor Needles, in 1879, and has been retained in it ever since. He is a Captain in the Illinois National Guard, having held that position since 1878. His society membership is confined to a collegiate society of Greek Letters. He has always been a staunch Republican. Captain Brinkerhoff is a very careful and competent gentleman, who is well adapted to the responsible duties of his position.

ALONZO McLAUGHLIN,

CLERK MUNICIPAL INDEBTEDNESS DEPARTMENT, AUDITOR'S OFFICE.

Mr. McLaughlin was born at Herkimer, New York, in the year 1839. He says his father was a Scot and his mother a Knickerbocker. His father was a farmer by occupation. When but one year of age, his parents removed to Burlington, Wisconsin. Mr. McLaughlin received a liberal education in the High School at Racine, Wisconsin, read law with Wentworth & Smith, and was admitted to the bar in 1868. He practiced his profession at Harvard and Woodstock, Illinois, at the same time editing and publishing a newspaper at the former place. He had previously practiced at Geneva, Wisconsin. Being a writer of considerable ability, he was soon engaged in political and general correspondence for numerous well known journals. His power as an organizer and canvasser is recognized by his party friends. He was elected Secretary of the Railroad and Warehouse Commissioners in 1873, and since 1877, has occupied his present position in the State Auditor's Office. He now resides in the Capital City.

HON. HENRY RAAB,

STATE SUPERINTENDENT OF PUBLIC INSTRUCTION.

Mr. Raab was born at Wetzlar, Rheinish Prussia, in 1837, his father being a currier, tanner and dealer in leather. His education was acquired in the Kindergarten, common schools and Royal Gymnasium College, of his native city. He was graduated in a scientific course from the last named institution, with the class of 1853, after having carefully studied the Latin, English and French languages. He came to the United States during the same year, and engaged in business in Cincinnati, later in St. Louis, and, afterward, became Assistant Teacher in the public schools of Belleville, this State. He was soon afterward made Principal of the Grammar School of that city, during the incumbency of Mr. James P. Slade, his predecessor in office, as Superintendent of the Belleville Schools. Mr. Raab had taken particular pains to inform himself in the various branches of study employed in our schools, and familiarized himself with the text books and methods in use. He has always been an active worker in educational conventions and institutes, striving for the advancement of national methods of instruction, and laboring to increase facilities for the improvement of teachers, and to produce the more beneficial results to be expected from their labors. In 1874, Mr. Raab founded the Belleville Kindergarten, now a flourishing institution, one in which he feels a great sense of pride. His connection with the Belleville Public Schools has endured for a quarter of a century, and he has been Librarian of the Sangerbund Library for twenty-three years. He is an ardent Democrat in politics, and was elected to his present office over Charles T. Strattan, of Mt. Vernon, by a majority of 2,869, in 1882, although the State is largely Republican. He will reside in Springfield during his term of office, and the citizens of the Capital will accept him as a learned and most valuable acquisition to society. Mr. Raab is one of the most thoroughly educated and substantially well informed men in the State, and his election to the all-important offices of which he is now the incumbent, was a stride in the direction of practical measures for educational reform. Being a gentleman of great intellectual power and polished education, his term of office cannot but prove both satisfactory and profitable to the schools of one of the greatest States in the Union. He is a man who will not hesitate taking up arms against all of those antiquated methods and fogy practices which have been a retarding influence in our educational affairs far longer than is consistent with the age of progress in which we live. With him, precedent is no guide, unless founded upon incontrovertible reason, and the fact that a given theory has long been accepted, without question, does not establish its correctness unless there be a more rational foundation for it than mere public acquiescence.

MR. WILLIAM L. PILLSBURY,

CHIEF CLERK OF THE OFFICE OF STATE SUPERINTENDENT OF PUBLIC INSTRUCTION.

Mr. Pillsbury was born at Derry, New Hampshire, November 4th, 1838, his father being at that time a farmer. He went to Andover, Massachusetts, in 1856, where he was prepared for college, at Phillips' Academy, and entered Harvard University in 1859, graduating in 1863. During the latter year he came to Illinois; taking charge of the model school in connection with the State Normal University at Normal. He retained that position for seven years, when he engaged in real estate and insurance business in Bloomington, and later in Springfield. In 1879, Superintendent Slade appointed him Chief Clerk in the office of State Superintendent of Public Instruction, and he was re-appointed by Mr. Raab in 1863. He is a gentleman of fine literary attainments, well suited to the position which he now occupies under Mr. Raab, and fully worthy of association with him in the educational affairs of the State.

HON. JAMES McCARTNEY,

ATTORNEY GENERAL.

The subject of this sketch was born in Perry County, Pennsylvania, February 14th, 1835. When James was about five years old, the family moved to Lawrence County, in the same State, and to Trumbull County, Ohio, about 1848. In 1857, they came to Illinois, locating at Monmouth. Mr. McCartney was educated in the common schools, principally; but attended the Western Reserve Seminary, in Ohio, one term. He began reading law in the office of Hon. Matthew Birchard, at Warren, Ohio, in 1856, and completed his course in the office of Harding & Reed, Monmouth, Illinois, in 1858, when he was admitted to the bar. He enlisted as a private in Company "D," Seventeenth Illinois Volunteer Infantry, April 19th, 1861, and was afterward commissioned First Lieutenant. He resigned in April, 1862; but re-enlisted in September following, as First Lieutenant of Company "G," One Hundred and Twelfth Illinois Volunteer Infantry, and was promoted to the Captaincy in April, 1863, serving in that capacity until mustered out, July 10, 1865. He was Acting

Compliments of James McCartney

Assistant Adjutant General of the Third Brigade of the Third Division, of the Army of the Ohio, from August, 1863, to May, 1864. He belongs to no church; but is a member of the Grand Army of the Republic and the Ancient Order of United Workmen. After the war, Mr. McCartney located at Fairfield, Wayne County, Illinois, where he entered upon a successful and profitable practice of his profession, which continued until his election to his present office, in 1880. He yet claims and recognizes that place as his home, although he has temporarily resided at the Capital, since entering upon the duties of his office. He is, and has ever been a staunch and unyielding Republican. He never held any civil office prior to his election as Attorney General, in November, 1880. At the polls, on that occasion, he defeated Hon. Lawrence Harmon, the Democratic candidate, by a majority of 42,112 votes. Mr. McCartney is an able lawyer, and a good natured, polite and obliging gentleman.

ELBERT S. SMITH,
ASSISTANT TO ATTORNEY GENERAL.

Mr. Smith was born at Twinsburg, Summit County, Ohio, March 8th, 1847. His boyhood was passed upon a farm. He is a graduate of Willoughby College, Willoughby, Ohio, where he received the degree of Bachelor of Arts. He came to Illinois in 1869, locating at Champaign, where he read law with Thomas J. Smith, Esq., being admitted to the bar in 1874, and practicing his profession in Champaign County until appointed Chief Clerk in the office of Attorney General McCartney, in January, 1881. Mr. Smith is a Free Mason and has always been a pronounced Republican. Since his appointment he has been a resident of the Capital City. Mr. Smith is a very capable and, industrious lawyer, and is an intellectual ornament to the responsible position which he now holds.

GILBERT L. MILLER,
ATTORNEY GENERAL'S SECOND ASSISTANT.

Mr. Miller was born on a farm near Canton, Illinois, June 8th, 1852, and educated in the common schools of his native county, after which he began reading medicine, at the age of eighteen, with G. W. Wright, a skillful surgeon of Canton. He attended one course of lectures, supporting himself meanwhile by teaching school in Winter. At the end of three years he espoused the law, reading in the office of an attorney, and teaching school in winter, as before. He entered the newspaper business in 1877, continuing until 1880, when he and a younger brother established a law office in Mills County, Iowa. Several months after, Gilbert left his brother in charge of the business and returned to Canton, where he remained until appointed to his present position, in December, 1882. He was married to Miss Eldora F. Slocum in 1878, and she died in December of the following year. November 19th, 1881, he married Miss Cora B. McCartney, daughter of the Attorney General. Mr. Miller is a Republican and Free Mason, but belongs to no church.

GEN. ISAAC H. ELLIOTT,

ADJUTANT GENERAL.

This gentleman is the son of a farmer. Indeed, among all of the prominent men mentioned in this work, there are few who are not. He was born in Bureau County, Illinois, in 1837, and his home is still on a farm near Princeton, in his native county. His education was acquired in the district schools of his county, by a two years' course of study at Knox College, Abingdon, Illinois, and a four years' course at Michigan University, from which he was graduated in 1861. He entered the army as Captain of Company "E," Thirty-third Illinois Regiment of Volunteers, served in that capacity two years, when he was promoted to Major, and, afterwards, to Lieutenant Colonel. He was brevetted Colonel soon afterwards, and, a little later, became Colonel of his regiment. He retired, after five years of service, brevetted a Brigadier General. In politics, he has ever been a staunch and unyielding Republican, and, as such, has served one term as Treasurer of his native county. With this exception he had devoted his attention to farming since the war, to the time of his appointment as Adjutant General of the State, by Governor Cullom, in 1881. Mr. Elliott is a brave and experienced soldier, of rare ability and tact. Entering the army at the age of twenty-four, and being rapidly promoted from one position to another, until he was a brevet Brigadier General, before attaining his thirtieth year, his military record stands with few parallels in brilliancy. He certainly is well qualified to control the military affairs of the State of Illinois. His administration of his office has been characterized by zeal and good judgment, as well as fearlessness and impartiality. Upon attaining the office, he found that more companies had been organized than the law permitted, and cut down the number accordingly. He also reduced the force of officers, in order to render the service more effective and less expensive, and while he expresses regret that the necessity for such action should exist, he applied the pruning knife freely and judiciously. The militia of our State is in better condition now than ever before, and much of the improvement, if not all, is due to his untiring efforts to render the service efficient.

PROF. AMOS H. WORTHEN,

STATE GEOLOGIST.

This well-informed and eminently scientific gentleman was born at Bradford, Vermont, October 31st, 1813, his father having been a farmer by occupation. The subject of our sketch was educated in the common schools of his native town, and Bradford Academy; but has probably acquired more knowledge by a course of careful reading and scientific research, than from his advantages in schools. In 1834, Mr. Worthen removed to Harrison County, Kentucky, where he taught school one year, at the end of which time, he located at Warsaw, Illinois, his present place of residence. After coming West, he became interested in the geology of the country, and studied it diligently and thoroughly. His opportunities for observation were excellent, and, taken in connection with untiring investigation, have rendered him a gentleman of preëminent qualifications for his scientific duties, as State Geologist. He was Assistant State Geologist of Illinois in 1851, under Dr. Norwood, the first man who ever filled the office in this State. He also served two years as Assistant State Geologist of Iowa, under Prof. Hall, the first officer of the kind in that State. In 1858, Governor Bissell appointed Mr. Worthen as Dr. Norwood's successor, and he had charge of the geological survey of Illinois, the official report of which is now deemed so valuable by scientists. Mr. Worthen is a straight

Republican in politics, and has never voted a Democratic ticket in his life. He is a truly scientific gentleman, excellently adapted to the position which he has ably filled for so many years.

HON. ETHAN A. SNIVELY,
CLERK OF THE SUPREME COURT, CENTRAL GRAND DIVISION.

The subject of this sketch was born in Cuba, Fulton County, Illinois, February 17th, 1845, his father being a merchant. His grandfather was an accomplished German and English Scholar, and was one of the Pioneers of Ohio. The father died in 1860, having held numerous and prominent positions as a Democrat. The mother died in 1879, both she and her husband closing their eyes in death, in the house where Ethan's first opened in life. The education of the subject was acquired in the common schools of his native village. His father desired to have him pass through a collegiate course and become a lawyer, but Ethan declared that he preferred to learn the printer's trade, and, his father consenting, he pursued it at Havana, commencing as "devil" at the age of fifteen, and becoming a full fledged journeyman at Canton. In 1866, he began publishing the *Times* at Rushville, Illinois, but soon sold it, having made it a success. He then established the *Galesburg Times* and soon sunk $3,000 in the enterprise. He edited the *Pekin Times* three months, and, in 1869, took the city editorship on the Peoria *Daily Democrat*, serving several years, during which he reported the proceedings of the Constitutional Convention of 1870, and the Twenty-seventh General Assembly. He was in charge of the *Macoupin Enquirer* from 1871 to 1877. It will be observed that Mr. Snively has kept up with the times, except during his residence at Galesburg, where the *Times* went down, but he still kept up. He was married to Miss Kate M. Dubois in 1876. She is a scion from one of the most prominent families in the State, and the union has proven fruitful of happiness to both parties. In 1878, Mr. Snively was elected Clerk of the Supreme Court for the Central Grand Division, as a Democrat, by a majority of 6,000, over four competitors. He is a most efficient officer, and a man of fine literary attainments and great political influence. He took editorial charge of the *Macoupin Herald* in 1879, and, during the same year, was elected President of the Illinois Press Association.

HON. GEO. W. JONES,

CLERK OF APPELLATE COURT, THIRD DISTRICT.

Mr. Jones was born in Boston, Massachusetts, in 1827, his father being a baker by occupation. The subject of this sketch came to Illinois in 1831, locating in Pike county, where he resided at the time of his election to the office which he now fills. His education was acquired in the common schools of Illinois. Mr. Jones is a Democrat, "boots, breeches and all," and is regarded as one of the prominent men in his party in Central Illinois. He has been actively engaged in politics for many years, and was elected Clerk of the Circuit Court of his county, in 1860, serving until 1864. In 1869, he again entered the office as deputy, discharging his duties as such until 1872, when he was again elected Circuit Clerk, which office he retained four years. In 1878, he was chosen Clerk of the Appellate Court for the Third District of Illinois, holding that responsible and honorable position at present. He is a comely man, in person, and was married in 1850, and now has two sons. Mr. Jones is deservedly popular. His kind and obliging manner, and whole-souled disposition have made friends of most of his acquaintances, and also many who have merely been brought into contact with him by business relations.

OFFICERS OF THE SENATE.

HON. WILLIAM J. CAMPBELL,

PRESIDENT OF THE SENATE.

This, one of the most prominent and popular Senators of the Thirty-third General Assembly, was born in Philadelphia, Pennsylvania, December 12th, 1850. His father is a farmer, and came West with his family in 1852, settling in Cook County. Mr. Campbell's education was acquired in the common schools and Lake Forest Seminary, of Cook County, and the University of Philadelphia, Pennsylvania, in which latter institution he remained two years. By profession, Mr. Campbell is a lawyer, having studied with W. C. Goudy, of Chicago, and admitted to the bar in 1875. He was elected State Senator in November, 1878, and, in January, 1881, was chosen President *pro tem.* of that body. He was, also, Chairman of the Congressional and Senatorial Apportionment Committees. In 1882, Mr. Campbell was again elected to the Senate, and was, a second time, chosen President *pro tem.* of that body in January, 1883, becoming President of the Senate and Acting Lieutenant-Governor by operation of law, when Governor Hamilton was called to the gubernatorial chair by the resignation of United States Senator elect, Shelby M. Cullom. Mr. Campbell has taken a lively interest in political affairs ever since attaining his majority, having frequently been made a delegate of his party to County and State Conventions, and having been one of the Illinois delegates to the National Republican Convention which nominated Garfield, in 1880. His place of residence is Blue Island, Cook County, Illinois. Mr. Campbell is tall and well proportioned, rather fair in complexion, wears no beard, and is pleasing in both features and address. He is a man of more than ordinary force of character. He has, both as Senator and presiding officer, earned and received the confidence and esteem of his fellow Senators.

JOHN F. DEWEY

John F. Dewey, Private Secretary for the President of the Senate, was born at Geneva, Illinois, in September, 1856. His father, John H. Dewey, was a physician and farmer by occupation, and was a native of Caldwell, New York. His mother, Maria Butterworth, was born in Lincolnshire, England. He was educated in the common school and printing office, having been connected with the press of Kane County since 1869, as apprentice, journeyman printer, foreman and editor. In 1878-80 he owned and edited the St. Charles *Review*. Was census enumerator in 1880; Senate Committee Clerk in 1881, and President's Secretary in 1883. He has always voted the Republican ticket, and is a liberal in religion. Resides at Batavia, Illinois.

LORENZO F. WATSON,
SECRETARY OF THE SENATE.

This gentleman was born September 26th, 1850, in one of the suburbs of Philadelphia, Pennsylvania. His parents were Quakers in religion, and his father was a farmer by occupation. In 1871, Mr. Watson came West, locating at Merom, Indiana; but, in 1877, he removed to Watseka, Illinois, where he now resides. His education is collegiate, and it is one which honors the man in a very great degree. He was graduated from the Pennsylvania Normal, when but eighteen years of age. Mr. Watson is a communicant in the Christian Church, an Odd Fellow and a prominent member of the Grand Lodge of Knights of Honor of this State. His private business is that of an abstractor of titles, and loan agent. During his residence at Merom, Indiana, Mr. Watson was Professor of Mathematics in the Union Christian College, resigning his position in 1877, previous to his removal to Illinois. He is a Republican in politics, and has held several public positions of honor and trust, among which may be mentioned Alderman of the city of Merom, First Assistant Secretary of the Senate of the Thirty-second General Assembly at its special session, and Secretary of the Thirty-third General Assembly, his present position. He was married in 1873; and has three children. Mr. Watson is well adapted to the honorable position which he fills with marked fidelity and ability. He is polite and obliging in demeanor, and pleasing and generous in disposition.

FREDERICK K. ROOT,
FIRST ASSISTANT SECRETARY OF THE SENATE.

Mr. Root was born in Chicago, in 1359, his father being a lawyer and politician of some notoriety. In 1861, he removed to the village of Hyde Park, where he now resides. He has a good education, acquired in the common and high schools of Hyde Park and the Chicago University. He also read law in his father's office. He has been Deputy County Clerk of Cook County, and was Secretary of the Committee appointed by the National Committee of the Republican party, to arrange for the convention of 1880. He is a member of the First Presbyterian Church, of Hyde Park. He was born a Republican, and remains one from choice. He was elected First Assistant Secretary of the Senate in the organization of the Thirty-third General Assembly. He is well qualified for his position and energetic and accurate in the performance of his various duties. He was married in August, 1881.

EDWARD E. MITCHELL,
SECOND ASSISTANT SECRETARY OF THE SENATE.

Mr. Mitchell was born in Williamson County, Illinois, where he now resides, his father being a farmer and local politician of considerable influence—one of the few Abolitionists of that locality at the commencement of the war. His education was acquired in the common schools of his native county. At fourteen years of age, he was employed in the Postoffice at Marion. He afterward served as Deputy Circuit Clerk of his county, Assistant County Treasurer and Deputy County Clerk. He was Postmaster of Marion for a short time, but resigned to resume his position in the County Clerk's office. He is an Odd Fellow, being a Past Grand in rank. In politics, he has always been a Republican. His former experiences adapt him to his present position most admirably.

ROSWELL W. GATES,
ENROLLING AND ENGROSSING CLERK, SENATE.

Mr. Gates was born at Antrop, Jefferson County, New York, August 29th, 1834. His father came to Illinois with his family in 1838, locating at Aurora, Kane County, where our subject was educated in the public schools. He has held numerous public positions of honor and trust in his city and township. He has spent two years of his life in California, where he cast his first vote for General Fremont. Since that time he has been a constant and active Republican. He is a member of the Free Masons and Ancient Order of United Workmen. He is a United States Commissioner in his city. He is a competent, genial, affable and good-natured man—one who has many friends and deserves them.

ROBERT W. WRIGHT,
FIRST ASSISTANT ENROLLING AND ENGROSSING CLERK, SENATE.

Mr. Wright was born at Belvidere, Illinois, July 19th, 1861, and has but little more than attained his majority. His father is a lawyer by profession, and Robert intends following in his footsteps, having been educated in the High School of his native city, and the college at Champaign, Illinois, and being now engaged in a course of study preparatory to his chosen calling. He is a young man of decidedly Republican proclivities, is bright and talented, and was honored with his present position in the organization of the Senate. We commit him to the future, hoping that some biographer of that period may be called upon to enroll and engross his history upon the scroll of fame.

F. B. HITCHCOCK,
SECOND ASSISTANT ENROLLING AND ENGROSSING CLERK, SENATE.

Mr. Hitchcock was born at Terre Haute, Indiana, and came to Illinois in 1866, locating at Louisville. He now resides at Flora. He is a graduate of the State University at Bloomington, Indiana. By profession, he is a lawyer and journalist. He enlisted, June 3d, 1863, his sixteenth birthday, in the army. He was captured at Red River, Tennessee, and paroled. He is a member of the Independent Order of Odd Fellows and Ancient Order of United Workmen. He has always been a staunch Republican, and was made Second Assistant Enrolling and Engrossing Clerk of the Senate, at its organization in 1883.

EDWARD I. BOIES,
BILL CLERK OF THE SENATE.

Mr. Boies was born February 19th, 1860, at Sycamore, DeKalb County, Illinois, his father being a farmer. He was educated in the Seminary at Woodstock, Illinois, and graduated from the Jacksonville, Illinois, Business College, in 1878. By profession, he is a rising young journalist. He is a Republican, by birth, education and choice, and was elected to his present position in the organization of the Senate, by a vote of forty-six to three. Some future biographer will probably be called upon to notice him at length, as his public career has just begun.

HON. PHINEAS W. WILCOX,

SERGEANT-AT-ARMS OF THE SENATE.

Mr. Wilcox is so well known to the people of Illinois, as the "Mendota Carpenter," that scarcely more than the plain facts in relation to his career is necessary. He was born in Belmont County, Ohio, March 29th, 1835, his father being a farmer; but afterward becoming a carpenter. The family removed to Jackson County in 1847, and, in 1855, the subject of our sketch located at Fairfield, Iowa. His education was acquired in the log school houses of his native State, and by a course of private study by the light of a pine-knot torch. His political education, which is, perhaps, as complete as that of any other man in Illinois, was acquired from the careful study of public documents and historical works, and the speeches of the great statesmen of our country. By occupation, Mr. Wilcox is a carpenter, he having learned that trade with his father, and worked in all of the principal cities of the Ohio and Mississippi valleys, from Portsmouth to New Orleans. In May, 1861, Mr. Wilcox enlisted in the army and served until October, 1865. Three years of his war experience was passed in the Secret Service Department, one of the most hazardous positions a soldier could occupy. His regiment was the Fourth Iowa Cavalry. Mr. Wilcox is one of the most eloquent orators in the ranks of the Republican party in Illinois, and has contributed both time and talent to the success of recent campaigns. He is a man of strong character and firm convictions. He is a prominent Odd Fellow. He was Door-Keeper of the House of Representatives in the Thirty-second General Assembly, and is Sergeant-at-Arms in the Senate of the Thirty-third.

MOSES W. ROBBINS,
FIRST ASSISTANT SERGEANT-AT-ARMS, SENATE.

Mr. Robbins was born in Davis County, Indiana, May 28th, 1828, his father being a farmer, who was a private soldier in the war of 1812. Moses' education was acquired in the common schools of Indiana, in the days of log cabin school-houses. Mr. Robbins is a carpenter by trade, having served an apprenticeship of three years, beginning in 1846, in Louisville, Kentucky. He served during the late war in the Fifty-fourth Illinois Regiment, entering the service as First Lieutenant and being mustered out as Major. He was appointed First Assistant Sergeant-at-Arms of the Thirty-third General Assembly, at the time of the organization of that body. He belongs to the Improved Order of Red Men and Knights of Honor, and resides at Charleston, Coles County, Illinois.

SIMON S. BARGER,
SECOND ASSISTANT SERGEANT-AT-ARMS, SENATE.

Mr. Barger was born in Pope County, Illinois, April 7th, 1844, his father being a farmer. The subject now resides at Eddyville, in the same county, where he is a Justice of the Peace, having held that office for the last fourteen years. His educational privileges were limited to a short course of study in the common schools of his county. He was First Sergeant of Company "K," Fifty-sixth Illinois, during the war, and was wounded in the thigh at the Battle of Corinth, and near the right eye, in a skirmish near Ressacca, Georgia. He has four children, and says his highest aim in life is to educate them properly. He is an Elder in the Cumberland Presbyterian church, and an Odd Fellow. He is a firm Republican and was elected at the organization of the Senate.

JAMES S. FREDERICK,
POSTMASTER OF THE SENATE.

Mr. Frederick was born August 25th, 1841, in Grafton County, New Hampshire. He worked at shoe-making, in Massachusetts, until 1861, when he removed to Milwaukee, Wisconsin, pursuing his trade in that city until August, when he enlisted in the First

Wisconsin Regiment of Cavalry as a private, serving until the close of the war, during which he lost his left arm, when he came to Paxton, Illinois, and was elected County Clerk of Ford County, and re-elected at the close of his term. He has not been a candidate for any elective office since. He has a good common school education and is well qualified for the offices he has filled. He was elected to his present position first, in 1881, again at the special session of 1882, and, again, at the opening of the present session. He is a Presbyterian and Odd Fellow, and an unswerving Republican. During his service he captured the horse and equipments of J. F. Crow, the dreaded Guerilla, after killing him. When his arm was broken by a musket at West Point, Georgia, he dropped his carbine and charged over the parapet with the storming party, firing his revolver. He was brevetted Captain for his bravery.

HENRY GINNETT,
ASSISTANT POSTMASTER, SENATE.

Mr. Ginnett was born at Aviston, Clinton County, Illinois, February 17th, 1847, his father being a farmer. Henry's education was acquired in the common schools of his native county. In 1862, he enlisted in the Sixtieth Illinois, serving seven months, when he was discharged, and re-enlisted in the One-hundred and Seventeenth Illinois, serving in the capacity of a musician until the close of the war. He is a farmer by occupation, an uncompromising Republican in politics, and a member of the order known as the Grand Army of the Republic. He was elected to his present position in the organization of the Senate of the Thirty-third General Assembly, and is well qualified for the discharge of its duties.

JAMES M. BREWER,
SENATE MAIL CARRIER.

Mr. Brewer was born at Bloomington, Illinois, April 12th, 1840, his father being a boot-and-shoe dealer, and dying when James was three years old. The latter received a good common school education, and entered the Wesleyan University, but was obliged to leave it before graduating, on account of ill health. He has served as Deputy Sheriff of his county, and was appointed to his present position in 1881, and, again, in 1883. Between sessions he has been a member of the force of State House janitors. He is a very trustworthy and assiduous man, and a sound Republican.

LIST OF PAGES, SENATE.

ELMER R. McDOWELL, President's Page,	Chicago
GIPP M. BREWER,	Springfield
EDWARD S. DAY,	Springfield
ADELBERT FULLER,	Springfield
ARTHUR H. GRACE,	Mound City
WILLIAM L. HONNOLD,	Camp Point
JOHN MARTIN,	Springfield
IVAN L. THOMPSON,	Peoria
HERBERT E. TORRANCE,	Pontiac
ERNEST E. WARREN,	Springfield
JAMES W. GUEST,	Springfield

SENATORS.

HON. GEORGE E. ADAMS.

This scholarly and excellently informed gentleman was born at Keene, New Hampshire, June 18th, 1840, his father being B. F. Adams, a noted manufacturer. His education was acquired at Exeter Academy, in his native State, the celebrated Harvard University, and the Dane Law School, at Cambridge, Massachusetts. He began his career, as a teacher, and followed that occupation until admitted to the bar, when he entered upon the practice of his chosen profession. In 1853, he came to Chicago, where he is now engaged in the practice of his profession—a practice which any other member of the State bar might be excused for envying. In politics, he is a strong, active and zealous Republican, one who advocates the cause of his party because he believes that it is founded upon the basis of pure republicanism in governmental principles, forms and affairs. He is a Unitarian in religion. In 1880, his party honored him by electing him to the State Senate, and, in 1882, he was elected to Congress from the 6th, Chicago district. He was one of the hold-over Senators under the law, and will probably resign his position in the State Legislature, before this sketch is in print, in order to enter upon his duties in Washington. He is said to be a very wealthy man, and is undoubtedly one of the best parliamentarians in the State Senate, if not in the entire Assembly. In person, he is tall and well formed, sedate, yet polite and obliging. He possesses a natural air of dignity, which creates a favorable impression—one in marked contrast with the assumed gravity of some of the members of this Assembly.

HON. HENRY A. AINSWORTH.

This gentleman was born at Williamstown, Vermont, September 28th, 1833. His father was a country merchant, when Henry was born. In 1853, the subject of this sketch came to Illinois, with his parents, who located in Henry County. His education was acquired in the district schools and some of the best academies of his native State. Mr. Ainsworth became a dry goods merchant at Geneseo, and followed that business for ten years, when, in 1870, he removed to Moline, and invested in stock of the Moline Iron Works, of which he is Secretary and Treasurer. In religion, Mr. Ainsworth is a Congregationalist, He is also a Free Mason. In politics, he is a Republican, having linked his fortunes with that party in the days of slavery, and never yet found good cause for changing his political affiliations. He has been a member of the State Board of Equalization for six years, and was elected to the Senate in 1882, by a majority of three thousand six hundred votes. Mr. Ainsworth is so extensively engaged in manufacturing, and has had such valuable experience as a merchant, that he may be looked upon as one of the men who will be a safe authority in legislative circles, upon questions relating to the commercial and manufacturing interests of the State. He will labor for the protection of the people against extravagant appropriations and over-taxation, and his championship will carry with it a great deal of weight and intellectual influence. He is of medium height, a very pleasant old gentleman, decisive in speech and action, and plain in dress and manners. Although a man of business, he is generous in opinion and purse.

HON. WILLIAM R. ARCHER.

This justly distinguished member of the Senate was born in New York City, April 13th, 1817. His father was a Gotham merchant. Mr. Archer was favored with a liberal and substantial education at Flushing, Long Island, and, unlike most young men of city extraction, who are favored with indulgent parents and superior educational advantages, it did not make a fool of him; but, on the contrary, increased his thirst for knowledge, and stimulated him to labor for honorable achievements in the never ending struggle for intellectual excellence and professional supremacy. Mr. Archer came to Illinois in 1838, and located at Pittsfield, Pike County, where he now resides. For three years prior to his emigration, he had been an untiring student of law in the office of the Honorable John L. Lawrence, of New York, and, contrary to the usual rule, was admitted to the bar for superior classical attainments, in three years, instead of four. He was licensed to practice his profession in the courts of Illinois in August, 1838, and soon afterwards in the United States Courts. He was a member of the Constitutional Convention of 1847, was Clerk of the Circuit Court in his county from 1856 to 1860, was a member of the Lower House of the Legislature in 1860–61, a member of the Constitutional Convention of 1870, was elected to the Senate in 1872, re-elected in 1876, and again in 1880. In 1877 he was made Chairman of a Committee or Commission on Damage to Overflowed Lands, and filed a report on November tenth, in which the Assembly concurred. Mr. Archer is an Episcopalian in religion, and an unswerving Democrat. He is one of the strongest men in the Assembly, and his words are generally heeded by his party friends. He is a very genial and agreeable gentleman, polite and affable to all. He is of medium stature, hearty, portly and full of vitality.

HON. ANDREW J. BELL.

Mr. Bell was born in Madison County, Ohio, May 25th, 1843· His father was a merchant, and his mother, formerly Mary Wright, was one of those good women who believe that a son, who begins life with proper impressions regarding the virtues and vices of society, will ever be found upon the roll of honor and integrity. Being left a widow when Andrew was quite young, Mrs. Bell spared no endeavor to rear him with proper views as to his duty toward mankind, and his privileges in well regulated society. Mrs. Bell and her family came to Illinois in 1844, locating in Marshall County. When twenty-two years of age, Andrew removed to Lacon, where he remained eight years, when he went to Peoria, where he now resides. His education commenced in the common schools of the various localities in which his youthful days were passed, was much improved by a course of study in Lombard University, Galesburg, Illinois, and he is finishing and polishing his mental acquirements in the stern school of experience. He read law with Richmond & Burns, and was admitted to the bar in 1866. He held the position of Deputy Collector of Internal Revenue during Andrew Johnson's administration, was City Attorney of the city of Lacon for three years, and was elected to the State Senate in 1880. He served as a Private of the Eleventh Illinois Infantry from 1862 to 1865. He holds no membership in the church, but is an enthusiastic Odd Fellow and a member of the Grand Army of the Republic. He is a pronounced Democrat and was elected over Harlan P. Tracy, a popular and wealthy gentleman, by a small majority. It is said that he is one of the strong men of his district. He is large and well proportioned in person, and kind, genial and gentlemanly in bearing. He is an admirable specimen of manly symmetry, and an influential and able speaker.

HON. AUGUST WERNER BERGGREN.

This prominent Senator was born in Sweden, August 17th, 1840. His parents were John and Catherine Berggren, his mother's maiden name being Larsan. The father, with six sons and one daughter, came to Knox County, Illinois, in 1856. His mother died in 1845. August had learned the trade of a tailor in his fatherland, and his first avocation in this country was that of his former choice. In 1869, he was elected Justice of the Peace, and afterward served as Sheriff of Knox County, four terms. He was elected to the Senate of the Thirty-second Assembly, during his last term as Sheriff, and reëlected as his own successor. He is a member of the Methodist Church, a Free Mason and a prominent Odd Fellow, being Past Grand Master of Illinois, in the latter order. He has been very desirous of introducing the order into Sweden; but during his visit to Europe, in 1882, made up his mind that the fraternity in Denmark, only an hour's sail from his fatherland, was in such good hands, that the efforts of Americans were unnecessary. He is President of the Covenant Mutual Benefit Association, of Galesburg, an insurance organization for Odd Fellows and their families. Mr. Berggren has accumulated quite a competency by his careful and assiduous attention to business, and excellent judgment in financial affairs. In person, he is large and portly, genial, yet dignified in disposition, and possesses those excellent qualities of mind and heart, which endear a man to his associates. He is slow and deliberate in speech and convincing in argument.

HON. FRANK M. BRIDGES.

This gentleman was born in Greene County, Illinois, July 27th, 1834, his father being a farmer. At the age of twenty-two years, he left home, going to Missouri, where he remained seven years, when he went to California, afterward visiting Nevada, Mexico and South America, and landing in New York City on his return journey, in 1866, when he returned to the old homestead, of which he is now the proprietor. His education was acquired in the common schools of Illinois, and by a partial course in Shurtliff College, at Alton. When in the far West, he was engaged in mining, but since his return to Illinois, has been pursuing the steadier but equally sure road to fortune which lies in the newly-made furrow. He belongs to no church or secret society. In political belief, he is an uncompromising and full-fledged Democrat, and has never been anything else. He was elected Sheriff and *ex-officio* Collector of Greene County, in 1874. His decision and determination were never more freely displayed than during this official term, when he levied upon a freight train of the Rockford, Rock Island & St. Louis Railway, for unpaid taxes, and chained it to the track at White Hall. He fought the company through the courts, and victoriously asserted the supremacy of the law, throughout his term. In 1878, he was elected to the House of Representatives, and to the Senate in 1882, over Smith, Republican, from the Thirty-seventh District. His majority was 2,300. In person, he is large and portly, light in complexion, fearless and determined, yet generous and kind in disposition. He is a man who will say precisely what he thinks, and says it plainly, whether it pleases his hearers or not. He is a man of considerable magnetism and great force of character.

HON. HORACE S. CLARK.

Senator Clark was born in Geauga County, Ohio, August 12th, 1840. His father, Captain Joseph M. P. Clark, was a farmer, and the earlier experiences of the incipient statesman were, as usual the result of farm life. Mr. Clark was educated in the common schools of his native county, the Western Reserve Seminary, Farmington, Trumbull County, Ohio, and the Iowa State University, at Iowa City. He began a course of legal study under the instruction of Judge William Miller, of Iowa City, but completed it with Smith & Page, at Circleville, Ohio, where he was admitted to the bar. Mr. Clark entered the army as a private in Company "E," Seventy-third Ohio Volunteers, and successively became Sergeant, Second Lieutenant and First Lieutenant. At the battle of Gettysburg he was severely wounded, and afterward commissioned Lieutenant Colonel in a new Ohio regiment; but never mustered into the service as such. In 1865, Mr. Clark came to Illinois, locating at Mattoon, Coles County, where he has since resided. His ability and merits as a lawyer were soon recognized by the people, and he has enjoyed a most profitable and successful practice. In politics, he is a clearly defined and uncompromising Republican, and, as such, has been recognized as a political leader in his district for a long time. He has served one term as Judge of the Circuit Court in his Judicial Circuit, and his official acts were endorsed as having been perfectly satisfactory to his constituents, by his election to the State Senate in 1882. He is a very able man, and occupies the prominent position of one of the recognized party leaders in the body of which he is an honored and honorable member. In person, he is of medium height and light complexion, kind, affable and obliging. He is a man of considerable firmness, and is very ready in wit, and quick to discover a vulnerable point in his opponent's arguments—quite shrewd, in fact.

HON. THOMAS CLOONAN.

Mr. Cloonan was born in Sufferns, New York, in 1851. His parents were Edward and Bridget Cloonan, and, at the time of the birth of our Senator, his father was a common laborer. Mr. Cloonan, himself, has risen from the humbler walks of life, by his own exertions and determined efforts to make himself worthy of the suffrages of his party friends. He emigrated to Illinois in 1855, and was educated in the public schools of Chicago. He has labored as a butcher and brick-maker until recently, when Mayor Harrison, of Chicago, appointed him a bridge-tender. He held that position from 1879 to March 16th, 1882, when he was transferred to the Water Department of the city government, retaining his position until last December, when he resigned to enter upon his duties as a State Senator. Mr. Cloonan is a devout Catholic, and member of the Ancient Order of Hibernians. He was elected to the House of Representatives from his district in 1880, and, in 1882, advanced to the honorable position of Senator by a plurality of 1,803 votes over three competitors for the office. In person, Mr. Cloonan is tall and well proportioned. He is what might truthfully be termed, a gigantic man. He is florid in complexion, broad shouldered, and manly. In temperament, he is a typical Irishman, full of vivacity, reckless of danger, and resolute in opinion. He possesses a fund of the characteristic mother wit of his race, which renders him a genial and agreeable companion, and a favorite among the laboring classes, which gave him the high office he now occupies. He is a fair sample of the self-made heroes of which our country is so prolific. It is scarcely necessary to add that he is an uncompromising Democrat.

HON. JOHN H. CLOUGH.

Mr. Clough was born in Maine, August 6th, 1830, his father being a farmer. When John was but nine years of age, the family removed to Farmington, in the same State, where it remained but one year, finally locating at Mt. Vernon, where he worked at farming until he attained his majority, attending school for a few weeks during each of two years at the Academy in Readfield. He taught winter schools for several years, also, but, in 1855, he came to Chicago, where he has since resided. He engaged in the produce trade and is yet an extensive dealer in provisions. In religious belief, he is a Congregationalist, but does not hold membership in any of the secret orders. He is a Republican in politics, and believes that his party advocates correct theories in relation to the affairs of a Republican form of government, as implicitly as one could adhere to any faith. He was one of the County Commissioners of Cook County from 1872 to 1875, serving in that capacity to the satisfaction of his people and his own honor. He was elected to the State Senate in 1882, by a very large vote, and is rapidly proving that he is a proper man in the appropriate place. He is a man of pleasing address and firm principles. He is an earnest advocate of party men and measures, and is respected and esteemed by his associates and constituents.

HON. LEANDER D. CONDEE.

Mr. Condee was born in Athens County, Ohio, September 26th, 1847, his father being a farmer by occupation, at that date. In 1854, the family came to Illinois, and settled in Coles County, whence Mr. Condee removed to Butler, Missouri, where he remained until 1868, then went to Kankakee, and afterward to Cook County, in 1874. His education is academic, except in professional matters, in which instance he is a graduate of the Law Department of the Michigan University. He also read law with Judge M. B. Loomiss, of Kankakee, being admitted about three months before he attained his majority. He is not a member, but attends services at an Episcopal Church. · He is both a Free Mason and Odd Fellow, and has attained high honors in both orders. In politics, he is a safe and constant-minded Republican, having espoused the principles of that organization long before he was able to emphasize his sentiments by casting a ballot. He has been Village Attorney at Hyde Park, Cook County, four terms. In 1880, he was elected to the State Senate, by a majority of about 4,600 votes, from the Second Chicago District, running ahead of the entire ticket. This is his Illinois record, and he has another, at Butler, Bates County, Missouri, where he resided from 1868 to 1873, equally as bright and promising, professionally and politically. In person, he is of average stature and dark complexion, his hair being quite gray, but his moustache as dark as ever. He is very kind, obliging and generous in disposition, and is respected and admired by his numerous friends.

HON. JAMES W. DUNCAN.

This gentleman was born in LaSalle County, Illinois, January 18th, 1849, his father being, at that time, a contractor and builder. He was educated at the school of Our Lady of Angels, Niagara Falls, New York. Mr. Duncan read law with E. F. Ball, attorney at LaSalle, Illinois, was admitted to the bar in April, 1871, and at once began practicing his profession in that city, where he remained until 1882, when he removed to Ottawa, where he now resides. Mr. Duncan has won an enviable reputation in his profession, and stands high in the LaSalle County bar. He is a Catholic in religion and does not belong to any secret society. In politics, he has been a Democrat from time, to him immemorial, and is more and more confirmed in the faith, as the years of extravagance in public affairs roll on. He has held many positions of a public nature during his professional career, among which may be mentioned City Clerk of LaSalle, two years; City Attorney, one year, and Mayor, five years. He was elected to the State Senate over Hart, Republican, in 1882, from the Twenty-third District, by a rousing majority, and this is considered a Republican District, too. He is President of the Union Coal Company, of Peru and LaSalle, and, also of the Twin City Gas Works. He is a large shareholder in the City National Bank, of LaSalle, and the Peru City Plow Works. As the reader will infer from these statements, he is a very wealthy gentleman and he is fully as generous and noble-minded as he is wealthy. He is a man of very fine physical proportions, although a little inclined to portliness, dark in complexion and hearty, genial, jovial and kind in his intercourse with the public. It is very safe to say that most of his acquaintances are his friends.

HON. JOHN C. EDWARDS.

This comparatively young gentleman, was born in Blount County, Tennessee, January 11th, 1849, his father being then engaged in farming. The family removed to Illinois in the following year, locating at McLeansboro, Hamilton County, where Mr. Edwards now resides. His education was acquired in the common schools of Illinois, and at McKendree College, of which he is a graduate. He read law with the Hon. John W. McElvain, of his city, and was, in due time, admitted to the bar. He is a Methodist in religious faith, and belongs to the order of Knights of Pythias. In politics, he is a Democrat, of life-long standing, and, as such, was appointed Master-in-Chancery of his county in 1874, elected Prosecuting Attorney in 1876, was Village Attorney in 1879 and 1880, and elected to the State Senate in the latter year. In 1882, he was reëlected, over Leslie Durley, by a majority of two thousand five hundred votes, from the Forty-sixth District. Mr. Edwards is a comparatively young member of the Senate, especially, when we consider the fact that he is now serving his second term as such; but he has made a good officer at both sessions, and his constituency would commit no error in returning him at the next election. He is a very honest, able and progressive young man, whose influence and power of conviction in debate cannot be disregarded by his associates. In person, he is tall, and dark in complexion. He is uniformly kind, affable and polite, and is well liked by all his intimate acquaintances.

HON. HENRY H. EVANS.

The subject of this sketch was born in Canada, March 9th, 1836, his father being at that time a millwright. His family came to the United States in 1840, locating at Aurora, Kane County, Illinois. The family is of Welsh extraction. Mr. Evans' education was acquired in the common schools of Illinois. He is engaged in dealing and speculating in real estate, and conducts other affairs of a like character. In 1862 Mr. Evans enlisted in the One Hundred and Twenty-fourth Regiment of Illinois Volunteers, as a private, and was mustered out of the service in the same capacity, at the close of the war. He does not belong to any church; but is a member of the Grand Army of the Republic. In political belief and practice, he is a Republican of life-standing and deep-seated convictions. Feeling, as he does, that his party organization is based upon principles, which lie at the very foundation of free government, he has never hesitated, in speech or vote, to give it his unqualified support. In 1876, he was elected to the House of Representatives, and promoted to the State Senate in 1880. He was reëlected to the latter honored station in 1882, by a majority of over 4,500 votes, from the Fourteenth Senatorial District. In person, he is tall and well proportioned, and has dark-brown hair and beard. In dress, he is very careful and neat—almost stylish, in fact. In disposition, he is jovial, witty, polite, obliging and generous, and his circle of friends is very large. He is a very careful, intelligent and apt legislator, and does honor to his official station.

HON. JOSEPH W. FIFER.

He was born in the Old Dominion, Staunton, Virginia, is the first town to which memory carries his recollections of men and things, and he cannot re-call anything which occurred prior to October 28th, 1842. His father was a contractor and builder in those days. The family emigrated to McLean County, Illinois, in 1857. Mr. Fifer enjoyed very excellent educational advantages, and, judging from the outpouring of his well stored mind, must have improved them as few young men do. He was graduated from the Illinois Wesleyan College with the Class of 1868. He had been pursuing his legal studies in the office of Bloomfield & Prime, in Bloomington, meantime, and was admitted to the bar soon after his matriculation. In August, 1861, Mr. Fifer enlisted as a private in Company "C," of the Thirty-third Illinois Regiment of Volunteers, serving until October, 1864. He was wounded by a shot through the right lung at Jackson, Mississippi. He is not a communicant of any church, but is a member of the Order of Knights of Pythias, of full rank and in good standing. He is a Republican, having espoused the principles of that party when he became a voter, and adhered to them ever since. He has served two terms as Prosecuting Attorney of his county, and was elected to the State Senate in 1880, by a very large majority. In person, Mr. Fifer is of medium height and dark complexion. He is a very fine lawyer, a strong debater, and a good conversationalist. He is dignified in bearing, and firm and aggressive, though generous and polite in disposition and deportment.

HON. JOHN FLETCHER.

Mr. Fletcher was born in Scotland, in August, 1831, his father being a house-carpenter. Ten years later, the family came to the United States, locating in Hancock County, Illinois. When asked the manner in which he acquired his education, he tersely answered, "I have none;" but we are very well satisfied that he is not so unfortunately situated, as his words imply. If he never enjoyed the privileges of good schools, he must have applied himself with unusual assiduity and perseverance; for he is certainly a very well informed man, possessed of exceedingly sound powers of reasoning, and a very excellent ability to form correct judgment at short notice. By occupation, Mr. Fletcher is a farmer, owning no less than three hundred acres of very fine farming lands, upon which he has numerous herds of well-bred swine. He is not a member of any church organization; but belongs to the Masonic Order. In politics, he is an enthusiastic and confirmed Republican, never having seen a tangible reason for being anything else. He has held minor offices in his city and county; but was never honored with one of very great prominence until elected to the State Senate from the Twenty-fourth District, in 1880,—a Democratic district. He is an honest farmer, who can brook no measure, which seems like a swindle on the people, no matter how cautiously it may be worded, or how plausible it may appear, as presented by its advocates. In person, he is plain, of medium height, and dark in complexion. He possesses a hearty good nature, is agreeable in conversation, and enjoys a joke very much.

HON. DANIEL B. GILLHAM.

When Mr. Gillham was born, there was no unusual disturbance
of the elements, or other phenomena as an omen of his coming.
Like all other men, who have been raised to positions of prominence and responsibility, he quietly began life in the usual way.
He was born at Wanda, Madison County, Illinois, April 29th,
1826, his father being a farmer and itinerant minister of the
Gospel. Mr. Gillham's education was begun in the common
schools of his county, prosecuted and further pursued in the
celebrated McKendree College, and will be completed when he
has become too old to learn. He is one of those progressive
agriculturalists and stock-raisers who take advantage of any
knowledge which is likely to assist them in intelligently pursuing
their most honorable occupation. He is a member of the State
Board of Agriculture at present, and has been President of that
body. He has been President of the Board of Trustees of
Shurtliff College for ten years. He is a Baptist in religious
faith, but does not belong to any of the secret orders. In
politics, he is a pronounced and uncompromising Democrat, and,
as such, was a member of the Lower House of the Twenty-
seventh General Assembly. He was elected to the State Senate
in 1882, over Brigeman, by a majority of three hundred and
fifty votes. He is rather short in stature and dark in complexion.
He is shrewd and witty, an entertaining conversationalist and
forcible debater. He is polite and generous in natural impulse,
and a man whom it is not difficult to like.

HON. LLOYD F. HAMILTON.

This gentleman, the Senator from the Capital District, was born in Meade County, Kentucky, April 25th, 1844, his father being, like most fathers of celebrated men, a farmer. The subject of our sketch came to Illinois in 1850, first locating in Tazewell County, but afterward removing to Springfield, where he now resides. His literary education was acquired at Eureka College, Woodford County, Illinois, his professional qualifications were the result of a course of law study under the instruction of Judge Scholfield, of the Supreme Court, and graduation from the law school at Ann Arbor, Michigan, and the Union College of Law, Chicago. He has served as State's Attorney of Sangamon County for four years, City Attorney of Springfield one year, and is one of the very best criminal lawyers in the State of Illinois. He has few equals and fewer superiors in this branch of his profession. He is a member of the Ancient Order of United Workmen, but does not commune with any church organization. In politics, he is thoroughly and indubitably Democratic, from core to circumference, being a candidate for presidential elector in 1880, and was elected to the State Senate, in 1882, by a majority of one thousand five hundred and sixty-five votes, over Dr. Jayne, his party opponent. In person, he is tall, gruff and dignified. He possesses many of those social qualities, however, which endear mankind to their fellow men, and has a firm hold upon popular favor. He is kind-hearted and generous to a fault, and is a powerful advocate of any measure which he chooses to endorse.

HON. MILLARD B. HERELY.

Senator Herely first opened his wondering eyes, in the State of New York, in the year 1857, and is, therefore, the most youthful member of the State Senate of Illinois, at this session. The family came to Illinois in 1863, locating in McHenry County, where the subject of our sketch remained until 1875, when he made a bee-line for Chicago, where he established hinself in commercial business. His literary education was acquired in the common schools of McHenry County, and, for purposes of personal interest and commercial information, he pursued a course of legal study in the Union College of Law, at Chicago. In religious faith, Mr. Herely is a Roman Catholic, but he does not affiliate with any of the secret orders. Politically, he is an uncompromising and unwavering Democrat, born, bred, educated and convinced. He has never for a single moment cherished the idea of forsaking the political organization which maintains that the people should be free in speech and religious belief, and that the government at Washington has no greater power than that expressly given it by the Constitution of the United States. He now occupies his first public office, having defeated Peter Kilbasse, his political opponent, by one thousand five hundred and eighty-one votes, for the State Senate in the Thirteenth District of Cook County. In person, Mr. Herely is of medium height and fair complexion. He is rather witty and apt in speech, possessing the genuine faculty of the Irish people for making tart replies to questions, or bandied words. He is very genial, kind and pleasant in disposition.

HON. DANIEL HOGAN.

Mr. Hogan is a noble son of Erin, who was born July 4th, 1849. His father cultivated the native heath for his daily bread and that of his family, and, being desirous of better opportunities, came to the United States with his family in 1852, locating in Pulaski County, Illinois, where Daniel now resides. Mr. Hogan's education was obtained in the public schools of Illinois, and the celebrated Bryant & Stratton Business College. Although he has been engaged, much of his time, as a telegraph operator and clerk, he has devoted a large amount of attention to farming, owning no less than three thousand acres of valuable lands. He also has an interest in a hotel in Mound City. He was a telegrapher and cipher-clerk in the army, during the rebellion. Mr. Hogan belongs to no church or secret order. He is a Republican, soul and body, from sole to crown, and has served as Sheriff of his county, two years County Clerk, nine years, and was elected to the Senate in 1882, over Youngblood, Democrat, by a majority of eight hundred and fifty-five votes. He has traveled over the greater part of the United States, in connection with various kinds of business, and has learned many valuable lessons from observation and experience. He has a family of three children, whom he keeps in the Capital during the session. This stamps him as a man of excellent qualities, with a heart, generous and noble in its impulses. Mr. Hogan has acquired his entire fortune by his own exertions, although he was penniless, when his independent career began. He is a first-class financier, and a good debater, and will impress the legislation of the sessions with the stamp of his handiwork.

HON. GEORGE HUNT.

Senator Hunt was born in Knox County, Ohio, in 1841, he came to Illinois, settling near Paris, in Edgar County. His education was acquired in the common schools and academies of Illinois, and has been very much improved by his diligent habits of study and observation. It is an education which is more practical and useful, than ornamental—one well calculated to serve him in the affairs incident to a public career. In July, 1861, he enilsted in the Twelfth Illinois Infantry, as a private, being mustered out of the service four years later, as Captain. He read law with practicing attorneys at Paris, and was admitted to the bar in 1869, since which time he has been engaged in business pertaining to his profession, and the public affairs of his county and district. He has been County Superintendent of Public Instruction, four years, and is serving his ninth year in the State Senate, having been elected to both of these offices as a Republican. He never held but one political faith, and has been as constant and faithful to the party whose cause he advocates, as a milk-maid to her best beau. In person, Mr. Hunt is quite a small man, quick, nervous and energetic in movement, and sharp and incisive in debate. He is very kind and polite in his intercourse with the public, and plain in dress. He is one of those little men whom God saw fit to create principally of heart and brain.

HON. LOUIS IHORN.

This gentleman was born in Saxe-Coburg, Germany, the Province in which the husband of Queen Victoria first looked upon the beauties of the world, January 31st, 1826. His father was then engaged in farming. In 1837, the family came to the United States, locating in St. Clair County, Illinois; but removing to Monroe County, ten years later. His education was acquired in the common schools of his native country, and he has obtained a very excellent knowledge of the English language, since coming to this country, by personal observation and persistent practice. Mr. Ihorn is engaged in various branches of business and trade, among which may be mentioned general merchandise, lumber trade and farming. He is an astute trader and successful financier. He does not affiliate with any of the secret orders, but is a member of the German Lutheran Church. In politics, he has been a Republican ever since he has been anything, and has, as yet, discovered no good cause for transferring his affections from his first love. He has been School Treasurer of his township for several terms, and was elected to the State Senate in 1880, defeating John T. McBride, of Randolph County, by seventy-two votes, in a Democratic district. His farm consists of five hundred acres of land, and, although he does not desire to boast of his wealth, and refused to particularize concerning it, when asked to do so, it is quite certain that he is a man of more than ordinary means. In person, he is short and heavy—a typical German, in fact. He is placid in temper, kind and obliging disposition, and jolly, social and generous in natural impulse. He is a man who does not hesitate to say just what he thinks, upon all proper occasions, and, while he says everything in a very pleasant way, it often cuts his opponent to the very core.

HON. MAURICE KELLY.

Mr. Kelly was born in the Emerald Isle, in March, 1830, his father then being engaged in farming. Not enjoying the form of government and circumscribed privileges incident to life in Erin, the family came to the United States in 1837, locating in Adams County, Illinois. Mr. Kelly's education was acquired in the common schools of Illinois, and by varied public experiences, since he has attained the age of mature manhood. He followed the choice of his father in selecting an occupation, becoming an honest farmer when he became a man. Owing to his energetic and observant habits, he soon arose in popular favor, and has held numerous positions of honor and trust in his county and district. He does not affiliate with any of the secret orders. He is and has ever been a Democrat in principle and practice, and the older he becomes the more firmly he is grounded in political faith. He has been Sheriff of Adams County for two years, and Supervisor for eight years, was a member of the Lower House of the Twenty-seventh General Assembly, and is now serving his third term as State Senator. He was elected over Joseph N. Carter by a majority of about six hundred votes. He owns a farm of three hundred and twenty acres, and devotes considerable time to the breeding of Cotswold sheep and Poland-China pigs. He is very proud of his fine stock, and, from information secured from other sources, we feel convinced that his pride is just and has its foundation in fact. In person, he is tall and dark in complexion. He is very decisive and eloquent in debate, and a shrewd legislator and kind, generous and obliging gentleman.

HON. GEORGE KIRK.

Mr. Kirk was born at Cairo, Greene County, New York, February 9th, 1824. He came to Illinois, May 21st, 1843, locating at Chicago, but in 1847, he removed to Waukegan, Lake County, where he now resides. His education has been acquired partially in the Dutchess County Academy, of New York State, and partly by a miscellaneous course of general and scientific reading. He was a foundryman and machinist by trade, being one of the early mechanics of Chicago, but he sold out that "plant" twenty-five years ago, and is now conducting an extensive lumber trade. He does not belong to any church denomination or benevolent or secret society. He has been a Republican in politics ever since the party came into existence, and he is proud of its record and determined to adhere to its cause, until some better reason for forsaking it than any which has ever yet been charged against it shall appear, and, even then, he would give it up as a child would leave the parental roof—with sorrow and regret. He has the utmost confidence that such an exigency will never arise, however. He was for ten years a member of the Committee on Public Buildings in the City Council of Waukegan; has been Chairman of the Board of Supervisors of his county, and, in 1882, was elected to the State Senate from the Eighth District, by a majority of seven hundred votes over the Honorable Merritt Joslyn. In person, Mr. Kirk is large and portly, dark in complexion and determined in position and spirit. He is averse to any effort at self-advertising, and so anxious was he to avoid being noticed in this work, that the facts upon which this sketch is based were ascertained with great difficulty, and partially from sources other than himself. He is very gentlemanly in appearance, and is a shrewd legislator and a noble and generous man.

HON. EDWARD LANING.

This gentleman was born in Clark County, Ohio, in December, 1837. His father was a merchant. The family came to Illinois during the following year, locating at Petersburg, Menard County, where Mr. Laning now resides. His parents are both now living, his father being eighty-four years of age. Mr. Laning's educational course consisted of a classical career of one year at the Wesleyan University, Bloomington, Illinois, and three years in Lombard University, Galesburg, Illinois, of which he is a graduate. He read law without any instructor, except his books, and was admitted to the bar in 1861. He has been engaged in an extensive and successful practice ever since. Mr. Laning is a Free Mason of the Degree of Knight Templar. In politics, he has always been a Democrat, and he is no less one to-day than he was years ago. His convictions are the force that controls his actions, and he is convinced that the principles of the Democracy are sufficiently numerous and powerful to commend them to the people. He was Superintendent of Schools of his county from 1864 to 1866, and was elected to the House of Representatives in 1868. In 1870, he was elected to the State Senate, and in 1880, he was reëlected to his present position, and, without questioning the propriety of the statement, we are informed that his legislative career has been an able and bright one. In person, he is a man of medium height; dignified, yet obliging in bearing and disposition, and a just and generous gentleman in his intercourse with the people. He is a man who wins friends without an effort to do so. He has traveled considerable in the Southern States.

HON. WILLIAM A. LEMMA.

This gentleman was born at Shawneetown, Illinois, in December, 1839, his father and mother being of Irish extraction. His education was acquired in the common schools of Illinois, and by diligent study of such valuable books as he was able to secure. He removed to Texas when quite young, remaining there four years, when he returned to Illinois, and located at Carbondale, Jackson County, where he read law with Judge Allen. He does not belong to any church or secret society. In politics, he has never espoused the cause of any party but the Democratic, of which he has been a consistent and unwavering member throughout his political career. His first public position was that of City Judge of Carbondale, an office which he held four years. He was elected to the House of Representatives in 1870, and re-elected in 1872. He was then chosen Mayor of his city, being re-elected to the office at the expiration of his first term. In 1876, he was made Prosecuting Attorney of Jackson County, and, in 1880, was made Senator from the Fiftieth District, over Joseph B. Thorpe, whom he defeated by a majority of about twelve hundred votes. Mr. Lemma's political career has been a mere repetition of his first success, inasmuch as he has scarcely been out of office since he entered the political lists in 1870. In personal appearance, he is large in both stature and circumference, dark in complexion, polite, affable and accommodating—in fact, a perfect gentleman. His political career has been untarnished by any species of jobbery or truckling. Not even a suspicion of his strict integrity and sterling worth has ever been whispered.

HON. WILLIAM H. McNARY.

This noble son of an industrious and patriotic ancestor, was born on a farm in Mason County, Kentucky, July 14th, 1821. His father was a soldier in the memorable War of 1812, and recollected when the Independence of the United States of America was promulgated. In 1826, the family removed to Greencastle County, Indiana, whence it came to Clark County, Illinois, in 1840. Mr. McNary's education was acquired in the public schools, and Asbury University, at his Indiana home. By profession Mr. McNary is a physician, of thirty-five years' experience, having read medicine with his brother, Samuel T., at Melrose, Illinois. In 1847, he joined the tide of humanity, which was pouring into the newly discovered gold-fields of California, and, after an eventful trip of five months across the plains, which were then peopled with Indians, and infested by wild beasts, reached his destination, where he remained through the exciting days between forty-nine and fifty-three. He is a prominent member of the American Medical Association, and the Æsculapian Society, both of which are professional bodies. He volunteered in 1847, going to the Mexican frontier; but, before reaching the front, the regiment was discharged and its members returned to their respective homes. Mr. McNary is a believer in the existence of God, but does not affiliate with any church or secret society. He is very wealthy, owning six excellent farms of Clark County land, aggregating about seventeen hundred acres. He is an unswerving and unterrified Democrat, and has always been one. He was elected to the Senate from the 45th District, in 1882, by a majority of 500 votes. He is one of the cool-headed, warm-hearted and wise old fellows, to whom the people may safely entrust their most vital interests, without fear or doubt.

HON. CHRISTOPHER MAMER.

Mr. Mamer was born September 10th, 1851, at Luxembourg, Germany. His father was a German watchmaker and jeweler, who was forty-eight years of age when Christopher came into the world. The family came to Chicago in 1852, and the subject of our sketch was placed in the College of St. Mary's of the Lake, at the proper age, for mental training. He was a very energetic student and made rapid progress, and is now a very finely educated young man. He engaged himself as an apprentice at the jewelry trade when seventeen years old, and, at twenty, began business for himself. He is not a member of any church or secret society, and has never held any public office prior to his election to the Senate in 1882. He has been a Republican ever since he became a voter, and knows of no good reason why he should be anything else, now or hereafter. Mr. Mamer has begun at the foot of the ladder and is rising to its summit with considerable rapidity. The people of the Fourth District made no mistake in sending him to the Legislature, and he will endeavor to serve them as he should, by voting for such measures, only, as they are likely to approve, and raising his voice in behalf of right and justice, on all proper occasions, which demand that his constituents should have a hearing. His majority over his opponent, Rogers, was over twelve hundred votes. In person, he is not above the average American stature, dark complexion, polite, affable and witty in conversation, and powerful, acute and incisive in debate. He is a man of generous nature and very estimable qualities.

HON. WILLIAM ERNEST MASON.

This gentleman was born at Franklinville, New York, July 7th, 1850, his father being a merchant at the time of this event. In 1857, the family removed to Bentonsport, Iowa, remaining for a short time and finally locating at Des Moines, in the same State. In 1871, Mr. Mason established himself in Chicago, where he has since been engaged in practicing his profession as a lawyer. His education is solely the result of attendance at common schools, and individual exertion. He acquired his professional knowledge by a course of reading under the instruction of practicing attorneys, for a period of no less than five years. He was admitted to the bar in 1870. Mr. Mason now is, and has been for the last four years, a member of the firm of Wallace, Mason & Medbury, Chicago. The combination of legal talent and energy is a very strong one, and the firm enjoys a lucrative and constantly increasing clientage. The subject of our sketch is not a member of any church, but is a Mason of the Knight Templar Degree, an Odd Fellow, and member of the Ancient Order of United Workmen. In politics, he is a faithful and earnest Republican, having entered his political career as such, and knowing of no reason sufficient to demand a change in his political affiliation. He is a man of recognized Legislative ability, and was a member of the Lower House of the Thirty-first General Assembly from the Fifth Chicago District. He now represents the Ninth District in the State Senate, although the Democrats carried the rest of the ticket by a large majority. His opponent in the canvass was Peter J. Thornum, who was defeated by over five hundred votes. In person, he is of medium height, dark in complexion, and a little inclined to portliness. He moves about with considerable agility, however, and enjoys a good joke as well as any Senator in this Assembly. He is very agreeable, kind and friendly in disposition, and enjoys the friendship of a great many people.

HON. THOMAS E. MERRITT.

Who has not heard of "Tom" Merritt, whose powerful voice and ready wit have chained the attention or tickled the fancy of the people of Illinois, for the last ten years? Of all of the members of the Thirty-third General Assembly, Mr. Merritt is, perhaps, most widely known and generally celebrated. He was born in New York, removing with his parents to St. Clair County, Illinois, in 1840. At fifteen years of age, the subject of this sketch went to St. Louis, Missouri, where he learned the trade of a carriage painter, which he followed seven years. His education was acquired in the common schools of the State, and, although his advantages were not great, "Tom" Merritt secured enough of the wares, in which they dealt, to give him a consuming ambition to acquire more. He studied men and events with his books, and, when he began reading law, in 1858, he was already well learned in the politics of his country. He was admitted to the bar in 1862, locating in Salem, Marion County, where he yet resides and practices his profession. He has been interested in most of the *causus celebre* of his section of the State, and is renowned for the earnestness and force, with which he pursues his cause. He is not a member of any church or secret order, but if you want to find a downright, upright, horizontal and incandescent Democrat, you need not pass him by. He, perhaps, holds greater political power in his district, and has held it for a longer time than any of the remaining members of either house. He was a Representative, prior to 1880, for no less than five consecutive terms, and, at that date was elected to the Senate, and re-elected by an overwhelming majority in 1882. He is as fearless as a lion and as persistent as a beaver. He is an accomplished politician, and, in the heat of debate, the slight impediment in his speech vanishes, and he deals with hard facts and amusing incidents in a manner unparalleled in the Senate Chamber, prior to his accession.

HON. WILLIAM S. MORRIS.

Mr. Morris is a native Illinoisan, having been born to O. B. Morris and Louisa, his wife, *nee* Enbanks, December 4th, 1842, on their farm in Gallatin County. He has never resided in any other State, and is content to live and die in the agricultural garden of the United States. His education was obtained in the common schools of his county, under almost insurmountable disadvantages, but, by close application and diligent effort, he has succeeded in qualifying himself for a successful career as a lawyer and Legislator. He studied law in a school conducted by Judge Duff, whose name is familiar to all of the older members of the bar in this State. He began his political career as a Justice of the Peace in Franklin County, in 1866, was States' Attorney of Hardin County from 1872 until 1876, and was a member of the House of Representatives in the Thirtieth and Thirtieth-second General Assemblies. Mr. Morris enlisted in the Thirty-first Regiment of Illinois Volunteers, in 1861, as a private, and, at the close of the war, was mustered out of the service as First Lieutenant. He was elected Senator in the Thirty-third General Assembly of his State, as a Republican, having adhered to that faith since his majority. He tersely declares, "I was never anything else." Although he is of Dutch descent in one line, and Welsh in another, he is thoroughly Americanized, and is a fair sample of the man which comes from a native "Sucker Boy," when he is born with intelligence, and taught perseverence by his early experience as a farmer. In stature, he is not above medium, has a light complexion and sandy hair. He is a good talker and earnest reasoner. His manners is that of a man, who knows his strength and is not afraid to try his mettle with the best. He is a Methodist in religious belief, and an ardent Odd Fellow.

HON. THOMAS B. NEEDLES.

This very well known gentleman was born in Monroe County, Illinois, ————. His father, James B. Needles, was a merchant when Thomas was born. He was born in Maryland and came to Illinois in 1830. He was a soldier in the Blackhawk War, and afterward served as Sheriff of Monroe County, six years. He was prominently known in Southern Illinois in the early days of that region, and identified with many of the public measures of Monroe, Madison and St. Clair Counties. Thomas B. has always lived in Illinois, with the exception of two years, which were passed at school in Keokuk, Iowa. With the exception of an academic course of the time and at the place mentioned, his education was acquired in the common schools of Illinois. His present place of residence is Nashville, Washington County. In politics, he is an active and prominent Republican. He was elected County Clerk of Washington County four consecutive terms, making sixteen years of service in that one office. He has been a member of the Republican Central Committee of the State for four years, and was elected State Auditor in 1876, serving four years. In 1880, he was elected to the State Senate from the Forty-second District. He is a Free Mason and a very prominent Odd Fellow. He was elected Grand Master of the latter order in 1870, and has served as one of the Representatives of the order in Illinois, to the Sovereign Grand Lodge, four years. He is above medium height, well proportioned and dark complected, grave in demeanor and dignified in bearing, but quite sociable and obliging in manner and disposition.

HON. LYMAN B. RAY.

Mr. Ray was born in Vermont, in August, 1831, his father then being engaged in the most honorable of all occupations—producing food for those who neither toil or spin. Mr. Ray's education was acquired in the public schools and academies of his native State, and, as he improved his opportunities, he possesses a mind well stored with valuable information. In 1852, he came to Illinois, locating at St. Charles, where he remained until 1854, when he removed to Morris, Grundy County, which he has since made his home. He is engaged in dry goods merchandising. His knowledge of commercial affairs is extensive and valuable, and he can and will illuminate the questions pertaining to such affairs, which may arise during his official incumbency. He affiliates with no secret order, but attends Congregational Church. In political matters, he became a Republican, when he became a voter, and has never wavered in his devotion to the principles of his party from that day to this. The party has, in return for his fidelity, honored him with various offices of honor and trust. In 1872, he was elected to the General Assembly, and was chosen State Senator in 1882, from the Seventeenth District, by a majority of about three thousand votes, over J. S. R. Sevirlle, his political opponent. He is descended from American ancestors. In person, he is of average stature, rather large, dark complected, and tidy in dress. He is polite, affable and generous in disposition and enjoys a pointed joke very much. He is inclined to be witty and sharp in speech, at times, as some of his associates know from experience.

HON. ISAAC RICE.

Hon. Isaac Rice was born in Washington County, Maryland, October 28, 1826. His father, Jacob Rice, was a farmer, who removed to Ogle County in 1837. Mr. Rice was educated in the public schools and Rock River Seminary, of Mt. Morris, Illinois, the school in which Shelby M. Cullom, United States Senator, received his intellectual training. He is also a graduate of Rush Medical College, of Chicago, but has never practiced medicine. He is a member of the Methodist Episcopal Church; but does not affiliate with any secret society. Mr. Rice is essentially a self-made man. He began farming in order to secure the means with which to obtain a medical library, and so liked the independent occupation of an agriculturalist, that he never forsook it. He is a total abstinence man in his habits, using neither weed or wine. He is a Republican of life standing, having espoused the cause of that party at its birth, and been an abolitionist before that, and has been twice elected to the House of Representatives, first in 1872, and again in 1874. In 1880 he was chosen to represent the Twelfth District in the State Senate. He has been a careful, temperate and prudent man all his life, and by his industry has acquired an ample competence. He is a very large and portly old gentleman, whose white locks contrast strongly with his vigorous physique and rudy complexion. He is kind, gentle and pleasant in his deportment and conversation, and enjoys a good joke as well as the next man. He says that a practice of these habits very much aids one in becoming immortal. He is a strong man in the Senate, and has the good will of his associates.

HON. ERASTUS N. RINEHART.

This gentleman was born in Effingham County, Illinois, February 29th, 1848, his father being a farmer and country merchant. Mr. Rinehart's education was acquired in the common schools of his county, and McKendree College, at Lebauon, Illinois. His professional education was acquired by a regular course of study in the office of Cooper and Kagay, a firm of practicing attorneys of Effingham, and in due time was admitted to the bar, and has been engaged in a successful and profitable practice ever since. He does not affiliate with any church organization; but belongs to the Improved Order of Red Men. In politics, he is unquestionably and very positively a Democrat. He has been one from "time whereof his memory runneth not to the contrary," and his convictions of the rectitude and advisability of his political preferences has grown stronger with each year, that has been added to his experience. He was a member of the Thirty-second General Assembly, and was reëlected to the Senate in 1882, by a plurality of about three thousand votes, over W. F. Leonard and Newton Gwinn. In addition to his legal business, Mr. Rinehart owns a well-stocked and nicely equipped drug store, in Effingham, and a farm of some three hundred acres in its immediate vicinity. He is quite comfortably situated, with reference to this world's goods, and takes life, as a man of his ability and surroundings should. In person, he is a large and powerful man, not only in physical proportions, but in mental force and personal magnetism. His hair is quite long and very black, and he is one of those men whose words tell at every motion of the lips. He possesses a faculty of presenting matters as hard facts, and convincing the mind of his audience of the truth, by apt illustrations. From this description, the reader might imagine him cold and indifferent in disposition; but behind all his strong manhood, there lies a heart as tender and sympathetic as that of a woman.

HON. JASON ROGERS.

Mr. Rogers was born in Lawrence County, Indiana, June 16th, 1833, his father, Lewis Rogers, being a farmer. The family removed to Greene County, in the same State, and the subject came to Illinois in 1860, and located at Bement, Piatt County, where he engaged in merchandising. In 1865, he removed to Decatur, where he has since resided. He continued merchandising and also conducted an extensive business in real estate brokerage, by which he has amassed a considerable fortune. At present, he should be classed as a retired merchant and broker, as he does little business, except that of overseeing his farms. He has always been a Republican in politics, and comes of a Methodist family, although he does not belong to any church. He has served as a member of the County Board of Supervisors of his county, two terms, and has held numerous minor offices of public trust. In 1880, he was elected to the House of Representatives, and to the Senate in 1882, defeating S. S. Jack, of the Decatur *Review*, by six hundred and sixty-three votes. Mr. Rogers ran five hundred and forty-nine votes ahead of his ticket, which is a very valuable circumstance by which to form an estimate of his·position among the people of his district. In person, Mr. Rogers is large and portly, his beard, once dark, is now becoming quite gray, and he is one of those whole-souled, genial men, who never lack friends. He is a successful financier, politician and legislator, and justly a popular man among his associates.

HON. WILLIAM H. RUGER.

Mr. Ruger was born at Plattsburg, Clinton County, New York, August 15th, 1841, his father being at that time, a sailor. In 1847, the family came to Illinois, locating in Chicago, where Mr. Ruger now resides. His education was acquired in the public schools of Chicago. In the autumn of 1861, Mr. Ruger enlisted in the United States Navy, serving on the Mississippi Flotilla until March, 1864. He has been a clerk in the Postoffice at Chicago, for sixteen years, and was Assistant Superintendent of Mails at the time of his election to the State Senate, in 1882, resigning the former position at the time of entering upon his duties in the latter. During his naval service, he participated in all of the principal engagements along the rivers, upon which the Flotilla operated, being at the first battle at Fort Henry, among others. He was mustered out of the service as Surgeon's Steward. He belongs to no church or secret society, but has always been a Republican, although elected to his present position as an independent candidate, from the Fifth Cook County District, which is Democratic by a majority of two thousand nine hundred votes. The regular Democratic nominee was defeated by Mr. Ruger by nearly one thousand votes. In person, Mr. Ruger is above medium height, fair in complexion and well proportioned. He is kind and polite in manner and jovial in disposition. He is very popular, and has a very large circle of friends wherever he is known. He is a very pleasant gentleman, who is worthy of his honors.

HON. CONRAD SECREST.

Mr. Secrest was born in North Carolina, May 3d, 1829. At the time of his birth, his father was engaged in farming, and the family moved to Indiana when Mr. Secrest was but three years of age. Conrad, at the age of twenty-one, came to Illinois locating in Iroquois County. The literary education of this gentleman was acquired in the common schools of Illinois, and, incidentally much improved by his professional studies at the Rush Medical College, at Chicago, of which he is a graduate. After a lucrative and successful practice of ten years, he added the duties of a druggist and pharmacist to his medical offices, and followed the combined occupations for some six years, when, to employ his own form of expression, he "became an honest farmer." His farm consists of about five hundred acres of land, and he devotes considerable attention to breeding Shorthorn cattle and Berkshire swine. He does not belong to any church, but is an active and esteemed Odd Fellow. In politics, he is a Republican, having espoused the cause of that party when it came into existence. He has held various offices of honor and trust in his township, was elected to the House of Representatives in 1876, and re-elected in 1878 and 1880, being chosen Senator in 1880, and re-elected over Dr. Spitter, by a majority of two thousand three hundred votes. In person, Dr. Secrest is large and portly, has light hair and a full beard, considerably streaked with gray. He is a gentleman of extended influence in the affairs of the Senate, and is one of those genial, shrewd, affable and generous men, whose acquaintances are generally their warm friends and enthusiastic supporters. He is a man, whose convictions are based upon sound reason, and who will put up with no rings, cliques or log-rolling political methods.

HON. HENRY SEITER.

This gentleman was born in the town of Lebanon, St. Clair County, Illinois, September 22d, 1845. He has never made his place of residence elsewhere. Mr. Seiter's educational advantages were excellent and well improved. In addition to as good public schools as there are elsewhere in Illinois, McKendree College stood almost at his door. He was graduated from the latter popular institution, and, also, from the Michigan State University. Mr. Seiter is a very wealthy and influential gentleman, owning no less than one thousand five hundred acres of very excellent farming lands, being President of the Illinois Live-Stock Company, which is largely interested in New Mexico cattle ranches, and the senior member of the private banking firm of H. Seiter & Company. He is not a communicant in any church; but is a Free Mason and Odd Fellow. He is a Democrat of long standing and confirmed opinions, and was a member of the lower house of the Thirty-first General Assembly. He was elected to the State Senate in 1882, by a small majority, in a very close district—the Bloody Forty-seventh. In person, Mr. Seiter is of the average stature, and is exceedingly neat and tidy in dress. He is polished in manners and affable, kind and generous in the natural promptings of his heart. He is rather inclined to wit, and enjoys a joke as well as any other member, if it be a pointed one. He is a very shrewd financier, and careful servant of the people of his great State. He does honor to the office which he fills, and his constituency can justly point to its Senator with pride.

HON. THOMAS M. SHAW.

Mr. Shaw was born in Marshall County, Illinois, to parents of German extraction, who were winning their food and raiment, and that of their family, by honest labor upon a farm, when their now distinguished son came to gladden their hearts, and urge them to more earnest efforts. Mr. Shaw has resided in the county of his birth, ever since that epoch in his history. His education was acquired in the common schools of Illinois and at Judson College and Rock River Seminary, the latter being the institution from which Senator Shelby M. Cullom was graduated. Mr. Shaw read law with William D. Edwards, of his native county, was admitted to the bar in 1867, and has practiced his profession at Lacon, Marshall County, where he now resides, ever since. He does not belong to any religious denomination or secret order. In politics, he is a firm and unwavering Democrat—one who feels that his party is based upon the true theories of a Republican form of government, and that it is his duty to adhere to it for the good of the country. He now holds the first public office, which he has ever been called to fill, having been elected from the Twentieth District over Cassel, Republican, by a majority of four hundred votes. Mr. Shaw owns a very valuable farm of one hundred and sixty acres. In person, he is large and portly, dark in complexion, but his hair is becoming quite gray. He is genial and kind in disposition, and polite and affable in his intercourse with the people. He is a man whose power is considerable, and friends numerous, in the Assembly.

HON. E. B. SHUMWAY.

This popular member of the Senate, was born at Jamaica, Vermont, June 27th, 1851, his father, Alvava Shumway, and his wife, formerly Miss Harriet N. Barber, then residing on a farm. Mr. Shumway was presumably very much the same kind of a boy that he is a man—one who laughed at the obstructions which lie in the way of aspiring genius, and immediately devised the plans and put forth the efforts necessary to overcome them. His early farm-life added experiences of inestimable value to his natural confidence and determination. His literary education was obtained at West River Academy, Londonderry, Vermont; Black River Academy, Ludlow, Vermont, and Chamberlain Females' Institute and Literary College, Randolph, New York. His professional education is due to individual effort, under the instruction of Dr. W. W. Mayo, of Rochester, Minnesota, and a full course of study in the celebrated Rush Medical College, Chicago, where he was graduated in 1874. After his graduation, he was selected, by competitive examination, as attending physician for the Cook County Hospital, where he remained for one year, when he returned to his original Illinois home, Peotone, Will County, and engaged in the active practice of his profession. He is a Free Mason, being Master of Peotone Lodge, No. 636. He is not a church member. Mr. Shumway is a Democrat, never having changed his political faith since he became a voter. He was a member of the Thirty-second Assembly, and having received the nomination of his party, for the Senate, determined to leave no stone unturned, which might reveal a means or furnish a vote with which to overcome the 2,000 Republican majority in his district. How well he succeeded is attested by his election, by a majority of 1,267 votes. Mr. Shumway is a man of noble physical and mental proportions, and is one of the most energetic and persevering Senators in the Thirty-third Assembly. He is a very able man, who seems to have begun a career of usefulness and honor, which may yet place his name high above his compeers, on the scroll of fame.

HON. W. C. SNYDER.

This gentleman was born in Cumberland County, New Jersey, in July, 1821, his father being a miller by occupation. In 1845, Mr. Snyder went to Lyons, Iowa, where he remained but a short time, removing to Whiteside County, Illinois. Owing to his being required to labor for the support of the family at a very early age, his educational wants were partially overlooked, and he was limited to a very irregular attendance at the public schools. He has supplied a great deal of what was denied him in youth, by extraordinary efforts since he has attained the estate of manhood, however, and enjoys a very excellent knowledge of mankind and its peculiar conditions and wants. He was apprenticed to a merchant, but afterward studied medicine and practiced his profession seven years. He was raised a Quaker in religious belief, and is a Free Mason. He is a Republican in politics, having linked his fortunes with that party, when it came into existence. He has served as Postmaster of the town of Fulton, for twenty-two years, only resigning the office when elected to the State Senate, in 1882. He has been Chairman of the Republican Central Committee of his party, for ten years, and Drainage Commissioner, twelve years. He is engaged in grain-dealing, and as a commission merchant, in connection with the Postmastership, and is largely interested in real estate transactions. Mr. Snyder is not above medium in stature, is, or rather has been dark complected, but is now quite gray, so far as hair and beard are concerned. He is polite and generous, and is a very practical and forcible speaker. He is one of the solid old men of the Senate, and will do his duty under all circumstances.

HON. DAVID H. SUNDERLAND.

This gentleman was born in Anderson County, Vermont, in 1822, and is now sixty years of age. His father was an honest and industrious blacksmith, from the sparks from whose forge and anvil, the youthful David, learned many lessons, which have had their effect in shaping his destiny and forming his character. Until he was past seventeen, the subject of this sketch spent most of his time in assisting his father forge and weld and file and grind, for the necessaries of life; but he afterward pursued his studies in a local academy. He came to Illinois in early manhood, and located at Freeport, where he now resides. He is a member of the First Presbyterian Church, of his city. In the early days of his residence in Stevenson county, he was a school-teacher. He is a Republican. He does not claim to be a politician, but has held several positions of honor and trust, among which may be mentioned, those of Mayor of his city, and Supervisor of his township. In 1880, Superintendent Walker, of the Census Bureau of the United States, appointed him Census Supervisor for the Second Census District. He was a warm advocate of the so-called Sunderland-Hinds bill, in relation to the liquor question, in 1880, and is said to have delivered the most eloquent address ever heard in the Senate Chamber of our State. He was congratulated by friends and foes, and was greeted with a shower of boquets from the ladies, who filled the galleries. He is short in stature, and crowned with a head of snowy white hair, which renders him very patriarchal in personal appearance. He is genial and kind in disposition, and is regarded as one of the most powerful men in the Senate of the Thirty-third Assembly. He possesses the friendship and regard of his associate.

HON. JOHN R. TANNER.

This gentleman was born in Warrick County, Indiana, April 4th, 1844, his father then being a farmer. In 1862. Mr. Tanner came to Illinois, locating at Flora, Clay County. His education was acquired in the common schools of his native State, his ex-periences with the Hoosier school-master, having been more lim-ited, however, than he desired. Mr. Tanner followed the noble example of his father in selecting his occupation, and is an es-teemed and popular farmer. His farm consists of about four hundred acres. In 1863, Mr. Tanner enlisted as a private in the Ninety-eighth Regiment of Illinois Volunteers, served untill June, 1865, when he was transferred to the Sixty-first Illi-nois, being mustered out of service at Springfield, in Sep-tember of the same year. He does not hold membership in any church, but is an Odd Fellow and member of the Ancient Order of United Workmen. In politics, he is a firm, prominent and active Republican, having become a voter as such, and never faltering or hesitating in regard to his political convictions since that time. In 1870, he was elected to the office of Sheriff of his county, and at the expiration of his term of office, was chosen Circuit Clerk. In 1876, he was appointed Master in Chancery, and, in 1880, elected to the State Senate, over Dr. Shirley, of Xenia, whom he defeated by a majority of nearly four hundred votes, in a very close district. He was appointed a member of the State Central Committee of the Republican party, in 1874, and has been retained in that capacity ever since. In personal appearance, Mr. Tanner is six feet, two inches high, and weighs two hundred pounds, dark in complexion, wears his hair quite long, and is hearty and jovial in disposition. He is large-hearted and generous, plain in speech, and a very strong and influential Senator. He is one of the honest farmers, who are the safe-guards of the people, against extravagant expenditure of State funds, and such misappropriation as they have a right to condemn.

HON. GEORGE TORRANCE.

This prominent and influential Senator was born in Fairfield County, Ohio, May 15th, 1847, his father being a carpenter and joiner, by trade. Mr. Torrance was educated in the public schools of Ohio, and his own incessant habits of study and observation. In 1864, the family came to Illinois, locating at Danville, from which place Mr. Torrance removed to Livingston County, in 1868. He espoused the law as his congenial calling, and studied under the instruction of Fosdick & Wallace, also Wyman, all of Chatsworth. He became a clerk in the Provost Marshal's office during the war, and, in 1864, when but seventeen years of age, enlisted in the One Hundred and Forty-ninth Illinois Regiment, serving until the close of the war. Prior to 1873, he had followed commercial pursuits for some time, but he then established the *Chatsworth Palladin*, and conducted it in connection with his profession, about eighteen months. He served as Village Attorney of Chatsworth for several years, being appointed to that position by the Board of Trustees. He is a born, bred and dyed-in-the-wool Republican in politics, and was elected to the State Senate in 1880. His present residence is Pontiac, Livingston County. In person, Mr. Torrance is not above medium height, a little heavy in proportion to his stature, polite, affable and obliging in demeanor, and kind, considerate and generous in disposition. He is not an orator, but he can turn loose a broadside of fact, sometimes, which will overcome all the flights of oratory, that can be brought to bear. He is a man who will not vote for appropriations intended to further private interests or provide free advertising for anyone at State expense.

HON. HENRY TUBBS.

Mr. Tubbs was born in Albany County, New York, December 12th, 1822. His father was a farmer of moderate means, and Henry was obliged to depend upon his own resources for education and support. After leaving home he devoted seven years to academic and medical study, teaching and working during vacation, for his support. Having become a physician, the twelve years of laborious practice which ensued, so impaired his health that a change became imperative. He therefore removed to Warren county, Illinois, in 1859, became interested in farming, and has resided there ever since. His domain was well managed, and, proving a productive investment, has continued to expand, until he is now the owner of a very large and valuable farm. During the last few years much of his time has been devoted to the First National Bank, of Kirkwood. He is the founder, President and principal owner of that institution. He is a pronounced and positive Republican; but never sought an office, or claimed the questionable honor of being a politician. He was a delegate to the National Republican Convention that nominated Grant and Wilson, and that which nominated our beloved and lamented Garfield. He has been President of the County Agricultural Society, and was, for many years, Chairman of the Board of Supervisors. Mr. Tubbs was a member of the State Constitutional Convention of 1870, and was elected to the State Senate in 1882, without a canvass, in what had been a Democratic District, during the four preceding years. He is a good-looking, kind, generous and benevolent gentleman, whose hair and beard are frosted with the threads of advancing years. He is an able and influential man, and is regarded as one of the Republican leaders in the Senate.

HON. WILLIAM T. VANDEVEER.

This gentleman was born at Taylorville, Christian County, Illinois, August 22d, 1842. His father, Horatio M. Vandeveer, was one of the most prominent lawyers of his day. He has held each of the county offices in Christian County, and was Circuit Judge two terms. William received a good common school education in his native city, after which he was a junior in Shurtliff College, at Alton, Illinois. After the completion of his collegiate course, he read law with his father, was admitted to the bar, and has since been engaged in the practice of his chosen profession. He transacts all of the business for his bank. He engaged in banking in 1868. The firm name of the establishment is H. M. Vandeveer & Company, and the institution is one of the strongest of its kind in Illinois. Mr. Vandeveer is an Odd Fellow, Mason, and Knight of Pythias, being the Representative of his lodge, in the latter, and High Priest of his Chapter, in the Masonic Order. He has held the latter position nine years. Ever since attaining his majority, Mr. Vandeveer has been a firm and ardent Democrat. He was one of the State House Commissioners for four years, has been Mayor of his city, and was elected to the State Senate in 1880, by the largest vote ever given a candidate in his district. He is the proprietor of about two thousand three hundred acres of excellent land, in addition to large banking and city real estate interests. In person, he is large and well-proportioned, neat, but plain in dress, polite and entertaining in conversation. He is one of the strong men of the Senate, and is generally admired, respected and beloved for his fairness and generosity.

HON. CHARLES A. WALKER.

He was born at Nashville, Tennessee, August 21st, 1830, his father being a merchant. His parents came to Illinois soon after his birth, locating at Carlinville. His education was acquired in the common district schools of Illinois, and Shurtliff College, at Alton. He studied law in Carlinville, and was admitted to the bar in 1858. He at once entered upon a successful practice of his profession, and is now in the very midst of its honors and glory. He is a Democrat of long and unswerving standing, and, as such, has held various offices of honor and trust in his city, county and district. He was the Mayor of Carlinville for several years, was a member of the House of Representatives in the Twenty-third General Assembly, and is now a member of the State Senate, having been elected by a large majority in 1882, from the Thirty-eighth District. In religious belief, he is a Presbyterian. In person, Mr. Walker is large and symmetrical, of dark complexion and prominent features. He is sharp and incisive in debate, and is a friend to be admired and an antagonist to be feared. He is one of the strongest men in the Senate, and possesses the respectful regard of his compeers and constituents. Mr. Walker is a man of plain habits and diffident demeanor, and, although a man of great force of character and considerable influence, rules rather by his personal magnetism and scathing methods of retort, than by a warmth of social disposition. He is admired for the leonine qualities of his mind, rather than the gentler promptings of his heart.

HON. GEORGE E. WHITE.

Mr. White was born on a farm near Milbury, Massachusetts, March 7th, 1848. In 1861, he left home to attend school at the Milbury Academy, and Wilbraham College, respectively. In 1863, he enlisted as a private in Company "I," Fifty-seventh Regiment of Massachusetts Veteran Volunteers, being at that time only fifteen years of age. He served until the close of the war in the same capacity, being present when Lee surrendered to Gen. Grant. In 1865, Mr, White came to Chicago, where he became a salesman in an extensive lumber yard, faithfully performing his duties until 1868, when, at the age of twenty years, he established himself in business as a dealer in hard wood lumber, an enterprise in which he is yet extensively engaged. He is an uncompromising Republican, and has been elected Alderman of his ward, three times in succession. He now represents the First District in the State Senate, having defeated Gustave De Mars, his opponent, in the election of 1882, by a majority of over four thousand four hundred votes. He is a Knight Templar. Mr. White is now a very wealthy man, owning no less than six fine farms in Illinois. He controls them through superintendents and tenants, and realizes an enormous income from them each year. On one of his three Will County farms, is situated his country residence. It is rich enough for the abiding-place of a king. It stands upon an eminence near the railway, and commands a view of the river for five miles. His landed estates will aggregate about three thousand two hundred acres. He also owns important railway interests, and is heavily interested in Chicago real estate, deriving a large income from its rental. He is one of the wealthiest members of the Thirty-third General Assembly. In person, he is of medium height, and dark complexion. He is quite handsome, winning and affable, and has a well-balanced and finely cultivated mind.

HON. L. D. WHITING.

Mr. Whiting was born among the hills of Oswego County, New York, November 17th, 1819. His mother was a lineal descendent of Cotton Mather, whose name is prominently mentioned in the history of Witchcraft, in New England, and his father was a farmer, lumberman and contractor on the Erie Canal. Mr. Whiting came to Illinois in 1849, settling in Bureau County, where he now resides. He has held nearly all of the township offices, from Justice of the Peace up, and was School Superintendent of the county. Prior to 1854, he was a Democrat, but July 4th, of that year, he helped to organize a convention in Bureau County, which was the foundation for the Republican party in Illinois, preceding all similar conventions, by at least six weeks. Mr. Lovejoy, one of the first of the martyrs of the party, was chief orator, and Mr. Whiting was the author of the resolutions adopted as a platform. He was elected to the House in 1868, Constitutional Convention of 1870, in 1869, and in 1870, 1872, 1874, 1878 and 1882, to the State Senate. He was the author of the proposition, afterward incorporated in the Constitution of 1870, that Railroads are public corporations, and should be controlled by law. Mr. Whiting is one of the oldest members of the Thirty-third General Assembly, and has the respect and confidence of all his associates. He is rather eccentric, but his head is a vessel, which contains a great deal of sound sense, and valuable information—more than some of his peers will be able to accumulate with double his years, and three times his advantages.

HON. JAMES S. WRIGHT.

This venerable Senator was born in Highland County, Ohio, August 4th, 1816, his father being a blacksmith at that time. Mr. Wright, the father of our Senator, was a member of the House of Representatives in Indiana, in 1825. In 1830, the family came to Illinois, locating in Champaign County, where the subject of our sketch now resides. His education was acquired in the common schools of Indiana, and by personal effort and close observation. He has been engaged in commercial enterprises a portion of his life; but gives his present occupation as that of a farmer. He owns seven hundred acres of rich farming lands, and is one of the most wealthy, intelligent and successful farmers of his county. He holds no membership in any church or secret order. His father was a Quaker in religious faith. In politics, he is a Republican, having affiliated with that party from the date of its organization, and never faltered in his political faith. He became Town Surveyor in 1837, serving for twelve years. In 1846, he was elected to the House of Representatives, serving one term. He was the nominee of his party for the State Senate in 1880, and in the election of that year, was chosen by a majority of six hundred votes, over Judge Cunningham, his political opponent, to represent the Thirtieth District in the honorable body of which he is a member. Mr. Wright is one of those honest old farmers who will not endure a legislative job or steal, in any form. In person, Mr. Wright is of medium height, slender and gray-haired. He is a very bright, shrewd, kind and generous man, whom all admire, when once acquainted with him. He is the oldest member of the Thirty-third General Assembly.

OFFICERS AND EMPOYEES--HOUSE.

---o---

HON. LORIN C. COLLINS, JR.,

SPEAKER OF THE HOUSE.

The subject of this sketch was born at Windsor, Connecticut, August 1st, 1848, whence, with his father and mother,—the Rev. Lorin Cone, and Mary Bemis Collins,—he removed, in 1852, to St. Paul, Minnesota. In 1868, the family removed to Illinois, locating in Cook County, where our subject and both his parents still reside. Speaker Collin's early education was carefully attended to by his fond parents, and, when performing the onerous tasks of a frontier farmer boy, his mental development was made to keep pace with the physical. Soon after settling in Illinois, he entered the Northwestern University at Evanston, where his peculiarly active, analytic and comprehensive mind gave him prominence, while his even temperament, candor and unaffected geniality won for him a warm place in the hearts of his teachers and fellow-students. He was graduated from the University in 1872, and at once gave his time and energy to the study of law. In 1874, he was admitted to the bar, in which well-chosen profession, he had abundant success. During his political life, he has been a staunch and industrious Republican, though never a narrow partisan, following blindly some temporarily self-appointed leader; but rather a true friend of the principles, by which he believes the party of his choice should be governed. Elected to a seat in the Thirty-first General Assembly, he bore his honors with becoming modesty, seldom using his excellent oratorical ability on the floor of the House: but before the session closed, he demonstrated to the observing ones, that he was a man of generous attainments, and a parliamentarian able to cope with any there. Naturally, on his reëlection he was looked upon by the Representatives in the Thirty-second Assembly as the parliamentary leader of the Republicans, a position he filled to the gratification of his party associates, and to his own credit. Long before his third election, he was singled out as the most available and suitable man for Speaker, and when the Republican members of the Thirty-third Assembly went into caucus, there was no opposition to Mr. Collins, who was nominated by acclamation—the youngest man on whom the honor and great responsibility of Speakership, had ever fallen. His conduct in the chair is the same as that which has characterized his entire political career. Always affable, never confused, ever firm, and seldom wrong in his opinions, yet ready to listen to reason, and reverse an erroneous decision, he has gained the confidence, respect and admiration, not only of his political confreres, but of the opposing party as well. Though by education and membership, a Presbyterian, he stands firmly on the eminence of belief that all creeds and dogmas are inferior to the great practical, warm-hearted religion of brotherly love. Although a Free Mason, Speaker Collins' fraternity of feeling has no prescribed limits, that do not comprehend all human kind.

WILLIS BROOKS HAWKINS,
PRIVATE SECRETARY TO SPEAKER COLLINS.

Mr. Hawkins was born at Aurora, Illinois, August 15th, 1852, his father being the claim adjuster for the C., B. & Q. R. R. He had held this position for thirty years, at the time of his death, in 1881. Willis removed to St. Paul, Minnesota, in 1873, and was there married to Miss Ophra E. Moore. He removed to Indianapolis, Indiana, in 1875, but returned to Aurora in 1876, and has made that city his place of residence since then. His education was acquired in primary schools, by individual effort, and by a careful study of good literature. He is an author of some note, and has had a varied experience as an editor and contributor to various newspapers and periodicals. He has been editorially connected with the *Tribune*, of Minneapolis, *Courier*, of Indianapolis, and Aurora, Illinois, *Daily News*, in which he owns a half interest, and of which he is nominally the editor, though his time has been so occupied with his manuscripts for projected books, that he has given the paper but little attention since 1880. He was Journal Clerk of the House, in 1879. He went with the boys in blue to the —— railway station, and this is his military record, complete. He has had a brief but brilliant theatrical career, which resulted in agony to his audience, and glory for himself. He is a jolly Republican.

JOHN A. REEVE,

CHIEF CLERK, HOUSE OF REPRESENTATIVES.

Mr. Reeve was born in Orange County, New York, December 7th, 1844, his father being a farmer. John came to St. Louis in 1866, remaining until 1873, when he located at Cairo, Illinois. His educational opportunities were very limited; but he was a dauntless student, and soon became an expert penman. He studied book-keeping by practical effort on his own part, and without an instructor, soon becoming so familiar with that branch of business as to render him a desirable acquisition to a business house. He served some of the best firms in St. Louis, in that capacity, and has kept the books of a number of prominent Cairo firms, since his removal to that city. He is now in business at his present home. He was a private in Harris' New York Cavalry, during the war, serving until crippled in the leg, at the Battle of Brandy Station, in March, 1864. He never performed active field duty afterward. After returning to Cairo, he was elected Circuit Clerk of his county, serving four years, has been Master in Chancery, was First Assistant Clerk of the House in 1881, and was chosen Chief Clerk, when the House was organized in January, 1883. He is quick and accurate in his work, and has many warm friends.

JOSEPH F. ALLISON,

ASSISTANT CLERK, HOUSE OF REPRESENTATIVES.

Mr. Allison is a Canadian by birth, having been born at Toronto, October 19th, 1838, on a farm. He came, with his family, to Dixon, Illinois, in May, 1840, but soon afterward removed to Carroll County, in the same State, where he was educated in the district schools, and Mt. Morris Seminary. At twenty-two years of age, he entered the army and served until January 1st, 1868. He entered the service a Sergeant, and was successively promoted to the Second and First Lieutenancies. After the war, he served in the Freedmen's Bureau, in North Carolina. He is an Odd Fellow and member of the Grand Army of the Republic. He was elected Circuit Clerk of Carroll County in 1868, and served until 1872. In 1873, he was elected County Treasurer, serving until 1882. He was First Assistant Clerk of the Twenty-eighth General Assembly, and, in the organization of the Thirty-third Assembly, was again elected for the same position. He is an active Republican, having espoused the cause of that party upon attaining his majority, and never having changed his mind upon that subject.

MISS CLARA E. PATTON,

ENROLLING AND ENGROSSING CLERK, HOUSE.

Miss Patton was born at Pana, Illinois. Her education was obtained in the city schools of Quincy, Illinois, where she was graduated at the age of sixteen, and took a commercial course in the Business College, of that city, where she now resides. She does not hesitate about saying that she is a Republican, and was elected to her present office upon that ticket. She is a very excellent scribe, and an accurate and neat copyist, well suited to the duties required at her hands. She is a lady of more than ordinary accomplishments.

WILLIAM I. ALLEN.

ASSISTANT ENROLLING AND ENGROSSING CLERK, HOUSE.

Mr. Allen was born at Williamsport, Maryland, his father being a teacher. William removed to Illinois in 1856, locating in Springfield, where he now resides. He has a good, substantial academic education. He was Deputy Sheriff of Sangamon County in 1867-8, and again in 1879-80. He was elected Assistant Enrolling and Engrossing Clerk of the House in the Twenty-sixth General Assembly, and Enrolling and Engrossing Clerk of the House, in the Twenty-eighth and Thirtieth General Assemblies, since which time he has been engaged in the insurance business in Springfield. He entered the army in 1862, as 2nd

Lieutenant, and was mustered out as Captain and Assistant Adjutant-General. He was a member of the first Post of the Grand Army of the Republic, and is Past Commander of the Stevenson Post, at Springfield. He has been an organizer of glee-clubs and writer of songs for Republican campaigns, doing the party good service.

ALLA R. DOW,

SECOND ASSISTANT ENROLLING AND ENGROSSING CLERK, HOUSE.

Mr. Dow was born in New York State, July 26th, 1859, his father being a jeweler. The family came to Illinois in 1868, locating at Belvidere, Boone County, where our subject now resides. He was educated in the High School of Belvidere, and a College at Beloit, Wisconsin, since which time he has been reading law with Hon. Charles E. Fuller, but has not yet applied for admission to the Bar. He has always been a Republican, and was made Second Assistant Enrolling and Engrossing Clerk in the organization of the House of Representatives, in January, 1883.

JOHN W. JANUARY,

POSTMASTER OF THE HOUSE.

Mr. January was born on a farm in Clinton County, Ohio, November 29th, 1847. He is descended from Puritanic and Revolutionary ancestors. He came to Illinois in 1855, and located at Henry, Marshall County. In 1861, he removed to Minonk, Woodford County, where he now resides. He received his education at the Soldiers' College, Fulton, Illinois, chiefly after returning from the war, where he served for nearly three years, being captured in 1865 and taken to Andersonville Prison, where he remained until so afflicted with scurvy, that his feet actually dropped off, about five inches above the ankles. He never had them amputated, but the limbs healed, after twelve long years of suffering. As he now expresses it, he wears " store feet." He came to the Union lines, clothed in a piece of a dressing-gown. At one time during his imprisonment, he was so emaciated that he weighed but forty-five pounds. Poor fellow! No wonder that the Republican caucus decided to make him Postmaster of the House of Representatives. He is very bright and jovial in temper, with all his misfortunes, and well qualified for his position. He has a picture of himself, which was made when he was at his worst. If shown to the public, it would almost elect him President of the United States.

MISS LIZZIE GILMER,

ASSISTANT POSTMISTRESS, HOUSE.

Miss Gilmer was born at Pittsfield, Illinois, her present place of residence, at a date, to the writer unknown. Her father was a lawyer, being at one time a partner of Hon. Milton Hay, now of the city of Springfield. Her father was a Colonel of the Thirty-eighth Illinois Regiment of Infantry Volunteers, and was killed during the Battle of Chicamauga. Miss Gilmer's education was acquired in the common schools of her city, and she is an accomplished young lady. General Grant, during his presidency, appointed her Postmistress of her native city, and, at the expiration of the term, she was re-appointed, her second term having expired last autumn. In the organization of the Thirty-third General Assembly, she was elected Assistant Postmistress of the House. She is a very amiable and agreeable young lady, probably past twenty years of age, and is admired and esteemed by all who know her.

WILLIAM H. SMITH,

MAIL CARRIER, HOUSE OF REPRESENTATIVES.

Mr. Smith was born at Berlin, Summerset County, Pennsylvania, December 14th, 1830. In 1865, he came to Illinois, locating at Bloomington. He has a good, common school education, and is a plasterer by trade. He enlisted, April 18th, 1861, in Company "A," Tenth Regiment, Pennsylvania Volunteers, and served during the war. He was appointed night watchman in the House, by Secretary Dement, in 1881, and is now mail carrier. He served as a private, during the war, and is now a member of the Grand Army of the Republic, and a Free Mason. He is of German extraction, and a good, honest man. He is very kind and benevolent in disposition.

LINDSAY STEELE,

DOOR-KEEPER, HOUSE OF REPRESENTATIVES.

Mr. Steele was born at Steeleville, Randolph County, Illinois, May 8th, 1837, his father being a farmer, after whom the town was named. His education was acquired in a log school house, from a teacher employed by his father. He was a farmer until 1861, in August of which year, he enlisted in Company "E," of the Thirtieth Illinois, serving until July, 1865, when he was mustered out as Captain. He was wounded in both arms and one leg, during the war; first, at Ft. Donelson, then at Vicksburg, and, later, at Kenesaw Mountain. His father was in the War of 1812, and his grandfather a Colonel of Dragoons, in the Blackhawk War. Mr. Steele is a member of a Lodge of Odd Fellows, and also, one of the Grand Army of the Republic. He has been Constable, Deputy United States Marshal, Justice of the Peace and Notary Public, United States Pension and Claim Agent, and was chosen Door-keeper of the House in its organization in January, 1883. He was Constable nine years, and Deputy Marshal, ten years.

EDWARD SMITH,

ASSISTANT DOOR-KEEPER, HOUSE.

Mr. Smith was born at Middletown, Maryland, June 4th, 1833, his father being a farmer. Mr. Smith removed from Maryland to New Madrid, Missouri, remaining two years, when he came to Bloomington, Illinois, where he has resided ever since. He attended school in Bloomington, two weeks, and has acquired a fair education by individual effort. He was in the army at New Madrid, Missouri, and, afterward, at Fort Pillow. He is a Republican in politics, and a Methodist in religious belief, being also a member of a lodge of colored Free Masons, at Lincoln, Illinois. He is a white-washer and kalsominer by trade.

REV. ARCHIE WARDE,

SECOND ASSISTANT DOOR-KEEPER, HOUSE.

Mr. Warde is the son of a farmer, having been born in Wilson County, Tennessee, December 25th, 1840. The family came to Illinois in May, 1875, locating at Peoria. His education was acquired in the common schools of his native State. He is now the pastor of a Baptist Church in Peoria. During the war, he was a cook for the Tenth Indiana Volunteers, serving until the close of the war. He is Master of a Masonic Lodge, and also a member of a society known as the Ladies' Court. In politics, he has always been a Republican. He is decidedly a portly, good looking colored man. He was married to Miss Annie Bou, colored, in 1862.

JOHN W. HEIDEMAN,

THIRD ASSISTANT DOOR-KEEPER, HOUSE.

Mr. Heidman was born in Prussia, in 1832, came to the United States in 1856, locating at Metropolis, Illinois, where he now resides. He served three years as porter in a St. Louis wholesale house, when he returned to Metropolis, where he has since been engaged in farming. He is now one of the County Commissioners of his county, having been elected in 1880. He was a soldier for three years and four months, during the late war, being Second Lieutenant of Company "D," Fifth Missouri Regiment, for three years of that time. He has always been a firm Republican, casting his first vote for Lincoln, in 1860. He was made Third Assistant Doorkeeper in the organization of the House, in January, 1883.

EVERARD H. DUGGER,

POLICEMAN.

Mr. Dugger's father was a soldier in the War of 1812, being actively engaged at the Battle of New Orleans. He was also in the Creek and Seminole Wars. Everard was born in Madison County, Illinois, in 1829, his father being engaged in farming, at that time. After leaving the parental roof, he located in Clinton County, where he now resides, pursuing the occupation of a farmer. He has been a country merchant, engineer and grain dealer, during his life. He is a Mason and a Republican, having been appointed to his present position by the Secretary of State.

DAVID JENKINS,

POLICEMAN, HOUSE OF REPRESENTATIVES.

Mr. Jenkins was born in Wales, July 9th, 1842, his father being a miner by occupation. David came to the United States in 1861, with his parents, and located at Alton, Ill., in 1853. He has a fair common school education. He served through the war as a private; He is a Presbyterian, Odd Fellow and Republican, and was appointed policeman by the Speaker of the House, in its organization.

JOHN STONE,

UNDER DOOR-KEEPER HOUSE OF REPRESENTATIVES.

Mr. Stone was born at Louisville, Kentucky, July 10th, 1840, his father being a cigar-maker. John came to Illinois in 1864, working for his support, and attending night-school for his education. He is a barber by trade, having served an apprenticeship of one year, and afterward worked in Washington, fourteen months. He was Messenger in the Lower House of Congress for two years. He has served as Messenger for the Doorkeeper of the House, for two years, and is now Under Doorkeeper in the House of Representatives. He is a member of the African M. E. Church, and also a member of a lodge of Odd Fellows, and one of Free Masons. His residence is Lincoln, Logan County, Illinois.

WILLIAM FINIS M'CLURE,

HOUSE POLICEMAN.

Mr. McClure was born in McLean County, Illinois, January 30th, 1839. He now resides in Ford County. He has a good common school education. He was engaged in farming prior or 1875, when he began dealing in stock and real estate. He is a Presbyterian, Mason and Knight of Honor. He has always been a Republican, and was appointed a Policeman by the Speaker, in the organization of the House, of the Thirty-third General Assembly. He is a very obliging and jovial gentleman.

JAMES B. SMITH,

JANITOR OF DEMOCRATIC CLOAK ROOM.

Mr. Smith is a very intelligent and industrious colored man, who was born in Amherst County, Virginia, May 1st, 1840. He came to Illinois in 1853, locating at Galesburg, where he received a fair common school education. He now resides at Peoria. He served in the Union Army during two years of the war. He is a member of the African M. E. Church, and of a colored men's lodge of Odd Fellows.

LIST OF PAGES,

HOUSE OF REPRESENTATIVES.

GORMAN F. B., - - - - - - - Chicago
ANDERSON, WARREN, - - - - - - Springfield
ANSLEY, JOHN, - - - - - - - Swedonia
BALLARD, EDWARD, - - - - - - Rock Island
BULL, GORDON, - - - - - - - Barry
COYLE, JOSEPH, - - - - - - - Barry
CREWS, FLOYD, - - - - - - Mt. Vernon
CURRY, WILL, - - - - - - - Springfield
NICHOLS, HARVEY, - - - - - - Carlyle
PATTERSON, WINTON, - - - - - - Chicago
PLETZ, BRUCE, - - - - - • - Springfield
RICHARDSON, WILLIE, - - - - - Springfield
RITTER, GEORGE, - - - - - - Springfield
SHEPPARD, WILLIE, - - - - - - Springfield
STUART, JOHN, - - - - - - - Springfield

REPRESENTATIVES.

HON. ISAAC ABRAHAMS.

Mr. Abrahams was born in Prussia, August 15th, 1834, his father being at that time, a tailor. In 1851, Mr. Abrahams came to the United States, locating in Chicago, where he remained until 1859, when he removed to Quincy, returning to the metropolis of the State in 1870, and residing there now. Thirty-one years ago, Mr. Abrahams was a peddler; to-day, he is one of the most respected members of the House of Representatives of his State. While in Quincy, Mr. Abrahams was Chief of Police for three years. In Chicago, he followed the provision and grocery business, until burned out in 1871. He then engaged in the wholesale liquor trade ; but, in 1874, was again tried by fire. He is a member of the following secret orders : Masonry, Odd Fellowship, Knights of Honor, Kesher-shell Bassell, and Sons of Benjamin ; but does not belong to any church. In politics, he is a confirmed and unrelenting Democrat. After the second destruction of his business, in 1874, he became Deputy Sheriff of Cook County, under the administration of Sheriff Kern. At the expiration of his term of office, he became a member of the City Board of Public Works, retaining that position until elected to the House of Representatives, in 1882, by the largest vote upon the ticket in his district—the Third Chicago, which is probably the wealthiest representative district in the United States. In person, Mr. Abrahams is of average stature and fine physical proportions. His complexion is quite dark ; but his hair is beginning to show the frosts of time, a little. He is an earnest and impressive speaker, and an amiable and agreeable gentleman, acute of perception and generous in disposition. He honors the office in the same ratio that he is honored by it.

HON. WRIGHT ADAMS.

He was born in Kendall County, Illinois, November 21st, 1842, to Earl and Deborah Adams, the maiden name of the latter having been Gifford. His father was one of the sturdy yeomen of pioneer Illinois. Mr. Adams followed in the footsteps of his father, and is yet engaged in the honorable and lucrative occupation of sowing and reaping, that the world may have food. He was educated in the public schools of his county, but, poor as were the educational advantages of those early days, his knowledge is extensive and his application of it most excellent. He enlisted in the Ninty-first Regiment of Illinois Volunteers, as a private, in 1862, and served three years in the time of our country's great travail. He was brevetted Lieutenant for gallant deeds, ere his term of service expired. He is a member of the Methodist Episcopal Church and a Blue Lodge Free Mason. Politically, he is a declared Republican, having been so since he attained the age of a voter. He was a member of the Board of Supervisors of La Salle County, for four years, and was elected to represent his district in the Lower House of the Thirty-third General Assembly, in 1882, by a large plurality. His farm consists of five hundred and twenty acres of excellent land, and he devotes considerable attention to breeding fine sheep. The Shropshire Down is his favorite family. In person, he is of medium height, dark in complexion and handsomely proportioned. He is genial, affable and entertaining in conversation or debate.

HON. J. M. ANSLEY.

The subject of this sketch was born in Westmoreland County, Pennsylvania, May 21st, 1833, his father being a farmer, at that date. Mr. Ansley came to Illinois in 1867, locating at Swedonia, Mercer County. The literary education of Mr. Ansley was acquired in the common schools of Pennsylvania and Glade Run Academy, at Dayton, in the same State. Professionally, he is a physician and surgeon, being a graduate of the Jefferson Medical College, of Philadelphia. He is reputed to be a very fine practitioner of the healing art. He does not belong to any church; but is a Mason and Odd Fellow. In politics he is a pronounced and unterrified Republican, who espoused the cause of the party in times of National peril, and, realizing that the blow aimed at the Union, was parried by its administration of the affairs of our government, he feels that duty calls upon him to adhere to its principles, and assist in perpetuating its civilizing influences. He has not been, nor is he now, a professional politician. Outside of the purely trust positions of School Director and Township Trustee, he had held no public office prior to his election to the House of Representatives, in 1882, from the Twenty-first District. He now resides at Swedonia, Mercer County. Mr. Ansley has been unfortunate in his domestic relations, having lost his wife and one of his two children. His living child is a page in the House of Representatives, at the present session. In person, he is large and well proportioned, neat in dress, wears a noble-looking beard, of great length, and is a very dignified man in bearing. He is earnest, forcible and positive in debate, genial, good-natured and generous in disposition. Since the above sketch was written, Dr. Ansley has taken unto himself a partner of his joys and sorrows.

HON. JOHN H. BAKER.

Mr. Baker was born in Moultrie County, Illinois, February 3d, 1855, and is now twenty-eight years of age. Joseph Baker and Mary Brown, his wife, were the parents of this gentleman, Like nearly all of his associates on the floor of the House, his life began on a farm, and his education was principally obtained from the common schools of his county. After he had left the parental roof, however, he entered the law school at Ann Arbor, Michigan, where he was graduated with honor, and afterward pursued his studies under the guidance of Hon. John R. Eden, of Sullivan, and Hon. Lloyd F. Hamilton and Rice, of Springfield. He had dealt in grain previous to adopting the law as his profession, so his character for good judgment was formed when he entered upon the practice of the law, and he had that advantage over most young men, who seek fame and lucre at the Bar. After his admission, he began practicing at Sullivan, Illinois, as a partner of Judge Meeker. This relation existed for three years, when Mr. Baker withdrew and launched his own legalship. He comes to the House as one of the Representatives from the Thirty-third District. In personal appearance, he is below the medium stature, dark complected, careful in dress and polished in manners. He is shrewd and incisive in debate, and very quick to perceive an advantage or avert a blunder.

HON. SOLOMON H. BETHEA.

This gentleman was born in Palmyra Township, Lee County, Illinois, in 1852. His father was the first, and at that time, only settler in Lee County, and his grandfather was a classmate of the celebrated John C. Calhoun, and, being a slave-holder, canvassed the matter in his own mind, and came to the conclusion that it would be right to set his slaves free. When a Bethea once makes up his mind that a given course of action lies in the line of duty, he does not hesitate to adopt it; so the blacks were called together, by their master, and given a deed of emancipation, which sent them forth in the world as free men and women. Mr. Bethea is a lawyer by profession, and has a very fine literary education, being a graduate of the Michigan State University. He read law with Judge Eustace, of Dixon, afterward becoming his partner, in the business of his profession. He does not hold membership in any church or society, except that of Free Masonry. He is a Republican in politics, and has always been one since he became a voter. He has not held any public office of note, until his election to the House of Representatives, in 1882, from the Nineteenth District. He is of Welsh descent, on one hand, and Irish on the other, thus forming a strong combination of perseverent characteristics, derived from his ancestors. He is a good lawyer, and a shrewd and successful politician. He is light in complexion, not above medium height, strong and vigorous, and will win his way to fortune and to fame, in the near future.

HON. GEORGE BEZ.

He is a German by birth, was born in the Southern part of Germany, August 9th, 1833. His father was both a miller and farmer. Mr. Bez came to Illinois in 1854, locating in Will County, where he now resides. He possesses a very excellent classical education, acquired in his native country, and has learned to speak and write the English language with great ease and remarkable correctness. He is engaged in brewing, and has succeeded in amassing a small fortune, by close attention to business and strict integrity in dealing with the people. August, 1862, found him enlisted in the One Hundreth Illinois Infantry, and he remained in the service until the result of his wounds compelled his resignation. The injuries, to which we refer, were received at the Battle of Stone River, near Murphysboro, Tennessee. Being disqualified for active army duty, he was placed in command of a battery, remaining in charge of the same until he resigned his commission as Captain, and returned to the more pleasant, but less exciting duties of civil life. He is not in communion with any religious denomination, although he inclines to the Lutheran belief. He is a Free Mason. Mr. Bez was a Republican until four years ago, when the political excesses of that party became so nauseous to him, that he sought refuge in the ranks of the Democracy. He has served as Postmaster of his town, Mokena, for eight years, was a member of the County Board of Supervisors for one term, and, in 1882, was elected a Representative to the Lower House of the General Assembly, by a very large majority. In person, Mr. Bez is tall, grave and dignified. He seems rather stern to a stranger, but, upon acquaintance, is known as a fair, generous and kind-hearted gentleman. He is always at his post, when the battle-cry resounds through our Legislative Halls, and will not flinch or shirk from his duty.

HON. HENRY O. BILLINGS.

The subject of this article was born at Alton, Illinois, September 20th, 1850, his father then being an active and influential attorney-at-law. In professional matters, Mr. Billings followed in the footsteps of his illustrious parent, and is a lawyer of considerable note and fine accomplishments. His literary education was acquired in the common schools of the city in which he was born, and Washington University, St. Louis, Missouri; his professional knowledge has been derived from careful reading and a course of study in the Albany Law School. He is not a church member, but affiliates with the following secret orders: Masonic of the degree of Knight Templar; Odd Fellows, and Knights of Pythias. In politics, he is a confirmed Democrat, from time, "whereof his mind runneth not to the contrary," and he will not "run to the contrary," so long as the principles of the party please him so well as they now do. He was elected to the General Assembly, as a Representative, in 1880, and reëlected in 1882) running considerably ahead of the regular ticket), from the Forty-first District. He is a man who appreciates the beautiful, in all that is done or said, and the inanimate and animate things that are. He dresses well and stylishly, is not above the average height of man, dark in complexion, and quite handsome in appearance, wearing a full beard. He is shrewd, polite and generous—a man who is best liked upon close acquaintance— thoroughly dignified, yet social in demeanor.

HON. THOMAS G. BLACK.

He was born in Columbia, Tennessee, June 1st, 1825, to William Black and Mary, his parents, the maiden name of the latter having been Vaughn. His father was a farmer, and, although this fact may attach to most of the sketches of his compeers in the House of Representatives, it adds to the evidences of worth of every other one of the number, even as it does to this one. He, who rises from the humble station of a farmer's boy, to a place in the Legislative Assembly of this State, has bridged a mighty chasm, yet few reach this office of honor, except they have had the noble experiences and suffered the pangs of self denial, which characterized the lives of farmer's sons, a quarter of a century since. He came to Illinois in 1804, and settled in Morgan County, finally making his home in Quincy, Adams County, in 1849. He possesses a very excellent education, the result of good schools and an inquiring mind. He is a graduate of the Louisville, Kentucky, Medical College, and is engaged in the practice of his profession at Clayton, Illinois. He enlisted, as Captain, in the Third Missouri Cavalry, during the war, served three years, and was mustered out as a Colonel. He is a member of the Christian Church, and a Mason and Odd Fellow, in good standing. He was a Representative in the Thirtieth, and now occupies the same position in the Thirty-third General Assembly, having been elected as a minority candidate. In person, he is large and portly, gruff, yet kind. He is a pleasant and convincing debater, and generally manages to get his bills, professional and legislative, safely placed among the things that are. He dreads defeat and enjoys victory, with the most extreme feelings of disgust or pleasure, as the case may justify.

HON. HENRY M. BOARDMAN.

Mr. Boardman is a very plain, affable, shrewd, honest and generous man, of positive opinions, good judgment and a calm temper. He was born at Pittsford, Rutland County, Vermont, December 12th, 1832. His grandfather was a ship-carpenter on board a man-of-war during the Revolution, and his father was a farmer. Mr. Boardman came to Illinois in 1854, locating at Joliet, where he remained but one year, removing to Paw-paw, DeKalb County, where he now resides. His education was obtained in the common school and Manchester High School, in his native New England State. He is a member of the Congregational Church, but not of any secret society. He is a farmer by occupation—a successful one, too, owning four hundred and thirty-seven acres of land in DeKalb County, and nearly as much in Iowa. He is a Republican in politics, and is not ashamed of the fact, or afraid to cross swords, metaphorically speaking, with any one, who opposes his party. He has served the people of his locality as Township Assessor, for eight years, and, as a member of the Board of Supervisors, five years. He was elected to the House of Representatives in 1882, as one of the majority members from the Seventeenth District. He is the very embodiment of energy and quiet, good humor, and, in personal appearance, bears a somewhat remarkable resemblance to General Ulysses S. Grant. He is one of the guardians of the people's interests, who will perform his duty well.

HON. WILLIAM H. BOYER.

The subject of this sketch, who represents the Forty-ninth District, in the Thirty-third General Assembly, was born in Spencer County, Indiana, February 5th, 1851. His parents were Lewis W. and Cynthia Ann Boyer, both of whom were Americans. His father, at the time of the birth of William II, was a well-to-do farmer. Mr. Boyer received his early education at the Glendale Academy, of his native county, and, later on, attended one term at the Hartville University, and, also, one term at the State Normal School, of Missouri. In 1874, he removed to Illinois, and located at Elizabethtown, where he began the study of law, in the office of Hon. W. S. Morris. In 1876, he was admitted to practice at the bar, and, soon afterwards, became the partner of his preceptor, W. S. Morris, who is a Senator in this General Assembly. Mr. Boyer has always been a Republican, and the present office is the first public position he has ever held. He was elected Representative over his competitor, Judge Bowman, of Shawneetown, receiving a clear majority of five hundred votes. Mr. Boyer is a member of the Ancient Order of United Workmen, and is, also, a Mason. In appearance, he is tall and shapely built. He is a talented speaker, and is a young man, who gives promise of a bright career in the political world.

HON. F. E. W. BRINK.

This gentleman was born in Prussia, March 17th, 1827, his father being at that time a farmer. He came to the United States in September, 1844, first locating in Illinois, but afterward removing to New Orleans, Louisiana. He remained in the South for seven years, finally returning to the Sucker State, and settling in Washington County, near Hoyleston, where he now resides. He was graduated at the College of Minden, Prussia. He is now engaged in milling and farming, having entered the milling business twelve years ago. Mr. Brink is a member of the Evangelical Church, but holds no affiliation with any secret order. He is a Democrat, in politics, having been one before the war, becoming a Republican in 1860, and returning to his first love in 1876, during the Tilden Campaign. The reasons for these changes are sufficient, in our opinion, in both cases, and our esteem for the man is much enhanced by the fact that he sought to vote for principles, and did not hesitate to forsake the parties, which failed to practice the principles by which he was guided. Mr. Brink has held several local offices of honor and trust, and was elected State Senator in 1876, serving four years. In 1882, he was elected to the House of Representatives, running five hundred votes ahead of the strongest man, other than himself, on the ticket. Mr. Brink bears a striking resemblance, in both form and feature, to that famous man of Illinois, Stephen A. Douglas. He is quiet, positive and commanding in bearing, and is generous and social in disposition.

HON. ALBERT F. BROWN.

This gentleman was born at Brimfield, Hampden County, Massachusetts, in September, 1819, now being one of the oldest men in either branch of the General Assembly. His parents removed to Ogle County, Illinois, in 1837, and his father, Dauphin Brown, was a member of the Sixteenth General Assembly of the Sucker State. Mr. Brown's education was obtained from the public schools and Wesleyan Academy, of Massachusetts. He has followed *the* occupation of occupations—producing food for the people—all of the many years of his life, even yet in his old age, directing the affairs of his highly-cultivated and excellently improved farm. His farm consists of six hundred and forty acres of land, and he is largely interested in stock dealing and breeding of fine stock. He is not a member of any secret society; but is a Congregationalist in religion. He is a Republican—was one of the founders of the first party organization, at Stillman Valley, his present home, and has never known any good reason for changing his convictions, or bestowing his suffrage elsewhere, since that date. He has been a member of the County Board of Supervisors, of Ogle County, for six years, two of which, found him filling the office of Chairman. He was elected to the House of Representatives in 1880 and 1882, from the Tenth District, and is one of the old men whose wisdom will be a necessary and proper check upon the enthusiastic measures of those who are yet in their youth. He is medium in stature, strong, hearty, kind and benevolent. He is very deliberate in both speech and action, and is as generous in heart, as a woman.

HON. BEN. F. CALDWELL.

The subject of this sketch, is a man of extensive wealth and political and financial influence. He was born in Greene County, Illinois, August 2d, 1848. His father was a farmer, and Ben followed the parental precedents, in choosing his occupation. Mr. Caldwell's parents came to Sangamon County in 1853, locating upon a tract of land, which is now a portion of his farm. He was educated in the public schools of the village of Chatham, and acquired some of the most valuable experiences of his life, upon the farm, where the principal portion of his youth was spent. May 27th, 1873, he married Miss Julia F. Cloyd, one of the most estimable young ladies of Chatham, by whom he now has two children—Mary Jane, born March 20th, 1874, and John Harvey, born September 9th, 1877. After their marriage, Mr. Caldwell and his wife made a tour to Europe, in which they traveled, visiting the principal points of interest, for a period of six months. He is a Past Master in Masonry, and a Past Noble Grand in the Independent Order of Odd Fellows, and he is greatly esteemed by the members of both these benevolent organizations. In politics, he is a pronounced Democrat, from conviction, rather than prejudice. He was elected to the House of Representatives in 1882, by a handsome majority. As a farmer and financier, Mr. Caldwell has been remarkably successful. His farm near Chatham, is one of the finest and best improved in his county. His residence is spacious in proportions, and palatial in furnishing and appointments. He also owns large interests in banking property, being President of the Bank of Chatham, and Vice President of the Farmers' National Bank of Springfield. He has served two terms as a member, and one term as Chairman of the County Board of Supervisors. He is liberal and obliging in disposition, handsome in person, and genial and kind in his intercourse with the public. With all of his financial and political cares, he loves his family dearly. His constituents are justly proud of him.

HON. WILLIAM F. CALHOUN.

Mr. Calhoun was born in Blaine, Perry County, Pennsylvania, November 21st, 1844. His father was a hard working and skillful cabinet-maker. In October, 1865, Mr. Calhoun came to Illinois, locating first at LaSalle, from which place he removed to Champaign, and from there to Farmer City, and, afterward, to Clinton, in DeWitt County, where he has since resided. He obtained his education in the public schools of Pennsylvania, being graduated from Mt. Pisgah Academy. Mr. Calhoun served an apprenticeship in dental surgery and mechanical denistry, under Dr. Joseph Smith, of Ottawa. He was engaged in practicing his chosen profession, when elected a Representative to the Thirty-third General Assembly. He was a member of the One Hundred and Thirty-third Regiment of Pennsylvania Volunteers, and reënlisted in 1864, in the Twentieth Pennsylvania Cavalry, serving under Gen. Phil. Sheridan until the end of the war. He is a member of the Methodist Episcopal Church, and Independent Order of Odd Fellows. Mr. Calhoun is a Republican, because he believes the enforcement of the principles of that party, to be in the interest of the whole people. He has served as Mayor of Farmer City, in his county, member of the Board of Education of his city, and was elected to the Lower House in 1882, by a very gratifying majority. In person, he is of average stature, sandy in complexion, except his beard, which is of a rich and beautiful reddish-brown color. He is a pleasant conversationalist, forcible debater, and a social and intelligent gentleman, who attends to his own affairs and expects everybody else to do likewise. He was married to Miss Blanche Derthick, in August, 1869, and now has three daughters, Maude, Nellie and Kate.

HON. WILLIAM J. CALHOUN.

Mr. Calhoun is tall and well proportioned, sandy in complexion, polite and social in his dealings with others, and able, kind and generous. He was born at Pittsburg, Pennsylvania, October 5th, 1848, his father being a merchant, at the time of this important epoch in William's history. The family soon afterward moved to Newcastle, Pennsylvania, where it resided for a few years, after which another removal established it at New Brighton, in the same State. William afterward removed to Mahoning County, Ohio. In 1869, he came to Illinois, locating at Arcola; but soon afterward removed to Danville, his present home. His education was acquired at Poland Academy, Poland, Ohio, and by unremitted personal effort. He is a lawyer by profession, having pursued his studies under the direction of J. B. Mann, his present partner. He passed through the last two years of the war, as a private, in Company "B," of the Nineteenth Ohio Regiment. His local reputation is excellent, and his constituents honored the office, rather than the man, when they elected him to the House of Representatives, in 1882. He is a Republican, of well-defined views, and is an excellent reasoner and fluent speaker. Mr. Calhoun holds no fellowship with any religious denomination. He is a Free Mason, of the degree of Knight Templar, and a Knight of Honor. He is a man who speaks and votes his convictions, irrespective of consequences, and is regarded as one of the safest, and most conservative partisans in the House. He is a man whom money or promises cannot influence against his impressions, when once formed.

HON. JAMES F. CANNIFF.

This gentleman was born in Orange County, New York, June 15th, 1850. His father was a farmer and stock-raiser. When James was but three years of age, his parents came West, locating in the city of St. Louis, where they remained but one year, after which, they established a home in Monroe County, Illinois. The education of James was something in which his parents were greatly interested, and, after the usual course in the public schools of his county, he was graduated from the College of the Christian Brothers, in St. Louis. The dreams of Jimmy Canniff were of libraries, orators, learned men, courts, judges and juries, and, after a careful course of study, he was admitted to the Bar in 1878. He then located at Waterloo, Illinois, where he now resides, and pursues the labors incident to his profession. He is an Odd Fellow and Knight of Honor, but holds no fellowship in any of the religious denominations. Although a young man, Mr. Canniff is very wealthy, owning three farms, which aggregate no less than eight hundred and seventy-five acres. He is a Democrat in politics, but has never held any public office, until elected to the House of Representatives in 1882, by a very handsome majority. In person, Mr. Canniff is below the medium stature, and rather slight in physical proportions, has dark eyes and hair, and wears a moustache. He is very cool and deliberate in conversation or debate, cautious in his movements and unalterable in a position, once assumed. He is friendly in his intercourse with the public, and dignified and manly in the performance of his public duties. He is as strong a man, when integrity and good judgment are in the balance, as there is in the House.

HON. WALTER E. CARLIN.

Mr. Carlin was born at Carrollton, Greene County, Illinois,. April 11th, 1844, his father being Circuit Clerk of the county, at that time. His father owned large landed interests in Greene County, and was a soldier in the Blackhawk War. His uncle, Thomas Carlin, was Governor of Illinois from 1838 to 1842. In 1870, Mr. Carlin removed from Carrollton to Mt. Vernon, from which place he returned to Jerseyville, in 1872, and has resided in that city ever since. His education began in the district schools of Greene County, and he afterward attended the school of the Christian Brothers, in St. Louis, and the University of Wisconsin, at Madison. He is now engaged in the banking business, at Jerseyville, the style of the firm being Carlin & Bagley. He owns a large farm, near his home. When seventeen years of age, Mr. Carlin enlisted in the Thirty-eighth Illinois Infantry, was made Second and First Lieutenants, successively, and commissioned Captain before he was nineteen; but declined the honor. He served on the staff of Gen. Carlin, his brother, in various capacities, being Adjutant at one time, and had two horses shot under him, at the battle of Chicamauga. He was commissioned Major of the Fifteenth Battalion, Illinois National Guards, by Governor Cullom, in 1878. He is a member of the Presbyterian Church, and a very prominent Odd Fellow, having passed all of the chairs in the Grand Encampment of Illinois, and is now serving his second term as Representative to the Sovereign Grand Lodge. He is a Democrat, and has held several local offices, having been Alderman of his City four years, and Chairman of the County Board of Supervisors, the same length of time. When he was chosen to the latter office, the county was $65,000 in debt, and, during his four terms, this debt was paid without increasing the tax levy. He owns considerable business property in Jerseyville, and extensive estates in Nebraska. He is rather small; but well proportioned; has light hair and a brown beard, and, although somewhat sedate, is polite and considerate. He is an excellent financier and parliamentarian.

HON. GRANDISON CLARK.

Mr. Clark was born in Marion County, Indiana, July 8th, 1829. His father was then a farmer and blacksmith. The subject of this sketch came to Illinois in 1850, and located a land-warrant, granted him for service in the Mexican War, in Jasper County. His education was acquired in the common district schools, and he followed his father's choice of a calling, and became a farmer, stock-breeder and stock-shipper. He does not hold communion with any church; but is an Odd Fellow and Free Mason. He is now a very wealthy man, owning over seven hundred acres of land, well improved and profitably stocked and cultivated. He was a volunteer in the Fifth Indiana Regiment during the Mexican War. He enlisted for a three years' term of service, but served until the close of the war. Mr. Clark is a very strong man, mentally and physically, and is one of the honest sons of toil, whom it is necessary to have in the Legislature, to keep the visionary schemes of lawyers and merchants within legitimate bounds, and to protect the State finances from misappropriation. Such Representatives as he is, lend a wholesome practicability to legislation, and are heard in behalf of the oppressed of the country in all cases, where corporations seek to exceed their powers and legal privileges. He is an old-time Democrat, and is proud of it. He is large and portly, and possesses an even, almost stolid temper. He has a kind and benevolent face, and is probably as generous and noble as he seems.

HON. MICHAEL CLEARY.

This gentleman was born in Ireland, February 9th, 1840, his father being a farmer. Soon after the birth of Michael, the family came to the United States, settling in LaSalle County, Illinois, where the public schools furnished this gentleman with an education. He was a very energetic and persevering boy, and largely supplied, by individual effort, what was denied him by fortune. He chose from all of the numerous avenues to fortune and fame, the rugged, but sure pathway, which leads across the fields of a farm. He realized that there could be no more independent occupation—nor one more honorable than that of the husbandman, so he bared his strong and vigorous arms, gazed for a moment upon the many obstacles in his way, and, with a hopeful heart and determined purpose set about winning gold and glory, by the sweat of his brow. He now owns no less than seven hundred acres of excellent land in the vicinity of Odell, Livingston County, and has it well improved and under excellent cultivation. This is a fair example of what can be accomplished by a young man of good health and true grit. Mr. Cleary is a Catholic in religion, and does not belong to any secret society. He has been a Democrat ever since he became a voter, and is just such a persevering and energetic politician as he is a farmer. He has been Supervisor of his Township for nineteen years, and was elected to the House of Representatives in 1882, over Joseph Berger, by four thousand majority. He represents the Eighteenth District. In person, Mr. Cleary is a very large and well developed man—one who is positively handsome because of his physical powers. He is a man of excellent humor, and genuine kindness of heart, but in debate and business, he is no less decisive and unwavering than he is good-natured in ordinary conversation. He is a strong and reliable Representative.

HON. HENRY C. CLEAVELAND.

Mr. Cleaveland was born in Woodstock, Windsor County, Vermont, October 25th, 1843. His father was a machinist by trade, and, in this regard, Mr. Cleaveland's birth is on a level with that of most great men of our day. The farmer and mechanic stand side by side in the parentage of brilliant minds and noble hearts. The subject of this sketch came to Illinois in 1864, locating in the flourishing city of Rock Island. His education was obtained in the common schools of the Green Mountain State, and he is justly proud of its practical and substantial character. Mr. Cleaveland is now engaged in the insurance business. He was one of the brave men who assisted in quelling the Rebellion. He enlisted as a volunteer, on the first call, and, at the expiration of his term of service, reënlisted in the Sixth Vermont Regiment, as a private. He was in some of the hottest battles of the war. In the Battle of the Wilderness, he was severely wounded in both thighs. He was mustered out in 1866, as Quartermaster. He is a Mason of high degree, being a Past Master, Past High Priest, Past Commander, and one of the Grand officers of the State jurisdiction. He is also a prominent Odd Fellow, Knight of Pythias, and United Workman, and is Deputy Great Sachem in the Improved Order of Red Men. He is a staunch Republican, and has held the offices of Township Collector, Supervisor, and member of the Board of Education, in his city. He was elected Representative, in 1882, by a handsome majority. Mr. Cleaveland is what is termed a self-made man. His boyhood was spent in incessant toil and voluntary study. The wounds, which he received during the war, made him a cripple for life, and, although he seems to move about with ease, he often suffers intensely from the indescribable aches and pains which they produce. In person, he is large, dark in complexion, and becoming. He is a man of broad charity in opinion, and liberal views. In his intercourse with the people, he is genial and common-place.

HON. MARK J. CLINTON.

Mr. Clinton's eyes first saw light on the Emerald Isle, June 2d, 1844. His father was a farmer, and came to Chicago when his son was but four years of age; so little Mark's experiences with the oppressive character of Irish land-lords is rather limited, but, being a man of noble sympathies and honorable motives, he is greatly incensed at the course of government affairs in his native country. His education, which is extensive and very substantial, was acquired in the public schools of Chicago. He has been engaged in mercantile pursuits ever since he attained a sufficient age to make his services desirable. He is a Catholic in religious faith, and is Secretary of Division No. 20, of the Ancient Order of Hibernians. To say that he is a Democrat, is but to state what the reader must have already inferred. As such, he was one of the Supervisors of Cook County, in 1869-70, occupying a place on each of some of the most important committees of that body. In 1882, he was elected to the House of Representatives from the Ninth Chicago District, by a majority of about two thousand votes. Mr. Clinton is possessed of much of the shrewdness and native wit, for which the Irish are noted, and does not hesitate to employ it in conversation and debate. His heart is with the laboring people, and his voice will not be drowned by the clamor of monopolists. In person, he is of medium height and sturdy, being, in fact, a well developed specimen of the *genus homo*. He is gentle and considerate in his intercourse with children, and suffering humanity of all classes and conditions, and possesses those noble characteristics of manhood—generosity of opinion and justice toward all men, which render an ordinary man, a giant in the eyes of the populace.

HON. JOHN H. COATS.

This gentleman was born at Petersburg, Pike County, Indiana, September 23d, 1843, his father being a farmer at that time. Mr. Coats suffered the misfortune of sustaining the loss of both father and mother at a very early age, and has been obliged to battle his way through the world without the protection of the former, or the kind counsel and noble sympathy of the latter— the best friend man ever possessed. He came to Illinois in 1844, locating in Pike County, where he resided until 1851, when he removed to Scott County, his present home. His education is such as the common schools of his day afforded, improved and extended by personal effort. He was a soldier in the late struggle between the North and South, serving during the war, and passing six months and twelve days of the time, in the environments of the soldiers' horror—Andersonville Prison. He is a Mason and Odd Fellow, and a Minister of the Gospel, in the Christian Church. He is a Republican, heart, brain and soul, because he believes it right to be so, and is the minority member from the Thirty-seventh District. He owns a grocery and queensware establishment, under the firm name of Coats & Graves. One of the incidents—or rather series of incidents—in his army life, which we deem worthy of mention, was his three efforts at escape from Andersonville, two of which resulted in his being run down by blood-hounds and re-captured; but the third enabled him to elude his pursuers and reach the Union lines, at Vicksburg. The reckless disregard of the dangers, attending an attempt at escape from that prison, confirm the belief that its horrors were more than death. Mr. Coats is a very generous and well posted man, who is not afraid to say or do what he conscientiously endorses as right. He is honest and moral, shrewd and witty.

HON. JOHN H. COLLIER.

One of the most active workers in the Thirty-third General Assembly, is the gentleman whose name heads this sketch. Mr. Collier was born in New York State, in March, 1844. He was the son of Joseph and Mary DeForrest Collier. His father, who was a farmer, together with his family, moved to Illinois in 1855, and located at Antioch, Lake County, and from there, in 1870, the subject of our sketch moved to Ford County, and engaged in the hardware business, and he is still following the same business, in that county. Mr. Collier's education was obtained in the common schools of this State. He has held many local offices, and was elected a member of the Thirtieth, Thirty-second and Thirty-third General Assemblies. In 1862, Mr. Collier enlisted, as a private, in the Ninety-sixth Illinois Volunteers. He served until the close of the war, in 1866, and, when mustered out of the service, he was Captain, commanding a company. He has always been a Republican. Mr. Collier is a Mason and Knight Templar, and is a member of the Grand Army of the Republic, at present is the Inspector for the Department of Illinois. Mr. Collier resides at Gibson City, Ford County, and represents the Eighteenth District, in the Legislature. His opponent for this office was Joseph Berger, Greenback and Prohibition candidate, who was defeated by a very large majority. In appearance, Mr. Collier is tall and portly.

HON. EDWARD DEAN COOKE.

Mr. Cooke was born in Dubuque County, Iowa, October 17th, 1849. His father was a farmer, and Edward was employed in working at the honorable avocation of his father, except during terms of school, until he had attained his sixteenth year, when he began clerking in various lines of business, finally becoming teller in a bank. He soon tired of this kind of employment, however, and determined to avail himself of an opportunity to acquire more than a limited common school education. He accordingly entered the law department of the Columbian College, at Washington, D. C., from which he was graduated in 1873. He was soon afterward admitted to the Bar, in the District of Columbia and Iowa, and has since been practicing in Chicago. The name of the firm is Beam & Cooke, He was elected to the House of Representatives in 1882, from the Fifth Chicago District. He is a Stalwart Republican, a Unitarian in religious views, and a Master Mason. In person, he is well proportioned, somewhat below the average in stature. He is not remarkable for warm social qualities, and is rather crisp in speech, and more or less moody in disposition. He is undoubtedly a very excellent lawyer and a studious man.

HON. EDWARD E. COWPERTHWAIT.

Mr. Cowperthwait was born in Philadelphia, Pennsylvania, his father and grandfather being farmers and extensive land owners near Morristown, New Jersey, at a village bearing the family name. In religious belief, his parents were Orthodox Quakers. The subject came to Illinois in 1870, and worked by the month, for Alexander Potts, and other prominent Christian County farmers, devoting his attention to books, whenever the opportunity was presented. He afterward taught country schools for five years, and finally pursued his studies in the Quaker City College, of Philadelphia, in branches, of which he had acquired some knowledge, when a boy. He afterward read law with J. M. Birse, of Assumption, Illinois, his present place of residence. He enlisted in the Second Regiment of Pennsylvania Artillery Volunteers, at the age of fifteen years, as a three years man, and served his full term, being twice wounded before Petersburg, Virginia, and receiving commendations from his commanders for his gallant conduct. He is a member of the Christian Church, and is also a Free Mason, holding membership in Morrisonville Lodge, No. 681, Morrisonville, Illinois. He is a thorough Republican in politics, and has held the office of Police Magistrate of the village, where he resides, and was elected to the House of Representatives in 1882, on that ticket. He believes in adhering to party measures in State and National affairs, but not so determined in local matters. He was the minority candidate from the Fortieth District, but the ticket was bolted by some Republicans, who combined to defeat him and elect John M. Miller, an independent candidate, but they failed by two thousand and thirty-seven and one-half votes, after the hottest campaign ever known in this section of country. Mr. Cowperthwait is essentially a self-made man—one of great energy—who does not shrink from duty, or despair under discouraging conditions.

HON. FLEMIN W. COX.

Mr. Cox is a Buckeye by virtue of his having first made his appearance among men in Coshocton County, Ohio, which event came to pass September 9th, 1833. His father and mother were farmers and Democrats, as well as Germans, by descent, as he jovially expresses it. His education was acquired in the ordinary public schools of his country, and improved by his experiences, as teacher and County Superintendent of Public Instruction, which last office he held in Lawrence County, Illinois, from 1873 until 1881. He is a farmer, by occupation, and a good one, too. He is not a member of any church or secret society. He is a Democrat by inheritance, education, and conviction that the principles of his party are the basis of a republican form of government. It is rather a significant fact in his favor, that his first majority for the office of School Superintendent, was eighteen, and his last two hundred and twenty-five. In addition to his farming interests and public duties, Mr. Cox deals in agricultural implements, in their proper season. His present place of residence is Bridgeport, Lawrence County, Illinois, in the Forty-sixth District, from which he was elected to the House of Representatives, by an overwhelming majority in 1882. In person, he is portly, and not above the average stature. He is dark in complexion, plain and neat in dress, hearty and generous in disposition, and uniformly happy and courteous.

HON. CLAYTON E. CRAFTS.

Mr. Crafts was born in Auburn, Geauga County, Ohio, July 8th, 1848. He does not differ from a majority of the members of his branch of the Assembly, in the occupation to which he was born. His father was a farmer, and his grandfather was a farmer in his day, being the first or second settler of the town in which Mr. Crafts was born. Grandfather Crafts was about the only man who was considered competent to draft legal documents in his neighborhood, and his services were in great demand. The father of our Clayton, was about the only Democrat in Auburn for some years, and had many a wordy war with his neighbors, as a result. Mr. Crafts was educated in what is now known as Hiram College, justly renowned for its association with the memory of the martyred Garfield, and is also a graduate of the Cleveland (Ohio) Law School, having been admitted to the Bar in 1868. A portion of his legal study was pursued in the office of Hon. John J. Van Allen, a somewhat celebrated lawyer and noted politician, of Watkins, New York. He is now engaged in the practice of his profession, in Chicago, but resides in the surburban village of Austin. Mr. Crafts is a member of the Christian Church, and of the Iroquois Club, a political and social organization of Democrats, in Chicago. He has held many minor offices of honor and trust in his county, and is held in high esteem by his party friends, being now a member of the County Democratic Central Committee. He has never been a member of any political party, except the Democratic, and did not, like some of his fellows, run after false gods, in off years. He lost his office and library in the Chicago fire, and, although well read in all branches of his profession, confines himself exclusively to civil cases. He is the minority Representative from his district, and polled a larger vote than any of his competitors. He is in comfortable circumstances, as a result of successful speculation in surburban real estate. He is above medium stature; wears a full beard, and bears himself in a dignified and gentlemanly manner. He is earnest and forcible in debate, and kind, considerate and generous in his social relations.

HON. JOHN H. CRANDALL.

In person, Mr. Crandall weighs one hundred and sixty-five pounds, and has a full red beard. He was born in Tazewell County, Illinois, June 9th, 1845, and is now in his thirty-eighth year. He is, in fact, in the very prime of excellent and estimable manhood. He does not differ from a majority of the members of the House of Representatives of the Thirty-third General Assembly, being essentially the sturdy product of a pioneer farm, and the valued progeny of one of the pioneer agriculturalists of the State of Illinois. He possesses a very good education, which he acquired in the common schools of his State, and the Normal University, at Bloomington. In choosing his occupation, he followed in the immediate footsteps of his parental ancestors, espousing farm life and engaging largely in rearing and dealing in fine breeds of live stock. He is not a church member, but is a member in good standing in a Lodge of Free Mason. In politics, he is an unswerving Democrat, having been one of the Board of Supervisors of his county, and held other local offices. He was a member of the House of Representatives of the Thirty-second General Assembly, and was reëlected in 1882 by a very satisfactory majority. His farm is a large one, consisting of no less than five hundred acres, upon which roam several herds of high-bred cattle. In disposition, he is very commonplace, affable and polite. He is an entertaining speaker, and is one of those men, who lengthen life by indulging their generous natures, and perpetrating harmless, but amusing jokes.

HON. SETH F. CREWS.

This, one of the most eloquent members of the House of Representatives, was born in Wayne County, Illinois, in March, 1847, being now thirty-six years of age. Andrew and Mary J. Crews, *nee* Vandeveer, his parents, resided upon a farm at the time of his birth, and were unable to afford their son a better education than that provided by the common school, in the immediate vicinity of their home. Young Crews was an ardent student, however, and, at the early age of seventeen, rose from the station of pupil to that of teacher, pursuing the latter profession until he had attained his majority, when he entered the law office of Hayward & Kitchell, at Olney. He was admitted to the Bar in 1870, and soon afterward became a partner with the present Attorney-General of Illinois, Hon. James H. McCartney, at Fairfield, in his native county. In 1874, however, this co-partnership was dissolved, and Mr. Crews established himself in Mt. Vernon, where he and Hon. Charles T. Strattan, who style themselves, Crews & Strattan, enjoy the largest and most valuable clientage of all like firms in the city. Mr. Crews, when quite small, lost one of his lower limbs by disease, and is obliged to resort to crutches, as a means of locomotion. Notwithstanding this misfortune, and his limited advantages in youth, there is not a brighter mind than that of Mr. Crews, in the Thirty-third General Assembly. He is a Methodist, Royal Templar of Temperance, Odd Fellow, and Knight of Honor. Of the latter society, he is Past Grand Dictator of this State jurisdiction. He is a sound Republican, and was elected County Attorney of his county, some years since, overcoming a Democratic majority of six hundred. He is the minority member from his district. He is of medium height, portly, and has sandy hair. He is polite and affable, and wins friends by his magnetism and eloquence.

HON. JOHN H. CROCKER.

The subject of this sketch was born at Derry, New Hampshire, July 9th, 1829. His father, John, and mother, formerly Miss Mary N. Pilsbury, resided upon a farm at that time, and little John's first experiences in life were calculated to give him a thirst for knowledge, and ambition to become an honored and respected man of influence. His dreams were dreams of wealth and fame, as are the musings of many other farmers' boys. In 1839, his parents came to Illinois, locating at Jacksonville, where their son was educated in the common schools and the Jacksonville College. His occupation is that of a banker and grain dealer. In religious belief, he is a Presbyterian, and he belongs to the Masonic Order, the Independent Order of Odd Fellows, and Royal Templars of Temperance. He is a very wealthy man, owning an undivided interest in one thousand acres of Illinois lands, and is the senior member of the firm of Crocker & Company, bankers at Maroa, Illinois. In politics, he is an unquestionable and unswerving Republican, having espoused the cause of that party upon attaining his majority, and never varied in political faith. He is a shrewd financier, a popular citizen and an intelligent and respected Representative in the General Assembly. He was elected from the Twenty-ninth District, by a majority of about eight hundred votes, over Doctor Miller, his political opponent. In person, he is of medium height, dark in complexion, polite and affable in his intercourse with the people, and firm, incisive and earnest in debate. His place of residence is Maroa, Macon County, Illinois.

HON. EDWARD L. CRONKRITE.

This prominent member of the House of Representatives was born in Rensaeler County, New York, in June, 1832. His father was a farmer, and his grandfather was one of the noble Sons of Columbia, who fought for American independence throughout the whole period of the Revolutionary War. Mr. Cronkrite came to Illinois in 1859, locating in Freeport, Stephensón County, where he engaged in merchandising. His education is academic, having been acquired at Troy Conference Academy, West Poultney, Vermont. He regularly attends services at the Presbyterian Church in his city, although he is not a member. He is a Thirty-second Degree Mason, and has been elected to the Thirty-third, the highest degree in the Order, which will be conferred upon him in September of the present year. He is an Odd Fellow of the Royal Purple Degree, and is the presiding officer of his lodge, and Uniform Degree Camp. He is also a member of the Patriarchal Circle, Ancient Order of United Workmen, and the L. of H., a Uniformed Degree of the last named order. He is a Democrat of the first water, and has been Alderman and Mayor of his city, and has also been a member of the House of Representatives since 1872, except in 1878, when he was the Democratic nominee for State Treasurer, against General J. C. Smith, the present incumbent. He is the minority Representative from his district, and is generally regarded as one of the very strongest men on the Democratic side, perhaps in the entire House. In person, he is large and portly, has an open and agreeable countenance, and is one of the most genial and affable members of the Legislature. He is a man of great social qualities, and has an intellect well adapted to his executive energies. He is a powerful speaker and a most convincing debater.

HON. ALFRED S. CURTIS.

The subject of this sketch was born in Ulster County, New York, December 9th, 1816. His father was a farmer at the time of this gentleman's birth. In 1858, Mr. Curtis came to Illinois, locating in Oneida, Knox County, where he resides at present. In education, Mr. Curtis enjoyed excellent advantages, being a graduate of that celebrated institution of learning, Yale College, of the class of 1838. In 1845, he read law and was admitted to the Bar in Ohio, where he practiced his profession for six years; but gave it up for the equally honorable and more independent occupation of a farmer, when he came to Illinois. In his efforts at farming, he has been extraordinarily successful, having been left fatherless at five years of age, and starting in life a few years later, with nothing but a sound physical constitution and a limited education as his capital stock. He is now a very excellent scholar, and a prominently wealthy man. He has now practically retired from business, doing a little private speculating now and then, "just to keep his hand in." He is a Congregationalist in religion, and a non-affiliating Free Mason. In political faith, he is a confirmed Republican, having cast his fortunes with that party, when it came into being, and been faithful to its principles ever since. He has served as Supervisor of his township, five years; Mayor of his city, twelve years; member of the District School Board, fifteen years, and was a Representative in the Thirtieth General Assembly. He was elected to the Thirty-third General Assembly by a majority over the Democratic candidate of nearly one thousand votes. He is careful in assuming positions on the various questions which arise in the Legislature; but when he once ascertains what he believes to be the proper view of a given case, he stands by it with the vigor of a much younger man. He is not above medium height, is hearty and jovial in disposition, and kind and generous of heart. He is one of the most valuable members of this Legislature.

HON. WILLIAM A. DAY:

This gentleman is one of the finest scholars in the House of Representatives. He was born at Wilmington, Delaware, in June, 1850. His father was a farmer, of Revolutionary ancestry, and a thorough-going, industrious and prudent one, at that. With that kind of ancestry, united with a strong heart, brilliant mind and willing hands, it is not wonderful that William has risen to eminence in the councils of his State. He is a lawyer by profession, having read law with Judge Cunningham, of Urbana, Illinois, and being graduated from the Law Department of Harvard University, in 1872. He has met with phenominal success in his legal undertakings, and is one of the leading lawyers of Illinois, to-day. He now resides in the city of Champaign, and owns valuable landed estates in the adjacent country, all of which he has made by his own efforts. He is an uncompromising Democrat; has been City Attorney of Champaign; was a member of the House in the Thirty-first General Assembly, and is now serving as the minority Representative of his district, in the Thirty-third. He was one of the delegates from Illinois, to the Cincinnati National Convention, which nominated Hancock for the Presidency, in 1880. He is a perfect gentleman in deportment, dress and carriage, and is considered one of the very ablest men in the House. Although dignified, he is courteous and generous, and is a great favorite with the members, who enjoy his intimate friendship and esteemed society.

HON. WILLIAM H. DeBORD.

This gentleman first saw the light October 1st, 1834, in Decatur County, Indiana. His father, Reuben DeBord, was a farmer, who removed to Shelby County, in the same State, where he resided until 1852, when he came to Illinois, locating in Jasper County. The education of the gentleman, whose name is now enrolled upon the journal of the House of Representatives, of Illinois, was acquired in the common schools of his native State, and the Seminary at Shelbyville, Indiana, he having received a certificate of qualifications, as a teacher, upon completing the stipulated course of study. He taught school for some time, then espoused the mercantile business. In August, 1861, he enlisted as a private, in Company "H," of the Thirty-eighth Illinois Volunteers. He served over three years, and was mustered out of the service, as a Second Lieutenant. He is a devout member of the Christian Church; but does not affiliate with any of the so-called secret societies. In connection with his military career, we cannot refrain from mentioning the fact that he was captured at the Battle of Chicamauga, and confined in nearly all of the worst military prisons of the South, except that at Andersonville. He says that the horrors of prison life have never been told, and that words are incapable of conveying an adequate idea of them. He is now engaged in farming, and breeding and dealing in live stock. He has a farm of two hundred acres in Cumberland County, where he now resides. He is a strong Republican, and has held various positions of honor and trust in his county and township. He has been Assessor of Jasper County, and Collector of Cumberland. He was elected to the House of Representatives, in 1882, by a very handsome majority, and is a solid and able advocate of the interests of the people. In person, he is not above the average stature, wears a full beard, and is kind and accommodating in disposition, and methodical in conversation and debate.

HON. JAMES E. DOWNING.

He was born February 19th, 1818, in Frederick County, Virginia. He is another of the great men, who have had an humble origin. His father was a sturdy Virginia farmer. His parents removed to Clark County, Indiana, in 1822, and came to Illinois in 1835, locating in Adams County. The subject of this sketch is also a farmer. He owns one thousand two hundred acres of tillable lands, and three hundred acres of good timber. He has retired from active farm labor, however, and his sons are conducting the business for him. Mr. Downing's education was of the good, substantial character, to be obtained in a well regulated country school. He does not affiliate with any church or secret society. He is a Democrat, born, bred and educated, and has held various positions of honor and trust in his township, county and district. He was a member of the County Board of Supervisors for four years, and served his first term in the House of Representatives in 1869. Mr. Downing is one of the wealthiest men in the county, and, unlike most wealthy farmers, possesses the esteem and good will of his neighbors, to a remarkable extent. He is not puffed up or self important, as many men of means become, but, on the contrary, is as social, plain and common as any one could desire. He is not miserly. He is generous in both purse and opinion, and does not deem it his duty or privelege to crush an opponent with the weight of his gold, or taunt a beggar with his poverty. He is a sturdy specimen of manhood, at an advanced age. He was elected to the Lower House in 1882, by a very large plurality. In person, Mr. Downing is a very hale, old gentleman, with snowy hair. Although sixty-five years old, he walks erect, and seems to be in full possession of his mental powers and physical senses. He is a hearty joker, and bids fair to live many years yet. His presence in the House is like that of Abra'am, of old, among his children of many generations. His father was ninety-two and his mother ninety-seven years old, at the time of their respective deaths.

HON. WILLIAM M. DUFFY.

Mr. Duffy was born in Ireland, January 30th, 1835, his father then being a landlord of a hotel. The subject of our sketch came to the United States in 1849, locating at Rahway, New Jersey, where he remained until 1853, when he removed to Illinois, establishing himself at Peoria, from which place he removed to San Jose, where he resided until he entered the army, in 1862. After the war, he settled at San Jose, Illinois, where he now resides. His education was acquired in the common schools of his native country. While residing in New Jersey he learned the trade of a harness-maker, afterward traveling extensively, while pursuing that avocation, as a journeyman. In 1858, he began cultivating his Mason County farm, and is still engaged in that noble avocation. In 1862, he recruited a company for the One Hundred and Eighth Illinois Infantry, and served as its Captain until the close of the war. He is not a member of any church; but is an Odd Fellow, possessing the Encampment and Rebekah Degrees. He was a War Democrat during the war, and has been a peace Democrat, ever since. His Democracy has been unfaltering and enduring. He has been a member of the Board of Supervisors for three years, and has held nearly all of the county offices in his county. He was a member of the Thirty-second General Assembly, and was reëlected in 1882, from the Thirty-fourth District, by the largest majority given any candidate upon his ticket. Mr. Duffy is a man of very great local popularity, and is one of the most uniformly successful politicians in the House of Representatives. In personal appearance, he is a man of medium height; dark in complexion; wears a full, black beard, and is one of the best natured, most generous and uniformly happy and jovial members of the Assembly. He is a man, who numbers nearly all his acquaintances as his friends, and will do what he conceives to be right, irrespective of consequences.

HON. JOHN F. DUGAN.

This gentleman was born at Gross' Point, Cook County, Illinois, February 18th, 1845. The thriving suburb of Evanston is now located at that place. His father was a wood dealer and farmer, who located there in 1836. The family removed to Wheeling, in the same county, when John was but two years old, and his brother William, established himself in the grocery trade, afterward engaging in pork packing, in the city of Chicago. Mr. Dugan afterward entered the firm which, conducted a large business on the Board of Trade, in pork and beef, and withdrew from it in 1873, at which time he engaged in the real estate business. He was educated in the public schools of Chicago and Wheeling, afterward being graduated from a Catholic School. He has been Deputy Assessor and Deputy Collector of Cook County. Mr. Dugan is a devout Catholic, and a member of the Ancient Order of Hibernians; also, the Order of Emeralds. He is an ardent Democrat, and has never done anything inconsistent with the interests of the party. He is a Representative in the Thirty-third General Assembly from the Thirteenth Chicago District, and is, also, a fair representative of the rush, bustle and business enterprise of the city in which he resides. He was elected in 1882, running ahead of his ticket, over a thousand votes. He is above the medium in height and stature, has dark eyes and hair and a light moustache. He is well proportioned and rather handsome in person; slow and deliberate in speech, and scholarly and dignified in carriage. He is very sociable and polite, and wins friends wherever he makes acquaintances. He is a man of and for the people, and has just such personal traits as are well calculated to redound to his honor and the advantage of his constituents.

HON. WILLIAM H. EMERSON.

Mr. Emerson was born at Richmond, near Cincinnati, Ohio, September 9th, 1832. His father died while William was very young. His mother was a grand-daughter of a Huegenot refugee, from France. He acquired his education by the exercise of privileges afforded by the common schools of his native State, in the early days of their history. Mr. Emerson's aspirations were commercial in their nature, and, at an early age, he removed to Cincinnati, where he engaged in mercantile pursuits, remaining until 1863, when he came to Illinois, locating at Ogle, Lee County, where he followed merchandising for seven years, when he finally settled at Astoria, his present place of residence. He is now chiefly engaged in milling and mining. He has been a very enterprising and successful business man, and is equally as enterprising in the Legislative body, of which he is an honored member. With the exception of one or two positions in the city government, Mr. Emerson has held no public office, prior to his election to the House of Representatives, in 1882, as a Republican. He is a Free Mason, of the degree of Knight Templar. In 1854, he was married to Miss Elizabeth P. Wilson, of Richmond, Ohio, and the union has been blessed with seven children. He is a large and portly man, whose hair is becoming gray, is actuated by pure motives and deep-rooted convictions; but is very polite and pleasant in his dealings with the populace.

HON. MILO ERWIN.

Mr. Erwin was born in Williamson County, Illinois, October 24th, 1847. At the time of the birth of young Milo, his father was in the army, which was prosecuting the Mexican War. Mr. Erwin attended the Normal University, at Bloomington, two years; but had made some progress in a collegiate course at the Carbondale College, prior to entering the former institution. Professionally, he is a lawyer, being a graduate of the Legal Department of the Michigan University. He has, perhaps, as fine an education as any other member of the House of Representatives, and is one of the ablest lawyers in his section of the State. He is a leading Republican, of Southern Illinois, and has served four years as City Attorney of Marion, the county seat of his county. In 1874, he was the nominee of his party for the State Senate, and, again, in 1878; but, the district being largely Democratic, he was defeated each time, though by small majorities. He was elected to the House of Representatives, in 1880, and reëlected in 1882. He is a Mason and Odd Fellow; but holds no membership in any church. Mr. Erwin is very wealthy, owning no less than nine hundred acres of good farming lands, besides very valuable milling interests. He possesses a fine literary education, and is the author of a history of his county, during the bloody period of the vendetta, which gave that locality such an unsavory reputation in 1873–74–75–76. He is a large and powerful man, physically and intellectually. He is dignified in bearing, forcible in debate, and kind and generous in disposition.

HON. JOSEPH H. EWING.

Mr. Ewing was born at Mattoon, Coles County, Illinois, November 30th, 1837. His father was a farmer in the day of prairie fires and deer chases. Mr. Ewing attended the public schools of his neighborhood in the winter, and labored on the farm in summer, during the years of his boyhood, completing his course of literary study at Gill's Academy, in the city of Mattoon. In 1871, he removed to Douglas County, where he purchased a farm of one hundred and sixty acres of soil, as fertile as the Garden of Eden is supposed to have been. He has resided there ever since, and is gradually extending the range of his operations, having had two hundred and forty acres under his control during the past year. In 1861, he enlisted, as a private, in Company " E," Fifth Illinois Cavalry, and was successively promoted to Sergeant, Lieutenant and Forage Master, the latter position being held under the command of Governor Baker, of Indiana. He also served as Quartermaster of his regiment for some time. He is a member of the Methodist Episcopal Church, and is a Mason and Knight of Honor. He is an avowed Republican, from conviction, and has been a Supervisor in Coles County; also, has held the same position in Douglas County, and was a member of the Lower House of the Twenty-eighth General Assembly. He is large and manly in physical proportions, has a prominent nose, beard well threaded with gray. He is cool and concise in debate, and grave and dignified in carriage.

HON. JOHN FAIRBANKS.

The subject of this sketch was born in the town of Holliston, Worcester County, Massachusetts, on the 17th day of November, 1848. His parents, both Americans, were George W. and Sarah L. Whitcomb Holliston. His father was a country merchant, and was an enterprising, industrious citizen, respected by all his neighbors. The mother of the subject of this article was distantly related to the Lincoln family. Two years after the birth of Mr. Fairbanks, his parents moved to Jangus, Essex County, and his father was station agent at this point for the Eastern Railway. Mr. Fairbanks attended the Grammar School and Academy, and, at the age of fourteen years, he was ready for college; but, the war breaking out, his father, who was forty-nine years old, and his brother, who was seventeen, enlisted, and John, the fourteen-year-old boy, was left to care for the family, of five persons. The railroad company gave the father's place, as agent for the road, to the subject of this sketch, who, with the aid of his mother, attended to the business of the office until the father returned from the army. Beyond all doubt, Mr. Fairbanks was the youngest railroad agent ever employed by any road. After the return of his father, young Fairbanks went into a book-store, as clerk, from which humble position he has worked his way up, until now he is a publisher of some note. In 1869, he moved to Chicago, and took charge of the Western Depository of the American Tract Society. Mr. Fairbank's parents were members of the Congregational Church, but he is now an attendant of the Reformed Episcopal Church. He has always been a Republican, and the position he now holds is the first public office he has ever filled. He is Representative from the First District, Chicago, Cook County.

HON. JOHN B. FELKER.

This gentleman was ushered into the mysteries of life, in Washington County, Maryland, in November, 1839. In the case of Mr. Felker, there is no variation from the histrionic origin of most of the members of the Legislature of Illinois. His father was a farmer. In 1855, the family came West, locating at Mt. Morris, Ogle County, Illinois. Mr. Felker removed to Lee County, where he now resides, in 1860. His education is comprehensive and substantial. He is a graduate of Rock River Seminary, at Mt. Morris, an institution which has contributed a number of its students to the Legislative Halls of the State. By profession, he is a physician and surgeon—a graduate of Rush Medical College, of Chicago—having begun the practice of his profession in 1863, in the city of Amboy. He is a Congregationalist in religion, and is a member of the fraternity of Free Masons. Politically, he is a Democrat of firm convictions and strong party preferences. He has served as an Alderman from his ward in the city of Amboy, for eight years, and has been its Mayor for the last five years. He is of German extraction, and his grandfather was a soldier in the War of American Independence. In 1882, he was elected to the House of Representatives over Johnson, Democrat, and Osborne, Greenbacker, by a plurality of about two thousand votes. He is large and portly in person, of dark complexion and a kind, affable and generous nature. He will sacrifice all else to duty, and is a man of excellent judgment and varied talents.

HON. EUGENE J. FELLOWS.

Mr. Fellows is now thirty-six years of age, having been born in New Orleans, Louisiana, March 17th, 1847.   His father was a wealthy Southern gentleman, who was engaged in banking. In 1867, Mr. Fellows removed from the metropolis of the South, to that of the Northwest—from the Gulf of Mexico, to the south-western shores of Lake Michigan, where he became a resident of the great and only original Chicago.   Mr. Fellows' education is collegiate, he being a graduate of the University of Louisiana, located in his native city.   He is an attorney, by profession, having received instruction in the office of Judge E. T. Fellows, of New Orleans.   Mr. Fellows is one of the most scholarly men in the Thirty-third General Assembly, and, although possessing a very diffident disposition, and being averse to any coarse ostentation or "spread-eagle display," he is an eloquent speaker and most forcible reasoner.   He is apt in repartee, and quick to cover a breach in the wall of argument of his opponents.   He is logical and methodical in his speeches, and will neither employ, or permit the employment of illegitimate premises or conclusions by his adversaries, without exposing them to ridicule, or utterly demolishing them by his crushing retorts and unimpeachable proofs of their want of adaptability.   He is a conscientious and unswerving Democrat, and was elected Representative to the Thirty-third General Assembly from the Second District of Chicago.   He is Episcopalian in religious belief, and is a member of the fraternity of Free Masons.   In person, he is of medium stature and well proportioned.   He is somewhat incisive and brusque in speech, firm as Gibraltar in his convictions, and neat, genteel and tidy in dress.   He is polite and sociable, and is really a handsome man.

HON. JOHN T. FOSTER.

The subject of this sketch made his appearance among men, January 25th, 1849, in McDonough County, Illinois. His parents, Henry and Eliza Ann, *nee* Kirkpatrick, were earning their bread by tilling the soil, prior to and succeeding his birth. On New Years day, 1877, Mr. Foster located in Logan County, Illinois. Prior to that time, he had acquired a fair common school education, but, determined to push his researches further, he entered Lincoln University, from which he was graduated with honor, in the class of 1872. Not being an ostentatious man, he did not seek to place his intellectual acquirements before the people in a professional capacity. He was content to apply his knowledge to a proper administration of the affairs of his farm and stock ranch, and is now regarded as one of the most intelligent and successful farmers of his locality. He is a member of the Cumberland Presbyterian Church and an Ancient Odd Fellow. In 1880, he was a Republican candidate for the Representativeship of his District, which was Democratic, being defeated by thirteen and one-half votes. He owns six hundred and eighty acres of good land, and knows how to make it productive. He was elected to the House of Representatives, in 1882, by a majority of four hundred votes. In person, he is dark complected, tall and well proportioned. He is kind and considerate in demeanor, and generous in both purse and opinion. He is a thorough gentleman in his intercourse with the public.

HON. CHARLES E. FULLER.

This gentleman was born in Boone County, Illinois, March 31st, 1849, and is now thirty-four years of age. Seymour Fuller and his wife, Eliza A. Fuller, at the time of the birth of their child, Charles, were engaged in earning their bread by tilling the soil. Charles' first experience was that of a farmer's son, as exemplified in the day when railways were scarce, and the scythe, sickle and flail were the most complicated pieces of machinery employed in the harvest of the few acres of grain and prairie grass, necessary for the maintenance of the family and its scanty herd of domestic animals. Mr. Fuller is a graduate of the Belvidere High School, and attended college at Wheaton for a short time; but did not matriculate. He read law with the Hon. Jesse S. Hildrup, and was admitted to the Bar in due time, when he began a successful and lucrative practice. He had served as City Attorney of the city of Belvidere for three years, when, in 1876, he became State's Attorney for his county, and resigned in 1878, to accept the office of State Senator, to which he had been elected. He served his district in this capacity for four years, when the new apportionment threw him into a district which contained a hold-over Senator, leaving no vacancy in that branch of the General Assembly; so he was elected to the Lower House, in 1882. He is a staunch Republican, and has been Chairman of the County Central Committee for several years. He is also a member of the Senatorial, Judicial and Congressional Committees of his party, in his districts. He is a member of the Subordinate and Encampment branches of Odd Fellowship, and, also, of the American Legion of Honor. In person, he is not above the average height; light complected and smooth shaven. He is cool and collected, and always thinks carefully before he speaks.

La-Fayette Funk.

HON. LAFAYETTE FUNK.

Mr. Funk was born in McLean County, Illinois, in January, 1834, his father being then extensively engaged in farming and stock raising. His education was acquired in the common schools of his county, and the Ohio Wesleyan University, from which he was graduated in 1858. He is a farmer, by occupation, devoting considerable capital and a great deal of time and effort to the breeding of short-horned cattle, and Berkshire and Poland-China swine. His farm consists of no less than two thousand, two hundred acres of land, all in one township. It is said to be worth $165,000, and he has a large stock interest in the First National Bank, of Bloomington, and the National State Bank, of the same city, in the latter of which he is Director. He is not a church member, but is a Free Mason, having attained the thirty-second degree in that Order. He is a Republican, in politics, unwavering and determined, and has been School Trustee, Commissioner of Highways, Town Clerk and Supervisor. He was elected to the House of Representatives in 1882, from the Twenty-eighth District, by a handsome majority. In personal appearance, he is a very large and hearty man; wears a full beard; is decisive in character, and quick of perception; honest, reliable and generous to a fault. He is a man, whose familiarity with the wants of the agriculturalist, fine education and sound judgment in financial matters, peculiarly fit him for the high position to which he has been elevated by the votes of his constituents.

HON. JOSEPH GALLUP.

This gentleman has an ancestry, of which he is justly proud. It is not because he believes that the blood of royalty courses in his veins, but for the simple reason that his family was established in this country by one of the companions of Governor Winthrop, of Colonial, Massachusetts. This was five generations ago, and John Gallup, one of the "Six Captains," was afterward slain in one of those horrible Indian massacres, which darken the pages of early New England history. The name is now one of the most common in Massachusetts and Connecticut, on account of the numerous progeny of this, one of the earlier settlers of that locality. A distant relative of Mr. Gallup occupied the honored station of Lieutenant Governor of Connecticut, a few years since. His father was Nathaniel Gallup, and his mother's maiden name was Sarah Barbour. Ben Adhem Gallup, his grandfather, was one of the brave band of Yeomen, who fought in the War for American Independence. Mr. Gallup was born in Windham County, Connecticut, September 4th, 1827, and is now fifty-five years of age. He came to Peoria County, Illinois, in 1850, and began farming upon lands owned by his father. He yet resides at the same place, and is one of Illinois' sturdy farmers. He received his education in Smithville Seminary and Plainfield Academy, in Rhode Island. The latter is one of the oldest places of learning in the country. He has held many positions of honor and trust in his county, and was elected to the House in 1880, and reëlected in 1882. He was once a Lieutenant of Militia, but prefers peace to war. He belongs to no church, but is inclined to the faith of Universalism more than any other. He has been a Democrat all his life, and was elected on that ticket, from the Twenty-sixth District, by a plurality of over one thousand votes.

HON. A. G. GOODSPEED.

This gentleman came into being in Clinton County, New York, in 1821, his father being a genuine downeast farmer. The family removed to Ohio in 1833; but left there in 1842 and came to La Salle County, Ill., the subject of this sketch afterward becoming, and now being a resident of the village of Odell, Livingston County. His education was derived from the public schools and personal effort, privately put forth. His business is as honorable as that of any other member of the Assembly, and equally as lucrative, perhaps. It is nothing more or less than plain farming. Mr. Goodspeed is a member of the Methodist Episcopal Church; a Free Mason and an Odd Fellow. He is a solid and unwavering Republican in politics, being, as it were, one of the charter members of the party. He has been Overseer and Commissioner of Highways in his township, and been its Assessor for fifteen consecutive years. He was elected to the House of Representatives in 1882, from the Eighteenth District, defeating his opponent by a majority of two thousand votes. He is tall, and his hair is snowy white. He is very patriarchal in appearance, in fact. He is one of those genial, good natured old men, whom everybody admires, and who always has a kind word or gentle deed for the humblest of his acquaintances. He is a fine speaker and an able legislator, who reflects honor upon himself, his constituency and the State.

HON. SIDNEY GREAR.

This prominent member of the House was born at Jonesboro, Illinois, March 20th, 1854. John and Cindona Grear, his parents, were serving the community as a skillful jeweler and tidy housewife, when Sidney came to honor the family's name. His great-grandfather was a graduate of the Edinburg (Scotland) University, though a German by birth, and served as a Surgeon in the British Army, during the Revolutionary War. His grandfather, George Grear, was an Ensign, afterward Major, under Andrew Jackson, in the War of 1812. He afterward became a Lieutenant, a Major, and was a Captain in the Blackhawk War. His father was born in Jonesboro, Illinois, where he now resides. Sidney's education is excellent, and was acquired more by close observation and careful reading than any systematic course of instruction, until he reached the age of fifteen years, when, having a talent for music, which had developed into a musical education, without extraordinary culture, he began traveling, as a musician, with theatrical companies. He also corresponded for various newspapers, during his wanderings, and, at the end of three years, came back to his home, and, in course of time, became a graduate of the Southern Illinois Normal University. He then became principal of the public schools of his native city, and, during his service in that capacity, read law with Gov. John Dougherty, who took great interest in him, and urged him to become a lawyer. He was admitted to the Bar in 1878, and became a partner of the Prosecuting Attorney of his county; afterward, in 1882, he became a partner with Judge M. C. Crawford, who had presided over the courts of his circuit for eighteen years. Mr. Grear defended the daughter of his preceptor in the law against an information for *quo warranto* in the Circuit, Appellate and Supreme Courts of this State, securing in the latter a decision that a woman may be legally appointed Master in Chancery of a Circuit Court. It is the first case of the kind on record in our higher courts, and young Grear has certainly accomplished an unparalleled success in it. He is a Democrat, defeating Thomas M. Logan, a brother of Hon. John A. Logan, by a plurality of 6,000 votes, for Representative, from the Cairo District. The firm of Crawford & Grear is one of the strongest in Southern Illinois.

HON. FRANCIS M. GREATHOUSE.

This prominent member of the House was born in Pike County, Illinois, in 1837, on the 26th day of March. His father was Bonaparte Greathouse, and his mother's name was Nancy. They were representatives of the early settlers of the State— generous, kind, hard-working, intelligent and thrifty. At his father's death in 1850, he left an estate worth $50,000. The subject of this sketch received a good, solid education in the common schools of his county, after which he entered the office of Senator Archer, of Pittsfield, in his native county, as a law student. He completed his course of legal study under the tutorship of Hon. N. M. Knapp, of Winchester, when he was admitted to the Bar, and at once entered upon a successful practice of his profession, at Hardin, Calhoun County. He has served as Master in Chancery, State's Attorney and County Judge of the latter County, resigning the last named office when elected Representative in 1882, from the Thirty-sixth District. He is a consistent member of the Christian Church and an enthusiastic Odd Fellow and Free Mason. His plurality was 5,000. In person, Mr. Greathouse is portly and dignified. His long, black, curling hair is sprinkled a little with gray. He is generous in purse as well opinion, and he is as genial a companion and talented a gentle. man as can be found in the House of the Thirty-third General Assembly. Judging from what we have observed, his presence at the sessions of his branch of the Legislature is no less gratifying to his associates than those, whose suffrages conferred the honor upon him. His future seems full of promise, and we have sufficient confidence in his good sense to feel sure that he will not fall into the tempting paths of error, which lie in the way of a rising public man.

HON. JAMES. M. GREGG.

Mr. Gregg was born in Hamilton County, Illinois, November 5th, 1846, his father being one of the early farmers of the State. His education was obtained in the common schools of Illinois, and by a course of study in a law office, as a result of which he was, in due time, admitted to the Bar, immediately entering upon a successful and profitable professional career. He is not a church member; but belongs to the Ancient Order of Free and Accepted Masons. In politics, he is a Democrat, of long standing and unquestioned fidelity. He was appointed Master in Chancery in 1871, and State's Attorney for Saline County, in July, 1872. He was elected to the latter office in November following, and reëlected in 1876. He was elected to the House of Representatives in 1880, and, in 1882, was reëlected to the same responsible position, which he fills with honor to himself, and the utmost satisfaction to the constituency, which raised him to power in the Forty-ninth District. His long experience as Prosecuting Attorney for his county, renders his services at this session of the Legislature peculiarly valuable, in the light of the changes in the Criminal Code of the State, which have been proposed, and are, or, at least, seem to be, necessary to a more stern administration of the penalties of the law. We venture the prediction that his knowledge of the methods of practice in criminal cases will prove largely beneficial to the people, by leaving its impress upon the legislation of the session. In person, Mr. Gregg is not above medium stature; fair, in complexion; a fine conversationalist and debater, and a leader on the Democratic side of the House. He is a very polite, intelligent and generous gentleman.

HON. ELIJAH M. HAINES.

Mr. Haines was born at Oneida, New York, his parents being natives of Connecticut. His father died when Elijah was but six years of age, and the son went to live with a farmer, remaining five years, after which, he and a brother came to Chicago, which was then a village of about five hundred inhabitants. He removed to Lake County, Illinois, a year later, and began farming. His educational advantages were very limited, and he procured books and began his struggle for knowledge. He soon acquired a fair understanding of ordinary studies, and of the German and Latin languages. During this time, he was obliged to provide for himself and his widowed mother. Owing to trouble arising from uncertain tenure of lands in his county, he. began reading law, and was admitted to the Bar in 1351. He practiced at Waukegan until 1860, when he removed to Chicago. He is the compiler of the Township Organization Laws of Illinois, and similar works in Michigan, Missouri, Wisconsin and Minnesota. He is also the author of a Treatise for Illinois Justices of the Peace, a work which was once very popular. He was originally a Democrat in politics; but espoused the anti-monoplist cause, and has since been an Independent. He was elected to the House of Representatives in 1858, 1860, 1862, 1874, and 1882. During the session of 1875, he was chosen Speaker, on account of a dead-lock, in which he held the balance of power. The history of that session, and his presidency, is yet fresh in the minds of the people of Illinois. He was, also, a member of the Constitutional Convention of 1870, holding the balance of power in that body. He is an excellent parliamentarian, exasperatingly cool and incisive in speech, and warmly cherishes his sentiments of favor or hatred. His recent filibustering process of obstruction, on the high license question, is a fair sample of his tactics on the floor of the House.

HON. JULIUS A. HAMMOND.

The subject of this sketch was born in Bath, Summit County, Ohio, April 25th, 1833. His parents were Ward K. and Sophronia Hale Hammond. They were of English descent, and the father was a farmer. When the subject of this sketch was ten years of age, his parents moved from Ohio to Illinois, and located in Knox County, at a point where there were, at that time, but few settlers. Here the father bought a fine farm of one hundred and sixty acres, and, during the six years following, young Hammond and the family worked very hard, tilling their fields. This farm of 160 acres, Mr. Hammond's father sold for $500, (to-day it is worth $15,000,) and moved to Hanover, Jo Daviess County, where he rented land. The subject of this sketch worked for the man who owned the farm his father had rented, for 25 cents per day and boarded himself. At the present time, Mr. Hammond owns the farm his father then rented, and the former landlord's son and daughter have been employed by him. He has erected on the farm a house costing $3,000, and he owns 480 acres of land in that County. Mr. Hammond had little or no advantages until he was 21 years of age. His education was derived from several different schools. He attended the Academic department of Knox College for one year, and was one year at the Rock River Seminary, at Mt. Morris. He also spent one year at the Northwestern University at Evanston, when he then returned to Knox College, where he remained six months. Mr. Hammond has held several local offices in his township. He has been School Director and School Trustee, and is Justice of the Peace. He now fills the position of Representative from the 12th District. Three of Mr. Hammond's brothers were in the army, and he was left at home to care for the remainder of the family. When the draft came, he was drafted ; but not being able to leave home, he hired a substitute, paying a man $800 to enlist for one year, in his stead. Mr. Hammond is a member of the M. E. Church. He has always been a Republican, and an active worker in the ranks of that party. In appearance, he is of medium height, and wears a full beard; is a pleasant gentleman and a sharp, shrewd member.

HON. WILLIAM HENRY HARPER.

Mr. Harper is one of those energetic young business men, whose energy, thoughtfulness and courage fit them for positions of honor and trust, and who wait for the office to seek them, rather than neglect more tangible matters, for the sake of pursuing a position, only to find that the people prefer that some less pretentious and more worthy gentleman shall fill it. He was born in Tippecanoe County, Indiana, May 4th, 1845, and, when very young, emigrated, with his parents, to Illinois, and became a resident of Woodford County. He was raised upon a farm, there forming habits of close attention and unceasing industry, which have proven invaluable to him in his more recent career as a grain dealer. At the age of nineteen, Mr. Harper enlisted as a private in the One Hundred and Forty-fifth Regiment of Illinois Volunteers, and remained in the service until the Rebellion was crushed. His education was obtained in public schools, and Eastman's Business College, Chicago. In 1872, he was appointed Chief Grain Inspector, and administered the affairs of that office to the satisfaction of the grain dealers of Chicago, until 1875. He is now largely interested in the immense Chicago, Milwaukee and St. Paul Elevators, as part owner and manager. He is a solid Republican, and his business experience has rendered him one of the most practical and far-seeing Legislators in the Thirty-third General Assembly. He is a perfect gentleman in appearance and bearing, and, although business to the core, is generous and considerate, withal. He is interested in numerous business enterprises other than those above named, and has accumulated a large fortune.

HON. WILLIAM S. HAWKER.

This gentleman was born on Long Island, State of New York, January 25th, 1834, his father being at that time industriously engaged in the responsible and multifarious duties of farm life. In 1845, the family came to Illinois, locating in Kankakee County, where Mr. Hawker now resides. The subject of this sketch modeled his professional choice after that of his father, becoming a farmer by occupation. He is the owner of a very fine farm of two hundred acres in Kankakee County, and cultivates it upon an intelligent and profitable principle. He is one of that better class of farmers, who do not simply think of the present; but are continually making substantial provisions for the future. His farm is well improved, and upon it are used the labor-saving appliances of this enlightened age. In fact, he has reduced farming to a system, which renders it no less remunerative than it is pleasant. He received his education in the common schools of New York and Illinois. He is not a member of any church or secret society. He has been a Republican throughout his voting career, and is no less warm in the faith now than in the beginning. He has been Township Collector, three years ; Road Commissioner, three years ; Supervisor, eight years, and is now serving his first term in the House of Representatives, having been elected in 1882, by a plurality of 2,500 votes, running ahead of any other candidate on the ticket. He represents the Sixteenth District. He is a man of average stature, dark in complexion, and believes that where there is a will there is also a way. On account of his energy and determination, coupled with good judgment, measures introduced by him seldom fail to pass. In disposition, he is kind, obliging and generous.

HON. JAMES A. HAWKS.

This gentleman was born in Oswego County, New York, July 19th, 1847, his father being a farmer at that time. Mr Hawks came to Illinois in 1869, locating at Atwood, Piatt County. His education was obtained at the Felley Academy, Fulton, New York, and the Hamilton Law School, of which he is a graduate. By occupation, he has been a jolly miller, ever since he began business for himself. In 1864, he enlisted as a private in the Third New York Artillery, although but seventeen years of age, and served until the close of the war. He was a prisoner at Libby Prison a month, being paroled the day before Grant captured the place. He is not a communicant in any church; but is a member of the Ancient order of Free and Accepted Masons. Mr. Hawks is quite wealthy, owning a mill and elevator worth $8,000, in Atwood, and two hundred and sixty acres of land in its immediate vicinity. He also has a half interest in a tile factory which is said to be worth at least $6,000. In politics, he is a sound and unwavering Republican, and has been a member of the Board of Supervisors of his County five years, two of which he occupied the responsible and honorable position of Chairman. In 1882, he was elected to the House of Representatives from the Thirtieth District, polling an unusually large vote. In person, he is of the average stature, fair in complexion; a good man of business, a shrewd legislator and careful financier. He has accumulated his entire property by individual effort and excellent management. He is dignified and manly in bearing, charitable in opinion and judgment, a clear and forcible speaker and a kind and generous gentleman. He is not ostentatious; but he is decidedly one of the sound, common sense Representatives of the State of Illinois.

HON. LOWRY HAY.

Mr. Hay is a native Illinoisan, who was born in White County, June 15th, 1838, to his parents, John and Hannah, who were engaged in earning their bread by the honest toil incident to farm life. Young Hay received an education in the common schools of his county, during the epoch of log-cabin school-houses. As his advantages in this respect were very limited, he did what every other young man who, under like circumstances, determines to make his mark in the world. He supplied, by extraordinary effort, what was denied him by necessity. He is a living illustration of the fact that an education is not entirely dependent upon the efforts of well qualified teachers; but more upon the energies of a willing and inquiring pupil. Mr. Hay is a farmer—one of the men who, having experimental knowledge of the needs of the majority of his constituents, is certainly a proper and worthy person to represent them in the Legislature of their State. He has always been a strict adherent to the Democratic party, and, in 1874, was elected Sheriff of Wayne County, where he then resided. After the expiration of his term of office, he returned to White County, and was quietly attending to the wants of his farm and family, in 1882, when the suffrages of his people were united in a successful effort to make him one of their Representatives in the Thirty-third General Assembly. His plurality was fully seven thousand, and the voters of the Forty-third District have no reason to regret their choice. In person, Mr. Hay is somewhat about the medium stature, and is possessed of an excellent physique. He has dark hair and wears a moustache of the same color. In manner, he is polite and affable, yet a little sedate. He is very genteel in his bearing and deportment, is an acute observer and shrewd politician. He is not hasty, yet he is quick to apprehend the errors of an antagonist or perceive the advantages of a position, or demerits of a pending question. He is a safe man to be entrusted with law-making powers and privileges. -

HON. THOMAS N. HENRY.

Mr. Henry was born in Shelby County, Illinois, on January 22d, 1837. His father was one of the pioneer agriculturalists of that part of the State, having settled at the above named place in 1829. On Sundays, the Reverend B. W. Henry ceased his farm labor and entered the log cabins of his neighborhood, to preach the Gospel. He was elected one of the County Commissioners of Shelby, in the good times when a five-dollar bill would defray the expenses of a very spirited campaign. To illustrate the perseverance and dauntless spirit of the pioneers of Illinois, we give space to the statement that Mr. Henry's father made a visit to the State of Virginia, when Thomas was very young, accomplishing the journey on horseback, and defraying the entire expenses of the trip with seven dollars and fifty cents. The son is a resident of Shelby County now, having engaged in merchandising at Windsor. Mr. Henry is a member of the Christian Church, a Mason and Knight of Honor. He is a conscientious Democrat in politics, and has been Chairman of the County Board for the last three years, and a member for five years, during which time a magnificent court-house was built, without the misappropriation or stealing of a single dollar. He was elected to the House of Representatives in 1882, by a plurality of four thousand five hundred votes. He is below the average stature, small and dark complected; has a very sharp, bright eye, which seems to penetrate one's inmost thoughts and motives at a glance. He is shrewd in business, and polite, social and generous in disposition. He is a trustworthy member, who will not be inveigled into a sacrifice of principle for the sake of so-called policy.

HON. JAMES HERRINGTON.

The eyes of Mr. Herrington first gazed in wonder upon the world, in Crawford County, Indiana during the year 1826. His father was at that time a merchant. The family came to Illinois in 1833, and located in Chicago. His education was acquired in a Chicago printing office, under the censorship of the celebrated character in Illinois politics—Long John Wentworth—where he was regularly apprenticed under the law; and served for seven long and weary, but profitable years. He is now a farmer and dairyman. He belongs to no church; but is a Free Mason and member of the Independent Order of Odd Fellows. In politics, Mr. Herrington is a Democrat, probably having become thoroughly disgusted with Republican methods and chicanery during his service under the baleful thumb of the above mentioned Long John. He was County Clerk of Kane County, eight years, and has been a member of the Lower House in the General Assembly of his State, for six consecutive terms. At the last election, in November, 1882, he polled the largest vote which he had ever received, and it begins to appear as if the Democrats intend keeping him in office as long as he desires it. They could not make a better choice, we are very sure. He is large and brusque in bearing, full of dignity, witty, has a remarkably powerful voice, and is one of the strongest debaters in the House of Representatives. He is very taciturn and distant at first acquaintance; but, upon more intimate association, appears, as he really is, a kind hearted gentleman.

HON. ROBERT S. HESTER.

This gentleman was born in Boone County, Kentucky, November 19th, 1825. His father was a farmer, and Robert followed his example in choosing the means by which he would win his way to fortune and fame. When the subject of this sketch was but a year old, the family removed to Ohio, where it remained until 1847, when it joined the tide, which was flowing to the fertile prairies of the Sucker State, locating in Marshall County, where Mr. Hester now resides. His education was obtained in the country schools of Ohio, and by careful observation and close study, since he has reached the estate of manhood. He is an Elder of the Christian Church, but does not belong to any secret society. He has been a Republican ever since that party came into existence, and feels that, until new issues arise and new party lines are drawn, it is his duty to remain faithful to the organization, which safely educated the government through the greatest crisis, which any Republic on earth has ever succeeded in bridging. He has served his constituents as Road Commissioner, Justice of the Peace, Supervisor and Sheriff, having been elected to the latter office on the ticket which was honored with the name of Abraham Lincoln, in 1860. He was elected to the House of Representatives in 1882, by the largest vote polled in his district at that election. His farm consists of six hundred acres of excellent land, and he is largely interested in breeding improved cattle and swine. In person, he is not above medium stature, is dark in complexion, has a great many gray hairs among the black, and is clever, generous and jovial in disposition. He is one of the men to be regarded as checks upon extravagant and visionary measures, and will labor to make the legislation of the session substantial and practical.

HON. LUTHER L. HIATT.

This gentleman was born in Henry County, Indiana, in August, 1844. His father is a physician and surgeon. In 1859, Mr. Hiatt came to Illinois, locating at Wheaton, DuPage County, where he now resides, and pursues the business of a druggist and pharmacist. He received a partial collegiate education ; but left the institution without being graduated. In 1862, he enlisted as a private in the One Hundred and Fifth Illinois Regiment, and was mustered out in the same capacity at the close of the war, conscious of having performed his duty, and faithfully served his country. He has been a Justice of the Peace for four years, and Postmaster of his village two years. He was elected to the House of Representatives in 1882, by an exceptionally large vote. He is a Republican in politics, solely from a conviction that that party is the proven friend of free government, and the enemy of repudiation, tyranny, and what he believes to be a baneful doctrine—State Sovereignty. He is a very cool and forcible reasoner, and is neither afraid or ashamed to make known his sentiments upon any question, in which he believes himself, his constituents or the people of the State, generally, to be vitally interested. He is a splendid man in physique, and a very polite gentleman in his intercourse with the public. He is determined in his position upon all topics ; but generous to a fallen foe, no less than a friend.

HON. JOHN HIGGINS.

Mr. Higgins, who represents the Forty-eighth District in the House of Representatives, was born at Middleton, Cork County, Ireland, November 22d, 1845. His family, consisting of his mother, four brothers and himself, came to the United States in 1852 and settled at Pittsfield, Massachusetts, where the subject of our sketch acquired his education in the common and high schools. In May, 1859, Mr. Higgins was apprenticed to a watchmaker and served his full time at that trade. In 1866, he came to Illinois and located at Du Quoin, Perry County, where he now resides and has been engaged in business since 1867. He is a Democrat in politics, and was elected to his present position in November, 1882. He is a member of the House Committee on Claims. Mr. Higgins is a somewhat peculiar man in deportment, although upright, honest and frank. One of his strong personal traits is diffidence, and it was with considerable difficulty that enough material for even this brief article could be obtained. He is a very firm and thoughtful gentleman, who commands both the respect and confidence of his associates and the highest regard of his constituents. He is a safe and able legislator and a very estimable man.

HON. GEORGE L. HOFFMAN.

Mr. Hoffman was born in Hesse Darnstadt, German Empire, December 1st, 1847, his father being a shoemaker by calling. The family came to the United States in 1850, locating at Chambersburg, Pennsylvania. Mr. Hoffman afterward removed to Lanark, Carroll County, Illinois, where he resided for some time, but finally made his permanent home at Mt. Carroll, in the same county. His literary education was acquired in the public schools of Pennsylvania and the Normal University of this State. He was professionally educated in the Wesleyan Law School being graduated in both that and the University in 1877. At the early age of fourteen, he had worked at the bench with his father, and acquired a very excellent knowledge of the trade, but that was not his kind of a bench, so he enters the Bar, that he might work at another, which he deemed better suited to his tastes. He is the junior member of the firm of Hunter, Hunter & Hoffman, attorneys, Mt. Carroll, Illinois—a firm which has few equals and no superiors in that part of Illinois. He is not a church member, but belongs to the Independent Order of Odd Fellows. In politics, Mr. Hoffman is a Republican, he voted for Greeley and Tilden in the campaigns of 1872 and 1876, but supported Cullom for Governor, in both of his campaigns. He is one of those men, who votes solely from a conviction of right, and it is pleasant to realize that the day for employing independence and pure and manly principles as an argument for the defeat of one, who exemplified them, is past. He was elected to the House of Representatives in 1882, from the Twelfth District, this being the first public office he has ever held. He is the owner of one hundred and sixty acres of land in Iowa. He is a very intelligent and obliging gentleman.

HON. J. M. HONEY.

This gentleman was born in Davis County, Indiana, October 27th, 1839. His father was then a clerk in a dry goods store. The subject of this sketch came to Illinois in 1847, locating in Jasper County, where he now resides. His education was acquired in the district schools of Illinois, and by observation and personal effort. He enlisted in the Eighth Illinois Regiment of Volunteers, in 1861, and served in the War of the Rebellion until 1864, when he was discharged. He afterward studied law with John H. Halley, a practicing attorney of Newton, in his county, and was admitted to the Bar in 1870. He is now engaged in practicing his profession, at Newton. He is an Odd Fellow and Free Mason, but not a communicant in any church organization. He is a pronounced Republican in politics, and, although a man of very great local prominence, had never held any public office prior to his election to the House of Representatives in 1882, as the minority candidate in the Forty-fifth District. He beat his prohibitionist opponent by about seven thousand votes, a political trifle, which few men could successfully overcome. Mr. Honey, in addition to his legal business, has a farm of about two hundred and ten acres, and owns a large interest in a flourishing and profitable dry goods establishment in his town. In person, he is of medium height and dark complexion; grave and dignified in bearing, yet generous and polite in his intercourse with the people.

HON. WILLIAM W. HOSKINSON.

This gentleman of the House of Representatives, was born in Ohio on the 15th of September, 1816.   His father was a foundryman and machinist by trade, so Mr. Hoskinson is another of the inumerable that has been born humbly, only to rise in the estimation of the people, by individual effort, and be chosen by their votes, to represent their interests in the Legislative Assembly of their State.   His education was acquired in the face of almost insurmountable obstacles, he being obliged to depend upon the subscription schools of the olden time, for its germ, and compelled to supply what they lacked of making it reasonably complete, by perseverent study of such books as he could obtain.   In 1825, the family come to Illinois, locating in Wabash County, at the village of Mt. Carmel.   Mr. Hoskinson became one of those indispensible elements of society—a tailor, following his business in that line until 1844, when he opened a large General Merchandize establishment and clothing house, in the affairs of which he was actively engaged until 1880, when he retired from active business life.   His life has not been a very eventful one, as he is one of those quiet men, whose innate merits are left to be discovered by the people, in their own good time.   He was never a candidate for any public office until in the autumn of 1882, when he was elected to the House of Representatives, as a Republican, by a very large vote.   Politically, he is not unreasonable; but is a staunch advocate of Republican principles, solely because he believes that they are based upon public policy and moral rectitude.   He has large real estate interests, and is said to be quite wealthy.   In religious faith, he is a Methodist.   He is a member of the Independent Order of Odd Fellows, also.   In person, he is spare and not above medium stature.   He is a shrewd financier and a generous hearted and generally amiable gentleman.   Although sixty-six years old, his hair is quite dark and beautiful, yet, time having dealt leniently with him.

HON. JESSE D. JENNINGS.

This gentleman is now serving his first term in the House of Representatives, having been elected as a Democrat from the Forty-third District, in 1882. He was born in Shelby County, Illinois, January 6th, 1831, and is now fifty-two years of age. His father owned one hundred and sixty acres of land, and, upon this Shelby County farm, Mr. Jennings began his career as a farmer's boy. In 1839, his parents removed to Fayette County, where they purchased some good farming lands. His father only recently died. He became a clerk in a store, remaining there for one year. He then married, purchased a three hundred and twenty acre farm, and became a husband and husbandman on his own account. He volunteered as a Second Lieutenant in the Thirty-fifth Illinois Infantry, and was soon promoted to the Captaincy of Company "K." In 1863, he was obliged to resign his commission on account of ill-health. Mr. Jennings says that his educational advantages were very limited, and significantly adds: "I have been acquiring my education since I became twenty-one, and, although I have paid dearly for it, I lack a great deal of having it all, yet." This is in marked contrast with some of the youthful collegians of the Assembly, who imagine that they know it all already. He is a pronounced Democrat, and has served as Sheriff and member of the Board of Supervisors of his county. He is a Free Mason, but not a member of any church. His opponent for Legislative honors, was Col. Sturgis, whom he defeated by a plurality of five thousand votes. Tall, raw-boned, as was Abraham Lincoln, angular in features, but a giant in bulk, is the way he appears to a stranger. He is as kind-hearted as a woman, generous as he is large, and as pointed in repartee as in features. He is one of the deceiving men of the House; one from whom little would be expected and much experienced.

HON. WILLIAM H. JOHNSON.

This gentleman is a native of the Sucker State, having been born in White County, Illinois, March 3d, 1840. He has spent his life as a resident of the county where he was born, receiving his education in its common and high schools. In March of 1861, he enlisted in Company "I," of the First Illinois Cavalry, serving one year as Orderly Sergeant. He became First Lieutenant of the Eighty-seventh Illinois Infantry, serving in that capacity until the close of the Rebellion. He is a Free Mason of the Royal Arch Degree, and a member of the Ancient Order of United Workmen. He is also a communicant in the Christian Church. He read law with John E. Whiting, of Carmi, Illinois, and was admitted to the Bar in 1867. He is an active and successful lawyer—one whom the people of his locality regard as able and influential, and, if the writer's judgment is worth anything as a guide to public opinion, the people of Illinois have no reason to regret that his birth-place and home—his professional career and political promotion are so intimately related to their proud State. In political belief, he is an avowed and uncompromising Republican—one who acts from convictions of right, justice and eternal fitness, in making his estimates of political merits. He never held a public office prior to his election to the House of Representatives, in 1882, and is not a professed or professional wire-puller in political matters. His election was based upon his intrinsic value as a man and lawyer. He is the minority Representative from his district. In stature, he is above the average. He is portly and yet neat in appearance; affable, gentlemanly and polite in deportment, and kind and generous in natural impulses.

HON. JOHN H. JONES.

Mr. Jones was born in Brown County, Ohio, on October 30th, 1823. His father was a farmer who removed to Warren County, Indiana, when John was a very small boy. Mr. Jones came to Illinois in 1851, locating in Iroquois County, where he has since resided. He received a limited education in the district schools of Indiana; but has been a close observer and untiring searcher after knowledge all his life, thus making amends for the disadvantages under which he has labored. He has devoted his life to the cultivation of the soil. He affiliates with no church or secret society. He is a lover of fine live-stock and has a great many rare specimens upon his farm. He is a staunch Republican, having cast his fortunes with the party in 1856, and stuck to it faithfully ever since. He has served his County as a member of the Board of Supervisors for thirteen consecutive years, and as Treasurer of Schools, for fifteen years in succession. He has no less than fourteen hundred acres of land in his County, and owns a large interest in the First National Bank, of Watseka, of which he is one of the directors. He is, perhaps, one of the wealthiest men in Iroquois County. He was elected to the House of Representatives in 1882, by a very large plurality of votes. In person, he is stout and heavy. He is a very hearty old gentleman, and one of the shrewdest financiers in the House of the Thirty-third General Assembly. He is good natured and generous in disposition, and practical in thought and speech.

HON. ROBERT BRUCE KENNEDY.

Mr. Kennedy was born at Roxbury, Delaware County, New York, November 25th, 1852. His father was a merchant by occupation. In 1875, Mr. Kennedy came to Illinois, locating in Chicago. His education is academic, he being a graduate of the Delaware Institute, in his native State. He is of Scotch descent, his mother having been a member of Dr. Chalmer's Church, in Glasgow, Scotland. His father was a Presbyterian. By occupation, Mr. Kennedy is a dealer in books and stationery, being connected with the J. M. W. Jones Company, of Chicago, which is one of the most extensive stationery and blank book houses in the United States. He is thoroughly conversant with his business, and has made it a financial success since the commencement of his commercial career. He is not a communicant in any church, although he is s regular attendant at Presbyterian meetings, and contributes to the maintenance of the organization. In politics, he is a firm and uncompromising Republican, having inherited his political affiliations, and confirmed them by study, practice and experience. He has never before held public office ; but, in 1882, was chosen to represent the First Chicago District, in the Lower House of the Thirty-third General Assembly. He is an ardent advocate of party measures, and a safe and perfectly reliable representative of the interests of his constituency. He ran about a thousand votes ahead of his ticket in his own precinct, which is a much stronger expression of the esteem in which he is held, than can possibly be placed upon paper. In person, he is above the average stature, rather dark in complexion, possessing a fine physique, and a genial and amiable temper. In speech, he is pointed and incisive, and the trust reposed in him by his constituency is not misplaced. Mr. Kennedy's father was a neighbor of Jay Gould during his residence in New York City.

HON. ERNREIS R. E. KIMBROUGH.

This gentleman was born in Edgar County, Illinois, March 28th, 1851. His father, Andrew H. Kimbrough, was a practicing physician and surgeon, when the subject of our sketch came into the world. Mr. Kimbrough has resided in the district where he was born, ever since his birth, and, perhaps his fidelity to the old stamping ground and the associations of his youth, had something to do with electing him to the House of Representatives. His education was acquired in the district schools of the State, and Normal University at Bloomington. He is a Free Mason and Knight of Honor, but is not a communicant in any church denomination. He is a lawyer by profession, and is said to be a very prominent and successful one. In politics, he is a regular, old fashioned, upright Democrat, from a conviction of the intrinsic worth of the principles, upon which that party rests. He was elected to the House of Representatives in 1882, and is also a member of the Board of Education of his city, Danville, in the Thirty-first District. He is quite a wealthy gentleman, being the proprietor of a very fine farm and holding considerable stock in the Gas Company and First National Bank, of his city, being a director in both of those corporations. He has accumulated his money by his own efforts and knows, by its cost in labor and anxiety, the full value of every dollar of it. He is tall and commanding in physique; fair in complexion; dignified in bearing and cool, collected and deliberate in speech. He is a forcible reasoner and a successful financier, whose services in the Legislature would be missed, were he to be called from his chair.

HON. EDWARD M. KINMAN.

This rising young Representative was born at Jacksonville, Morgan County, Illinois, April 2d, 1856, to William and Ann Kinman, a wedded pair which had cast their fortunes in what was then known as the far west. His father was a Lieutenant Colonel in the One Hundred and Fifteenth Regiment of Illinois Volunteers, and became a martyr to his cause and country, upon the gory field of Chicamauga. Mr. Kinman possesses a very excellent education, being a graduate of the Northwestern University, of the class of 1878. He read law with the firm of Brown, Kirby & Russell, in Jacksonville, and is now considered a very prominent member of the Morgan County Bar. He is a member of the Methodist Church, and is a brother in good standing of one of the Jacksonville Lodges of the Independent Order of Odd Fellows. He yet maintains his connection with the *Beta Theta Pi*, a secret literary society in the University, where he received his education. He is a prominent Democrat, has never been anything else, politically, within the range of his memory, and seems to be held in high esteem in the Thirty-eighth District, of which he is one of the Representatives. He was elected in 1882, by a plurality of over two thousand votes. In person, he is very trim and well proportioned. He is a little above medium height, and inclined toward a dark complexion, though not in a very pronounced degree. He is prepossessing in both manners and appearance, and the young ladies of Springfield are unanimously agreed that he is a good looking young gentleman. He is a fluent speaker, and will make his mark with the first good opportunity that offers.

HON. GREGORY A. KLUPP.

This gentleman was born at Golawoz, Prussian Poland, on the 10th of April, 1849, to Joseph Klupp, a contractor and architect, and Anna, his wife, whose maiden name was Smarzynski. In 1868, Mr. Klupp came to the "land of the free and home of the brave," locating at Berlin, Wisconsin, from which place he removed to Milwaukee, thence to St. Louis, and finally locating in the City of Chicago, which is now his home. He was educated in a graded school of his native country, and has acquired his knowledge of the English language by close observation and frequent experiment. He was a distiller prior to his emigration from Poland, and followed that business during his residence in St. Louis. He is now actively engaged in business connected with Chicago and Western real estate. He is said to be the owner of real estate valued at twenty-five thousand dollars. He is a devoted Catholic and holds no fellowship with any secret society. He is a Democrat from crown to sole, and was elected to the House of Representatives in 1882, by a plurality of nearly three thousand votes. His life has been rather an eventful one, he having been compelled to contend against adversities in many forms. This has given him a determined air, which is calculated to inspire an opponent with a full conviction that the task of overcoming his objections to a given measure is one of no mean dimensions. In person, Mr. Klupp is small and fair. He is polite and affable, and a shrewd reasoner. He is very plain and unassuming in dress, no less than in speech, and he will keenly watch all measures, which may threaten the interests of his constituents. He possesses all of the ingenuity as a Legislator, for which the people of his father-land have always been noted as artisans.

HON. JOHN LACKIE.

This gentleman is of Scotch descent, and is the son of Andrew and Elizabeth Waddill Lackie. He was born in Barnet, Caledonia County, Vermont, on the 26th of December, 1823. His father was a sturdy farmer of the Green Mountain State. John's education was obtained in the Academic Schools of his native State, where he remained until 1844, when he removed to this State, and settled in Stark County, where he commenced farming. He here served afterward as a Justice of the Peace for four years, and was a County Supervisor for about twenty years. In 1882, he was elected to the Lower House of the Legislature from the Twenty-fifth District, on the Republican ticket, defeating his opponent by about one thousand three hundred votes. Mr. Lackie is a Master Mason. He is comfortably situated in life, and owns about three hundred acres of good land in this State, and the same number of acres in the State of Iowa. He is a man of large build—a hale, hearty farmer. He is a clear and logical thinker, and, though reticent at times, he is one of the active workers in the present body of Legislators. He resides at Osceola, Stark County, and his worth as a man is recognized by his friends and neighbors, as his handsome majority at his last election bears evidence.

HON. JOSEPH F. LAWRENCE.

He is a native New Englander, having been born at Lee, New Hampshire, December 6th, 1836. His father was a farmer, and Mr. Lawrence, himself, labored upon a farm until he was thirty years of age, thus gaining some of the most valuable experiences and most useful information, which it is the lot of man to enjoy. He received his education in the district schools of New Hampshire, completing his routine of studies in the Academy of New London, in the same State. After leaving his farm, Mr. Lawrence engaged in business, pursuing and achieving in the realms of commerce, five years, when, at the age of thirty-five, he came to Chicago, where he has since been engaged in loaning his own capital, and that of Eastern friends. His Chicago residence is situated at 373 Park Avenue. He is a Republican of life standing, practically speaking, and was for six years County Commissioner of Strafford County, in his native State, and a member of its Board of Agriculture for five years. He has held no public offices in Illinois, except that of West Chicago Park Commissioner, which he resigned upon his election to the House of Representatives, in 1882, from the Fourth Chicago District. Mr. Lawrence is a very practical, common-sense gentleman, whom those who are unacquainted with his amiable traits of character, might mistake for one who is sour and morose. Although a careful financier, and a confirmed man of business, there is a generous and pleasant side to his nature, which greatly endears him to his constituents and acquaintances. He is a tall man, of excellent physical proportions, dark in complexion, and his hair and beard are quite gray. He knows his duty and will do it.

HON. DAVID T. LINEGAR.

This prominent member of the House of Representatives, was born February 12th, 1830, at Melford, Clermont County, Ohio. His parents removed to Hamilton County, Ohio, in 1831, remaining there until 1840, when they located in Spencer County, Indiana. In 1858, Mr. Linegar came to Wayne County, Illinois, whence he removed to Cairo, where he now resides. His literary education was acquired in the district schools of Indiana. He read law with Hon. L. Q. DeBuler, of Rockport, Indiana, but acquired most of his knowledge, requisite to his admission to the Bar, by close application to his books at odd hours and of evenings, while engaged in teaching school. Prior to 1873, Mr. Linegar was a Republican, believing in the principles which that party had prominently advocated from its birth. He was Postmaster of Cairo for two years, and, in 1872, was one of the Republican electors for the State at large. He became disgusted at the excesses of the administration, soon after the accession of General Grant, however, and, in 1874, joined the Democrat party, because he believed it to be right that he should do so. He was elected to the House of Representatives in 1882, by a large foreign vote, which was almost all cast in his favor. Mr. Linegar is one of the leading spirits of the Democratic side of the House of Representatives, and is one of its ablest members. He is large in physical proportions, of fair complexion and wears a very long, light colored beard. He is a powerful debater, and a gentleman of large heart and generous disposition. He is a man loved by his friends and feared by his foes.

HON. DAVID T. LITTLER.

The subject of this sketch was born at Clifton, Greene County, Ohio, February 7th, 1836. His father was a teacher, by profession, and died at the early age of thirty-nine, when David was but four years old. The widowed mother was thus left with seven children, of whom David was the youngest son. The family was supported by the older brothers until David attained his majority, when he continued to maintain her until she died, in 1875, in the seventy-fifth year of her age. Poverty drove him to Illinois at the age of twenty-one, and he settled at Lincoln, in Logan County, where he worked at the carpenter's trade for two years, saving enough money to support him during a course of study in the office of S. C. Parks, now Judge of a Federal Court in Montana. He was admitted to the Bar in 1860, soon after which, he was elected Justice of the Peace, and, later, appointed Master-in-Chancery for Logan County, by Judge Scott, now Chief Justice of the Supreme Court of Illinois. Prior to his course of law study, he had received a fair common school education in Ohio. He held the above office until 1868, when he came to Springfield, and formed a law partnership with Henry S. Greene. This firm remained as first organized nearly two years, when the Honorable Milton Hay was admitted into it, and the firm name became Hay, Greene & Littler. This firm was regarded as a very strong combination of legal talent, and continued until 1881. Mr. Littler has enjoyed some very important offices of honor and trust. In 1866, Andrew Johnson, the President, appointed him Collector of Internal Revenue for the Springfield District. He held this office until 1868, when he resigned. He has amassed a considerable fortune, by bold speculation and close attention to business, and he now spends most of his time in his private business, when not engaged in official duties. He is a Mason and Knight Templar, and a rock-ribbed and firmly-rooted Republican. He was elected by a vote of 9,600, as the minority candidate from the Capital District. In 1868, he was married to Miss Kate Logan, who died in 1875. He has one child, a boy, aged twelve years. In person, he is portly and noble looking, gruff in conversation, but kind and generous, nevertheless.

HON. AUGUSTUS N. LODGE.

Mr. Lodge is a Hoosier by birth and a Sucker by adoption. He was born in Madison, Indiana, January 31st, 1831. His father's ancestors were Quakers, and his mother was a relative of Daniel Boone, the celebrated Kentucky Indian fighter. His father was a merchant at the time of the birth of Mr. Lodge. In November, 1856, Mr. Lodge came to Springfield, Illinois, and left that city for Williamson County, a year later. He was educated in private schools and a Naval Academy, located at Annapolis, Maryland. He was graduated from the St. Louis Medical College in 1858, and began practicing his profession at Marion, Illinois, where he now resides, soon afterward. He was a midshipman in the United States Navy, appointed by President Polk, in 1846. He resigned his position in the Navy in 1850. He is and has always been a Democrat in politics, and served his county in the capacity of Superintendent of Public Instruction, from 1869 to 1877. He was elected as the minority Representative of the Fifty-first District, in 1882. Mr. Lodge is an Episcopalian and holds membership in lodges of Masons, Odd Fellows and Knights of Honor. He is a public spirited gentleman, of varied accomplishments, and is worthy of the honor conferred upon him by his constituents in electing him to the honorable station, which he so ably fills. In person, he is below the average stature, and well proportioned, dark complexion. He is quiet and undemonstrative in disposition, and is possessed of a happy vein of humor, which often crops out in conversation, when least expected. He is very sociable and agreeable in his intercourse with the people. During his Naval experience, Mr. Lodge performed garrison duty on the west coast of Mexico, and was present at the siege of Vera Cruz.

HON. ROBERT W. McCARTNEY.

This Representative was born in Trumbull County, Ohio, in 1843. His father was a farmer, of Scotch descent, who had linked his fortunes with those of Miss Jean Brown. In 1867, Mr. McCartney came to Metropolis, Illinois. His education is of wide range and good quality. He is a graduate of a Commercial College, and of the Ohio State and Union Law College. In 1861, he enlisted as a private in the Sixth Ohio, and came out of the service as a Captain. He was twice wounded, and is no less proud of his scars than his country is of the gallant deeds which resulted in them. He adheres in belief to the Methodist Episcopal Church, and is a Free Mason and Knight Templar. He is a Republican throughout, and has served his city in the capacity of Prosecuting Attorney for three years. He was elected County Judge of Massac County in 1866, and held the office for nine consecutive years. In 1892, he was chosen to represent his district in the Lower House of the Thirty-third General Assembly, and is engaged in doing his duty, with marked ability and rare good judgment. Although a lawyer by profession, he is also a member of the Wm. Towel Lumber Company, saw millers and boat-builders, of Metropolis, Illinois, and owns valuable farm lands, amounting to over three hundred acres, near his home. He is above medium in stature, and sandy in complexion. He is keen of perception, and seems ever on the alert for some development, which may give affairs a different turn from that which seems to be generally anticipated. He is sedate and grave in demeanor, dignified in bearing and intensely practical in conversation, illustration, comparison or debate.

HON. JOHN R. McFIE.

Representative McFie was born in Washington County, Illinois, October 9th, 1848. His father was a farmer at the time of his birth, and taught school in the winter. Mr. McFie received a very fair common school education, under rather unfavorable auspices. Two or three years after his birth his parents removed to Coulterville, Randolph County, where he has since resided. During the Summer of 1863, his father died, and, in December of the same year, young McFie entered the army, enlisting as a private in Company "E," of the Thirtieth Illinois Infantry, serving until the close of the War of the Rebellion. He was with Sherman's Army on its memorable March to the Sea. After the War, he returned to Coulterville, where he engaged in merchandising. In 1868, he began reading law under the instruction of Gen. J. Blackburn Jones, of Sparta. He was admitted to the Bar in 1870, and began practicing his profession at his present home. He was elected to the House in 1878, was made Secretary of the House Caucus in 1879, and was appointed Chairman of the Committee on Commerce at the same session. He was chosen in the House Caucus to second the nomination of Gen. John A. Logan, for the United States Senatorship, for the Southern part of the State, performing his duty with satisfaction to his party and honor to himself. He is a member of the United Presbyterian Church, but does not hold membership in any secret society. He is a Stalwart Republican, and was elected from the Forty-eighth District by the largest vote polled by any one of the six candidates in the field. In person, he is of average stature and light in complexion. He is mild and generous in disposition, forcible, earnest and convincing as a debater, and a shrewd and successful politician. He is one of the leading men upon the Republican side of the House, and possesses no superiors and few equals among its members.

HON. THOMAS J. McNALLY.

This gentleman was born in New York City, June 24th, 1847, his ancestors being of Irish extraction. The subject of this sketch came to Illinois in 1850, locating in Chicago, where he now resides. His education was principally acquired in the common schools of New York. He served his apprenticeship as a machinist in New York City, and became quite an adept in the trade, which he followed for some time afterward. He now owns an interest in the Chicago House, a very prominent and well patronized hotel in that city, where he resides. He is not a member of any church or secret society. In politics, he is a Democrat, but has never held any public position, prior to his election to the House of Representatives in 1882, from the Third Chicago District. His residence in the city is as 323 South Clark Street. Mr. McNally is a large and portly man, of strongly marked characteristics, and a somewhat peculiar, but very polite and obliging disposition. He is of light complexion, free and generous in spirits, jovial and light hearted in conversation, determined and persistent in intention and execution, and fertile in imagination and resource. He is one of those men, who prefer broad and sweeping positions to those, which appear to deal with minute details, and, following that general plan, is not burdened with detail in either conversation or discussion. He states the broad fact, and accepts a plain fact without indulging particulars upon the one hand, or requiring them upon the other. This is one of his virtues, which has its weight in the formation of character, and its effect upon the estimation placed upon him by others.

HON. JOHN G. MANAHAN.

Mr. Manahan was born in Lancaster County, Pennsylvania, May 12th, 1837. His father was a merchant. The family came to Illinois in 1846, and John attended Knox College, at Galesburg, one term. He read law with Hon. E. N. Kirk, deceased, and was in due time admitted to the Bar. May 24th, 1861, he enlisted in the Thirteenth Regiment of Illinois Infantry Volunteers, as a three years' man. After a service of two years and four months, he was wounded in the attack on Vicksburg and transferred to the Invalid Corps, in which he served the residue of his term. He is a member of the Presbyterian Church, and Ancient Order of United Workmen. He has always been a Republican, having cast his first vote for Fremont, in 1856. He was Alderman of Sterling, his place of residence, for six years; City Attorney, three years; Supervisor of his township, two years, and Mayor three years, and was elected to the House of Representatives in 1882, by a large majority, from the Nineteenth District. He has acquired a considerable fortune by close attention to business, and judicious speculation and investments. He is a director of the Sterling Gas-Light Company, and, also, of the Orton Manufacturing Company, of his city. He also owns a valuable farm. His father is still living, at the advanced age of Seventy-six years. He is of average stature, has a sandy beard, with hair a few shades darker. He is a gentleman of fine talents and varied accomplishments, and honors his office and the constituency, whose votes elevated him to it. He is regarded as a first-class lawyer in patent cases, making that branch of practice a specialty.

HON. TREVANYON L. MATHEWS.

Mr. Mathews was born at Florence, Washington County, Pennsylvania, March 1st, 1849. In 1865, he came West, locating in Fulton County, where he remained four years, then removing to Beardstown, in Cass County, where he resided until 1876. He then located at Virginia, in the same county, where he now resides. His education was acquired in the common schools of Pennsylvania, but the printing office contributed much, which he failed to obtain by more scholastic, but less practical training. He was apprenticed to a carriage manufacturer, and worked at the trade thus learned, for six years, after which he clerked in various county offices, and, finally became editor of the *Virginia Gazette*. He likes journalism better than anything else, and proposes reëntering the profession at the expiration of his term of office. He was a candidate for Circuit Clerk, of his county, at one time, but, he being a Republican and the county largely Democratic, he missed connection, and, in the phrase of the railroader, "got left." He was elected to the House of Representatives in 1882, as the minority candidate from the Thirty-fourth District. He is a Methodist, Odd Fellow and member of the Ancient Order of United Workmen. In person, he is of medium stature, dark in complexion; has straight, black hair, and is as energetic and perseverent as any one could desire. He is polite to all with whom he is brought in social intercourse, and is an able and worthy Representative. He is generous and kind in disposition.

HON. JOSEPH B. MESSICK.

He is a native of Illinois, having been born in Macoupin County, January 29th, 1847. His father was a farmer, and his early experiences have had their influence in the formation of his character for strict integrity and undaunted perseverance. He removed to St. Clair County, Illinois, in 1872. His education was obtained in the public schools of the "State of Macoupin," and Shurtliff College, at Upper Alton. He enlisted as a private in Company "I," One Hundred and Forty-fourth Illinois Infantry Volunteers, in 1864, and served until the close of the Rebellion. He is not a member of any religious denomination or secret society. In politics, he is a staunch Republican, having espoused the cause of that party when it was but an infant among political organizations, and faithfully adhered to it ever since. He is a lawyer by profession, and enjoys the enviable reputation of being a very excellent one. He is one of the attorneys of the Indianapolis & St Louis Railroad Company. He was Judge of the City Court of East St. Louis, from 1875, until that tribunal and he, who presided over it, were legislated, the one out of existence, and the other out of office, in 1878. He is now the minority Representative from his district, elected in November, 1882. In person, he is dark and gigantic. He is an able debater; witty and incisive, and the members of his branch of the Assembly would enjoy being hauled over the coals by any other member full as well as by Mr. Messick. He is exceedingly entertaining as a conversationalist, and is generous and kind in disposition.

HON. AUGUST METTE.

His father was a musician, by profession, in the Province of Hesse, Germany, when this gentleman was born, in 1844. The family came to the United States in 1854, locating in Baltimore, Maryland. Mr. Mette came to Illinois in 1870, establishing himself in business, as a manufacturer of soda-water, ginger-ale, mead, cider, etc., in Chicago. His education was acquired in the public schools of Baltimore, he being instructed in music, at the same time. In the early part of the War, he enlisted in the Sixth Maryland Regiment, was wounded, and, in 1863, honorably discharged from the service. He is an Odd Fellow, as such being also a member of the Degree of Rebekah, and belongs to the German Order known as Harigari, but holds no membership or relation of communion in any church. In politics, he is a Democrat, having affiliated with that party about two years since, from motives of public policy. He feels that the Democratic party is the party of the people, and that the interests of the people demand its supremacy in the affairs of the government. He is now an occupant of a public office for the first time, having been elected to the House of Representatives, by the largest vote cast for any candidate upon his ticket, from the Eleventh Cook County District, in 1882. In personal appearance, he is short, and light in complexion. He is quiet and dignified in bearing; polite and generous in his intercourse with the public; firm in opinion and incisive in debate. He is a man, who cannot be coerced into measures, but is obliging and generous when treated as a gentleman should be.

HON. THOMAS F. MITCHELL.

This prominent Representative was born at Hillsborough, Highland County, Ohio, December 28th, 1828, his father then being a brawny blacksmith and farmer. In 1849, Mr. Mitchell removed to Kentucky, coming to Illinois in 1853, and locating at Bloomington, where he now resides. His education was acquired in the common schools of his native county, and Ripley College, Brown County, Ohio. He has been a carpenter, lumber dealer and grain dealer, and has also read law. He is a prominent Odd Fellow and Free Mason, having held the offices of Grand Master and Grand Representative of the Grand Lodge of Illinois, in the former order. In religious belief, he is a Methodist; in politics, a firm and unterrified Republican. His party and people have honored him with many offices of honor and trust, and he has filled each of them with marked ability and to the full satisfaction of his constituents. He has been Superintendent of Streets in his city for two years, a member of the City Board of Education, five years, and is now Treasurer of the State Board of Education. He is now serving his fourth term in the Lower House of the General Assembly, preferring that position to one in the Senate, which he might be filling, if he had chosen to do so. In the first session of which he was a member, he was Chairman of the Committee on State Institutions; Chairman of the Committee on Appropriations in the second; Committee on Penitentiaries in the third, and is now Chairman of the Railroad Committee. He is of Scotch and Irish descent. Mr. Mitchell is one of the leaders on the Republican side of the House of Representatives, and is regarded as one of the ablest men in that branch of the Assembly. He is tall and commanding in person, his hair and beard are quite gray, and he is a very forcible speaker in both conversation and debate. He is very liberal, obliging and kind in disposition, and is generally esteemed and admired.

HON. JOHN W. MOORE.

Mr. Moore was born near Bloomington, Indiana, August 15th, 1847, his father then being a farmer. The family came to Illinois in 1849, locating in Adams County. In 1877, Mr. Moore removed to Mound Station, Brown County, where he now resides. His education was acquired in the common schools near Beverly, and the college at Abingdon, Knox County, where he was graduated, receiving the degree of Bachelor of Science. Mr. Moore taught school for a time after the completion of his scholastic career; but is now engaged in farming, and breeding and shipping live stock. He is particularly proud of his two families of fine short-horns, "Mazurka" and "Waterloo J." In religious belief, Mr. Moore is a Christian, being a member of the denomination indicated by the word. He is not a member of any of the secret orders. Politically, he is a confirmed and uncompromising Democrat, having become one when he first arrived at man's estate, and continued true to the faith ever since. It is said that his father was in Nauvoo when the celebrated and notorious Joseph Smith, so-called prophet of the Mormon Church, was slain by the indignant populace. The subject of this sketch was elected to the House of Representatives in 1882, over A. B. Allen, his opponent, by a majority of about five thousand votes, from the Thirty-sixth District. Mr. Moore is a quiet, genteel and unobtrusive gentleman, having a well cultivated intellect, and being possessed of rare good judgment. He is not one of those men who speak upon all occasions and questions; but one who bottles his thoughts—to use a metaphor —for an opportune moment. He is below medium height; dark in complexion; pleasant and agreeable in his intercourse with the people, and generous and kind in disposition. His pride in the fine cattle, which he breeds, is said to be fully justified by facts.

HON. ISAAC L. MORRISON.

Isaac Lafayette Morrison was born in Barren County, Kentucky, in 1826. His ancestors, in both branches of the family, were American patriots. His grandfather on his father's side was a soldier in the Revolutionary Army, and lost his life in the cause of free government, at the Battle of the Brandywine. His grandfather on his mother's side, was also a Revolutionary Soldier, who served in the campaigns of the Carolinas and Virginia. The father of Mr. Morrison was a farmer, and the earlier lessons of patience and perseverence taught our subject, were the result of farm experience, as they have been in so many other noted instances. Mr. Morrison was educated in the common schools and Masonic Seminary of his native State, and, upon completing his course, entered into the study of law with commendable zeal. He was admitted to the Bar, and, in 1851, came to Illinois; locating at Jacksonville, where he is now the senior member of the celebrated firm of Morrison, Whitlock & Lippincott, one of the strongest legal combinations in the West. Mr. Morrison is one of the foremost men in his party in Illinois. He helped organize the first Republican Convention in Illinois, at Bloomington, in 1856; was a delegate to the Baltimore Convention, which re-nominated Lincoln for the Presidency, in 1864, and has been a recognized leader of his party for many years. He is now serving his third term in the House, having been elected over Cowen, his opponent for the minority office, in 1882, by a very handsome majority, in the Thirty-eighth District. Mr. Morrison is the leader of the Republican party in the House. He is a very kind and agreeable gentleman, and an able and fearless debater

HON. GEORGE W. MURRAY.

Hon. George W. Murray, of Sangamon County, Illinois, was born at Covington, Miami County, Ohio, July 7th, 1839. Mr. Murray's education was acquired in the common schools and High School of Dayton, Ohio. He is a lawyer by profession, having commenced the studies necessary to qualify him for his profession, in the office of General Moses B. Walker, of Dayton, Ohio, in 1868. He was admitted to the Bar at Dayton, in 1870. He was a member of the City Council of the above named city from 1869 to 1872, and came to Illinois in 1874, locating in Springfield, where he at once entered upon a successful practice of his chosen profession. He holds membership in no church, but is a member of the Independent Order of Odd Fellows. Mr. Murray is a man of pleasant address and genteel manners. He is tall and slender, dark in complexion; keen of perception; careful, cool and grave in debate, although inclined to perpetrate a dry joke occasionally, which is the more amusing for being presented in his inimitably droll manner. He is one of those cautious and deliberate men, who seldom give way to the promptings of passion or avarice. He is noted for his strict honesty and unimpeachable fidelity to all trusts confided to his keeping, and is a safe man to entrust with legislative authority. He is a Democrat in political faith, and was easily elected upon the majority ticket, to represent the Thirty-ninth District in the House of Representatives of the Thirty-third General Assembly. He is a shrewd politician, without the reckless disregard of moral principles, which sometimes characterize the career of men of his opportunities and ability. Mr. Murray will be heard, when questions of importance are under discussion.

HON. GEORGE W. MURRAY.

This gentleman is known as George Murray, of Scott, to dis-
tinguish him from George W. Murray, of Sangamon. He was
born in Greene County, Illinois, in 1850. His father was a
cooper at the time of George's birth, but is now engaged in
farming in Missouri. The subject of this sketch located in
Scott County in 1870, on his farm of one hundred and fifty acres.
He received a substantial education in the district schools of
Illinois, and has turned his knowledge to agriculture and the
ministry. He is an ordained Minister of the Baptist Church,
and Moderator of the State Association of his denomination. He
is a firm Democrat, and was made Superintendent of the Pauper
Farm of his county, by the Board of Supervisors, in 1879, continuing to manage that institution until elected to the House of
Representatives in 1882, from the Thirty-seventh District.
There was no especial opposition to his candidacy, and he ran
ahead of his ticket. Mr. Murray has risen by his own efforts
and intrinsic worth, from the station of a farmer boy, to that of
a Legislator of his State. He possesses the unqualified confidence of his constituents, and has a hold upon the hearts of his
people, which is worth more than all of the chicanery and wire-
pulling ever practiced. He was elected without the expenditure
of a dollar for electioneering purposes, and his friends were much
disappointed when he refused to retain the Superintendency of
the County Farm, for the reason that he could not give it proper
personal attention during the session of the Legislature. In
person, he is of average stature, well proportioned, and plain in
dress. He is incisive and aggressive in debate, and plain and
sociable in ordinary conversation.

HON. REVILO NEWTON.

Mr. Newton was born at Tonica, LaSalle County, Illinois, April 11th, 1842. His father was a native of New York, and a Major in the State Militia, prior to his removal to Illinois. He was also a soldier in the Blackhawk War. In 1868, the subject of this sketch went to Iowa, remaining until 1872, when he returned to this State, settling at Minonk, Woodford County. His education was acquired in the common schools of this State. By occupation, he is a merchant. In 1862, he enlisted in the Eighty-eighth Regiment of Illinois Infantry Volunteers, as a private, serving two years, when he was discharged on account of sickness. He is a Methodist in religious belief, and a Master Mason. In politics, he has been firmly adherent to his early convictions, which were most decidedly Democratic. He has served as a Justice of the Peace for four years, and as a member of the Board of Education of his city, for six years. He was, also, Mayor of his city, two years, and Treasurer, four years. In 1882, he was elected to the House of Representatives from the Twentieth District, running with the ticket. Mr. Newton is one of those quiet, unostentatious men, who are the safety of the people's interests, in our Legislative halls. He abhors all forms of peculations under the name of appropriations, and will make himself heard upon some of the private bills, which amount to nothing more or less than a misappropriation of the people's money, now pending consideration. In person, he is of medium height; rather light in complexion; quiet and dignified in demeanor; kind, generous and obliging. He is a man of considerable influence in the House.

HON. JOHN L. NICHOLS.

The gentleman, whose name heads this sketch, was born in
Clinton County, Illinois, on the 21st day of December, 1837. He
is the son of Turner L. and Mary Johnson Nichols, both Americans. His father was a well-to-do farmer and stock raiser, of
Clinton County. Mr. Nichols is a dealer in agricultural implements. He was a Justice of the Peace in Clement Township, for
two years. At the commencement of the War for the Union,
Mr. Nichols responded to the President's call for Volunteers,
and, on the 15th day of July, 1861, he enlisted as a private in
the Thirtieth Illinois Volunteer Infantry. He was promoted
several times, and, when mustered out, August 11th, 1865, he
was Captain of one of the Companies in the Thirtieth Regiment.
Before the War, he was a Democrat, but since the close of the
Rebellion, he has voted and acted with the Republican party.
The present is his third term in the Lower House of the Legislature. He was elected at the last election by a very handsome
vote. Mr. Nichols is a pleasant, affable gentleman, is of medium
height and dark complexion. He is a sharp, shrewd Representative, and is a most earnest worker. He ably represents his
district in the Thirty-third General Assembly. In secret society
circles, Mr. Nichols is a leader, being a member of the Masonic
fraternity and of the Ancient Order of United Workmen.

HON. THOMAS NOWERS.

Mr. Nowers was born in Oneida County, New York, February 12th, 1834. His father, whose Christian name was also Thomas, was a farmer, when little Tom was born. In 1869, the family came to Illinois with him, settling in Mercer County, where they remained for two years, when they removed to Rock Island County, remaining five years, finally reaching Henry County, where he now resides. His education has been wholly acquired in the common schools of his various places of residence, and by observation, experience and persistent personal effort. Mr. Nowers' occupation is that of a private banker and merchant. He belongs to no church or secret order. Mr. Nowers is a man of rather remarkable energy and business tact, and has no such vanity in either dress or reputation, as so often actuates men in the affairs of life. He is strictly a man of business, and does not meddle with other men's affairs, so long as he can find employment in his own, and the time never comes, when a man of his executive ability and personal characteristics does not feel that his affairs demand attention. He is a staunch Republican, having voted and acted with that party ever since he has attained his majority, and he cannot see that his party is guilty of anything, not sufficiently general in its evils, to have excited the cupidity of its political opponents and involved them in the maelstrom of excesses, which is charged upon Republicanism, as deeply as it has the devotees of the party in power. He feels that his party is as pure to-day as in the days of national tribulation, and that it does, can and will punish the light-fingered gentry, Democrats and Republicans, who have formed rings and cliques to defraud the government. He has been a member of the Board of Supervisors of Henry County, at various periods-for eleven years, and was elected to the House of Representa, tives by a respectable majority, in 1882. He is above the average height, kind, shrewd and generous, yet firm and dignified.

HON. JOHN O'CONNELL

His name is the index to his nationality.   He was born in
Ireland, in 1836, to his father, Michael, who had married Miss
Ellen McCarty.   His father was an industrious farmer, and little
John soon became an adept with the implements usually employed in agriculture, on the Emerald Isle.   Mr. O'Connell came
to the United States in 1860, locating in New York City, where
he remained, until he came to Illinois, some ten years ago.   He
now resides at Joliet, Will county.   Mr. O'Connell received his
education in private schools in his native country.   He is an intelligent and industrious laborer, and is not ashamed of the fact.
He is principally employed in the mills of his city.   He is a
lineal descendant of the patriotic statesman, Daniel O'Connell,
famous in the annals of Ireland's struggle for liberty.   Mr.
O'Connell is Catholic in religion, and is a member of each of the
following named secret societies: Ancient Order of Hibernians,
Ancient Order of United Workmen, Knights of Labor, Independent Order of Odd Fellows, and the Amalgamated Association of
Iron and Steel Workers.   He is an avowed anti-monopolist in politics, and may ever be found battling in the cause of honest labor.
He was elected by a fusion of the Labor and Trade, Anti-monopoly,
Greenback and Democratic parties, in 1882, to the House of
Representatives, the first office he has ever held.   His majority
was the largest ever given a candidate on any ticket, in his
county. In person, Mr. O'Connell is above medium height, sandy
in complexion, and intelligent in countenance.   He is as kind-
hearted as a girl ; yet bold as a lion.   He is a man of the people,
and will fight for them and stand firmly in his place as an advocate of their rights.   He possesses a large fund of that wit, for
which the Irish people have such a widespread reputation.

HON. PATRICK O'MARA.

This gentleman was born in the County of Galway, Ireland, August 21st, 1848. His father was a farmer, and little Pat learned to dig and delve in the soil of his native isle, only in play, for when he was but three years of age, his parents came across the surging ocean, and became denizens of the land in which the footprints of John Bull do not exist upon the necks of a nobility-ridden Nation. The family first made its home near Lancaster, Pennsylvania; but did not tarry long there, finally locating at Rock Island, Illinois. The education of this gentleman is very excellent. He attended one year at Knox College, Galesburg, Illinois, and was graduated at the Soldiers' College, Fulton, Illinois; and the law department of the State University, Iowa City, Iowa. It is scarcely necessary to state that he is a lawyer, and a good one, too. He has battled down adverse circumstances, and triumphed over all of the obstacles to intellectual and political progress, as only a determined Irishman can. He is a Catholic in religion, and holds no membership in secret societies. He is an unterrified and faithful Democrat, was elected a member of the House of Representatives in 1880, and re-elected in 1882. He served three years in the army during the Rebellion, as a private in Company "I," of the One Hundred and Twenty-sixth Regiment of Illinois Infantry Volunteers. He is a man of average stature; dark in complexion, and dignified in bearing. He possesses a powerful mind, and a fair share of the characteristic wit of his race. He is a genial and entertaining conversationalist, and a generous and free-hearted gentleman.

HON. JOHN O'SHEA.

Mr. O'Shea is one of the most youthful members of the House of Representatives, having been born in Chicago, December 15th, 1859. At the time of his birth, his father was largely interested in a firm of bridge builders, now known as the American Bridge Company. He probably had little thought that his Johnny would be one of the Solons of his State before he had seen twenty-four summers, but such is the case. Mr. O'Shea has never resided out of his native city, having been educated in its public schools and St. John's Academy. He is a laboring man, having been engaged at the Stock Yards in Chicago, at the time of his election. He knows that the workman is worthy of his hire, and, in all Legislative matters, which may interest that class, directly or indirectly, his voice and vote will be recorded in its behalf. He is a devout Catholic and a member of the Ancient Order of Hibernians. In politics, he is a Democrat, born, bred, educated and confirmed, and was elected from the Eleventh Chicago District, on that ticket, by a very pronounced majority, running ahead of McNeal, some fifteen hundred votes. He is a very sensible and dignified young gentleman, whose head has not been turned by his political success. He is beardless, at least closely and cleanly shaven; dark in complexion, and possesses such a disposition to do what is right, that he will not be led astray by the exciting incidents, which sometimes characterize the sessions of his branch of the Assembly. He is shrewd, gentlemanly, polite and amiable.

HON. JAMES L. OWEN.

James Lakin Owen, eldest son of Francis Owen and Keziah Wright, was born September 19th, 1824, near Winchester, Clarke County, Kentucky. He removed, with his parents, to Putnam County, Indiana, in 1827, thence to Will County, Illinois, where he has since resided, with the exception of a few years in California, about 1849, when the gold fever was at its height. To the subject of this sketch, belongs the honor of erecting the first steam saw-mill and sawing the first lumber ever sawed by steam, in the State of California. Strange as it may appear, Mr. Owen found a wife on the Golden Coast, having there been married to Miss Catherine Madden, a lady widely known among the early Californians, for her beauty and accomplishments. The father of our subject, was a farmer and local preacher. His grandfather was a Chaplain in the Revolutionary War, subsequently being the Private Secretary of General Washington. He was present at the surrender of Yorktown. His great uncle, Edward Cullom, was a member of the first Constitutional Convention of Illinois. Mr. Owen is a relative of Hon. Shelby M. Cullom, United States Senator. Our subject was educated in "Brush College," being "graduated with honor." He is a farmer by occupation, having made stock-raising a specialty for the last twenty-five years. He is a member of the Methodist Episcopal Church. He was a Henry Clay Whig prior to the organization of the Republican party, when he cast his fortunes with the new venture, to which he has never been unfaithful. His present place of residence is Mokena, Will County, Illinois, in the Fifteenth District, from which he was elected to the House of Representatives, in 1882.

HON. HILON A. PARKER.

Mr. Parker was born at Plessis, in the town of Alexandria, Jefferson County, New York, in 1841, his father being a genuine New England farmer of the old school, and his grand-father having fought for his country in the Revolutionary War. In 1862, Mr. Parker enlisted as a private in the Tenth Regiment of New York Artillery, being mustered out at the end of his three years service, as First Lieutenant. In 1866, he removed to Iowa, remaining in the Hawkeye State most of the time for ten years, when he came to Illinois, locating at Englewood, Cook County. His education was acquired in the common schools and academies of his native State. He is, by occupation, a civil engineer, having probably patterned after the illustrious Father of his Country in this regard, although we have no account of any hatchetted cherry-tree in his father's garden. However, Mr. Parker's character for truth and veracity needs no circumstance of this nature to give it weight. He is regarded as a truthful and upright man, wherever he is known. In religious belief, he is a Presbyterian; but he is not a member of any of the secret orders. He is a thorough Republican in politics, and was elected to the House of Representatives in 1882, from the Second District of Cook County. He is a shrewd and energetic guardian of the interests of his constituency, and a strong man in the House. He is noble and commanding in physique, dignified in bearing and polite in his intercourse with the people. He is a man, who is generous enough to be courteous to all, irrespective of race, sex, age, color or social position. He is quiet and unostentatious in demeanor, except when laboring under strong mental excitement, when he at once becomes eloquent and impressive in carriage, gesture and speech.

HON. JOHN L. PARISH.

Mr. Parish was born in Chicago, February 22d, 1854. His father was a ship-carpenter by trade, and many a craft, which rode the billows of the great lakes, bore the marks of his handiwork. The family removed to Fulton, Illinois, in 1858, and, afterward to Ottawa, returning to Chicago in 1866. Mr. Parish is one of the best educated young members of the Lower House, and nothing but the common schools of his State, and the generous efforts of himself are responsible for that most gratifying state of affairs. He began reading law in 1873, was admitted to the Bar three years later, and practised his profession for the ensuing three years; but the law was not sufficiently exciting to gratify his ambitious nature, and, in March, 1882, he began his career as a journalist, by becoming a correspondent of the *Chicago Daily News*, and has been in the service of that paper ever since. He says that his military career was confined to a 1st Lieutenancy in a torch-light brigade, during the last presidential campaign. Mr. Parish is a member of the Baptist Church ; a Free Mason; member of the Royal Arcanum and Ancient Order of United Workmen. He has been a strong Republican since he has attained his majority, and was elected to the Lower House of the Thirty-second General Assembly in 1880, and re-elected in 1882, receiving the highest vote polled in the district, each time. He is essentially a self-made man, having left the parental roof at the youthful age of thirteen; he made so much of a success that five years later, he found himself able to support a wife; so he married a handsome little lady, and they are now the proud parents of four children. Mr. Parish is a noble specimen of manhood. Tall and well proportioned, dark in complexion, and neat in dress. It is little wonder that the ladies pronounce him "*the* man of the Legislature." Added to his magnificent personal appearance, are such qualities of mind and heart as have created for him a large circle of warm friends.

Since the above sketch was written, Mr. Parish has been appointed Consul to Chemnitz, Germany. Fortunately he will not be compelled to resign, as a member of the House, as he will probably not be required to leave for Chemnitz until about the first of June. The Consulate at Chemnitz will have in Mr. Parish a representative who will be a credit to the service.

HON. ISAAC N. PEARSON.

Mr. Pearson was born in Mercer County, Pennsylvania, in July, 1842, his father being a merchant, and member of the State Legislature at that time. When Isaac was but three years of age, the family removed to Lawrence County, in the same State. He came to Illinois in 1850, locating in McDonough County. His education was what he terms very limited, being derived from the common and high schools of his time, and more than all by personal exertion out of school, and away from its privileges. At eighteen years of age, he became Deputy Circuit Clerk of McDonough County, serving four years; clerked in a bank four years, when he was elected Circuit Clerk, serving four years in that capacity. At the expiration of his term of office, he was made Cashier of the Union National Bank, of Macomb, Illinois, resigning his position upon being elected to the House of Representatives, in 1882, and having been elected Vice President of the bank, which position he now holds. He owns a fine farm of one hundred and thirty acres, and is worth over $25,000, accumulated by his own industry and caution. He belongs to the following named orders, the charters of the last three of which, bear his name: Masonic, Odd Fellowship, Degree of Rebekah, Uniformed Patriarchs, Ancient Order of United Workmen, and Knights of Pythias. He has been an Odd Fellow for twenty years. He is not a member of any church. In politics, he is soundly and safely Republican. In person, he is tall, and dark in complexion. He is pleasant in address, and dignified; yet agreeable in demeanor. He is a man of noted generosity, of both purse and opinion, and has many warm personal friends.

HON. JOHN M. PEARSON.

Mr. Pearson was born in Newberryport, Massachusetts, in 1832. His father was a ship carpenter at that time. Mr. Pearson came to Illinois in 1849, locating at Alton. His education was acquired in the common schools of the Bay State, and by personal effort, and a wide range of general reading. He was engaged in the manufacture of agricultural implements in Alton, and, being familiar with the wants of the agricultural and manufacturing classes, may be looked upon as a very valuable acquisition to the Lower House of the General Assembly. He is a member of a Congregational Church, and a Free Mason of the degree of Knight Templar. In politics, he is a Republican, having espoused the cause of that party, when it came into existence, and being faithful to its principles on all occasions, where political action is required. He was a member of the Railroad and Warehouse Commission from 1873 to 1877, by appointment of the Governor, and, in 1878, was elected to the House of Representatives, and reëlected in 1880, and again in 1882, from the Forty-first District. His residence is at Godfrey, Illinois. Mr. Pearson has had considerable experience in Legislative affairs, and is a strong man in the House. He is of medium stature, and well proportioned in physique; genial, courteous and pleasant in his conversation; incisive and apt in debate, and noble and generous in the promptings of his heart. He is a man, generally admired and respected, and is worthy of the high office which he so ably fills.

HON. JULIUS PEDERSON.

Norway has but one son in both branches of the Thirty-third General Assembly of Illinois, and that one is the subject of this sketch. He was born in the above named country, in August, 1832. His father was a farmer. Mr. Pederson came to the United States in 1855, first locating at Chicago, from which city he removed to Racine, Wisconsin, where he resided for nine years. He again came to Chicago at the end of that time, and it is his present home. His education was acquired in the common schools of Norway; but he has been such a close student of American customs and the English language, that he is a very proficient gentleman in both. By trade, Mr. Pederson is a carpenter and joiner, and, until the last four and a half years, has earned his food and raiment, and that of his family, by the sweat of his brow. In religious belief, he a Lutheran. He is also a member of the benevolent Order known as the Royal Arcanum. He is a plain and unassuming, but incorrigible Republican in politics, believing that his party was founded in brotherly love and human justice, and feeling that the record of its opposite, does not justify him in even thinking of a transfer of his political affections. He was Supervisor of the Town of West Chicago in 1877 and 1878, after which he became an Internal Revenue Storekeeper in Chicago, and was elected to the House of Representatives from the Ninth District, in 1882, polling a very large vote. In person, he is tall, and dark in complexion. He is very keen in perception, and is a shrewd and reliable Legislator. He is plain, generous and accommodating in conduct and bearing, and has a strong, but pleasant foreign accent in speech.

Isaac L. Pratt.

HON. ISAAC L. PRATT.

The flowing white beard and snowy locks of this old gentleman, give him quite a patriarchal appearance. He was born in Easton, Bushton County, Massachusetts, August 4th, 1817. His father, Seaver Pratt, was a farmer, who linked his destinies with Miss Charity Lothrop, many years ago, and the marriage was blessed with at least one child, who has since risen to the station of honor in the council of State. Five generations of Pratts have lived and died on the old Massachusetts homestead, and Isaac, the sole survivor of the last, is still its proprietor. In April, 1841, Mr. Pratt came to Roseville, Warren County, Illinois, where he secured some valuable farming lands and began in earnest, the life of a husbandman. He is now dealing in cattle, and, at the same time, has a large interest in an excellent banking establishment, of which he is President. He has served as Justice of the Peace in his county for fifteen years, and has held other minor offices of honor and trust. He was elected Representative in November, 1882, as a Democrat, his plurality being over three thousand. Although in his sixty-sixth year, Mr. Pratt is robust and strong in physique, and cheerful and vigorous in conversation or debate. He is a teetotaler in regard to intoxicating drinks. His presence is inviting, and, at the same time, tempered with a quiet, dignified and polite bearing, which will win him friends among all classes of people with whom he may associate.

HON. JAMES E. PURNELL.

He is a native Illinoisan, who was born in the City of Quincy, April 26th, 1848. He has never changed his place of residence, and was elected to the Thirty-third General Assembly from the district in which he was born. His parents were James Purnell and Martha, his wife, *nee* Brotherson. His father was a Quincy Merchant. His education was acquired in the public schools of his city, and improved by untiring and continuous personal effort, since he has attained the estate of manhood. The youthful dreams of Mr. Purnell were of courts, and lawyers, and judges, and statutes, and precedents, and juries. They were accepted as an omen of his future, and he espoused the law as his profession. He has served two years as City Attorney of Quincy, and was elected to the House of Representatives in 1882, by a plurality of five thousand votes. He is a Democrat, born, bred, educated and augmented with each additional year. His parents were of English extraction, and the subject of this sketch is somewhat English in his physical appearance. He is of medium stature, and dark complexion—decidedly a handsome gentleman. He is self-possessed and cool, ordinarily, but, upon the proposal of any measures, which fails to fully meet his approbation, the fires of his intellect are immediately aglow, and he defends his position with all the earnestness, effectiveness and vehemence peculiar to a man of his temperament. He is polite, affable and dignified in demeanor, yet, a whole-souled, large-hearted man, when anything occurs to excite compassion or sympathy. Generosity is one of the first impulses of his nature.

HON. MICHAEL C. QUINN.

Mr. Quinn was born in Ireland, in the year 1840. His father was a farmer, at that time, and "he was a farmer, too." The family came across the ocean in 1845, locating in Massachusetts, where Michael remained until 1864, when he removed to Illinois, making his home in Peoria, where he now resides. His education was derived from the schools and academies of the Bay State. He read law with Judge Morris, of Springfield, and W. B. C. Pearsons, of Holyoke, Massachusetts, and was in due time admitted to the Bar. He is an attorney of more than ordinary accomplishments, being very much aided in his business by the ready wit, which is a distinguishing characteristic of the people of his native country. In religion, he is a Catholic, and holds no membership in any of the so-called secret orders. He is a Democrat in politics, and has never been anything else. He has been City Attorney of Peoria, five years, and a member of its Board of Education, ten years. He was a member of the Lower House of the Twenty-eighth General Assembly, and was again elected to the office in 1882. He seems to be a man of great popularity, not only in his city and district, but, also, in the honorable body, of which he is a member. He is a glib talker and ready debater, and does not fear to speak his sentiments upon proper occasions. In person, he is smooth shaven, and not above medium stature. He is rather corpulent, and is a good conversationalist, an amiable, agreeable and generous-hearted gentleman. He is a very shrewd man in debate and political tactics.

HON. DAVID RANKIN.

Born in Sullivan County, Indiana, in 1825, he had the usual experiences of a country boy in ancient Hoosierdom. His father was a wheel-wright and farmer, who believed that man was intended to earn his bread by the sweat of his brow, and little David had his share of the ups and downs incident to his station in life. In 1836 the family came to Warren, now Henderson, County, Illinois, where the subject of this sketch became a thrifty and respected farmer, on his own account. He had received a fair common school education in Indiana, and improved his mind by close observation and general reading, as opportunity was offered. He is a shrewd financier, and has accumulated money, until he is one of the wealthiest farmers in the State. He owns 30,000 acres of land; 5,000 acres in Illinois, and 25,000 in Iowa and Missouri. He is a member of the United Presbyterian Church, but holds no affiliation with any secret order. When the Whig party ceased to be, Mr. Rankin became a Republican, and he has voted with that party ever since. He was a member of the Lower House in the Twenty-eighth and Twenty-ninth General Assemblies, and was chosen as Representative from the Twenty-fourth District in 1882. He has large monied interests, owning three large banks, in addition to his landed estates. He is above the average in stature, slender in form and wears a full beard. He never suffers any measure to go to vote, without first familiarizing himself with its provisions. He always votes from conviction, and is firm and undemonstrative in his demeanor. Though cautious and somewhat reserved, he is not morose, and is as affable to the humblest page or most importunate interviewer, as to his fellow Legislators.

HON. ROBERT B. RAY.

Robert Brown Ray, one of the Representatives from Vermilion County, was born in Dearborn County, Indiana, February 18th, 1830. His father was a farmer and native of Kentucky, of Irish descent. Mr. Ray's grandfather on his father's side, died at the advanced age of one hundred and four years. The mother of our subject, is a relative of Hon. Richard M. Johnson, once Vice President of the United States. Her maiden name was Mildred Johnson Watts. Robert's father died, when the former was but eight years old, when his mother came to Vermilion County, Illinois, settling on a small farm, where he was raised, acquiring some of the most valuable experiences of his life. He attended winter schools in log school houses, until he had passed his majority, and subsequently studied in an academy at Danville, for two years. He then taught several terms of school, meanwhile reading medicine with Dr. James H. Farris, of Danville, after which he was graduated from the Rush Medical College, of Chicago. He received his diploma in 1860, locating in Macon County, Missouri, where he remained practicing his profession until the beginning of the War, when he left that State and settled at Fairmount, fourteen miles west of Danville, where he now resides. In 1859, Dr. Ray was married to Miss Fannie Beecher, of Adair County, Missouri. He has a very bright record as a physician and surgeon, his practice being very extensive. His professional standing in his county is very high. He is a member of the County Medical Association, having been its President in 1880. With the exception of that of Village Trustee and School Director, the Doctor held no public office until elected to the House of Representatives in 1882. He is a member of the Committee to visit the State Charitable Institutions, also those on Highways, Bridges, Mines and Mining, and Warehouses. He is an influential and active Republican, being thoroughly devoted to the cause of his party. He is a member and Trustee of the Methodist Episcopal Church. Dr. and Mrs. Ray have three children, the eldest, Beecher B., being a scientific and classical graduate of an Institution at Valparaiso, Indiana, and Agnes and Robert being now engaged in pursuing their studies at home.

HON. FRANCIS M. RICHARDSON.

This gentleman first lightened the hearts of his parents and raised his voice in behalf of the fettered and oppressed, at Feesbury, Brown County, Ohio, July 24th, 1831. His father was a farmer; but, being a skillful veterinary surgeon, the calls of his neighbors upon his time were so frequent that he found little time to cultivate the soil. His father was a Corporal in the English Army, during the War of 1812. In 1869 the subject of this article came to Illinois, locating at Sumner, Lawrence County. He did not remain in Sumner very long, leaving there to establish himself in Neoga, which he has since made his permanent home. He obtained his education in the common schools of Ohio, and the Eclectic Medical Institute, of Cincinnati, of which he is a graduate. Previous to his Eclectic course, he attended an Alapathic school for a single term. He is engaged in practicing medicine at his home. He belongs to no religious denomination, but is a member of each of the following named secret societies: Odd Fellows, Royal Arch Masonry, Knights of Honor and Knights and Ladies of Honor. He volunteered as a private in the One Hundred and Eighty-fourth Ohio, serving on detached duty most of the time, in the Commissary Department. He was also a prescribing physician at sick-call, and served as Hospital Steward. He was also a Lieutenant in the Home Guard, a drill corps for preparing men for the service. He was what is termed a War Democrat, voted for Douglas, and has never forsaken the old party. He was elected to the House of Representatives in 1880, and reëlected in 1882, from the Thirty-second District. In person, he is tall and dark. He is cool, sedate and deliberate in debate, and collected amidst exciting surroundings, and a polite and entertaining conversationalist.

HON. JOHN B. RICKS.

Mr. Ricks was born near Cadiz, Trigg County, Kentucky, November 14th, 1833. His father was a farmer and stock-raiser, and Mr. Ricks is a good judge of horses and cattle to-day, as the result of his observations during his early years of existence. In 1836, the family came to Illinois, locating in what was then Montgomery County, now Christian. The father was a member of the Illinois House of Representatives in 1845, and was instrumental in having enough of Montgomery, Shelby and Sangamon Counties cut off to form Christian County. He died near Springfield, and rests in the family burial ground on Bear Creek. After a residence of thirty years in this State, Mr. Ricks removed to Kentucky; but he did not remain there very long, returning to this State, and locating at Morrisonville. His education was partially obtained in a veritable log school-house, which he avers was not much higher than his head; but he afterward attended other schools and McKendree College. The family then resided twenty-one miles from a physician, post-office, or voting place. He jocosely remarked that he would gladly have run away, had there been any place to go without danger of starving or freezing before getting there. He then herded cattle in the summer-time, and occasionally secured a copy of the *Sangamon Journal*, and some Chicago paper, which he read with only the avidity of which a starving mind in an active body, is capable. Mr. Ricks is a Mason, of the degree of Knight Templar, and an Odd Fellow. During the war, he raised a company of soldiers, and was commissioned Captain; but he could not get into the service, as he desired. He is a Democrat, born and bred, and has held so many important offices that to enumerate them would render this sketch far too statistical to be interesting. He was a member of the House of Representatives in 1867, and was on all of the committees to consider plans and specifications for what is now the great, unfinished, yet magnificent Capitol of Illinois. He deals extensively in short-horn cattle, of which he is a celebrated shipper. In person, Mr. Ricks is above medium height, compactly built, and well knit. He is a man of apparently unlimited physical strength, and mental vigor. His hair is very black. He is noble and generous in spirit, and convincing and practical in debate.

HON. CHARLES L. ROANE.

Mr. Roane was born in Loudoun County, Virginia, October 3d, 1820. His father was a farmer at that time. In 1854, the subject of this sketch came to Illinois, making his home at Sullivan, Moultrie County, where he now resides, and is engaged in merchandising. His education was acquired in the common schools and Flint Hill Academy, in his native State. He has quietly pursued his course as a dry goods merchant, for twenty-one years, and by close attention and cautious conduct, has amassed a competency. In addition to his stock in trade, he owns about ten thousand dollars worth of city real estate, and recently disposed of a farm at good figures. Mr. Roane is a Presbyterian in religious faith, and has been a member of the Independent Order of Odd Fellows for the last thirty years. He is probably the oldest Odd Fellow in either branch of the General Assembly, and is one among the oldest in the State. In politics, he is a sound Republican, who was one of the first members of that political party. He adheres to its principles with unwavering fidelity, but is not a politician in any sense of the word, except that of personal preference in political belief. He was County Clerk of his county from 1857 to 1861, and was much surprised, when he received the nomination for Representative in 1882. His selection was undoubtedly partly due to the fact that he was not a chronic office-seeker, and that he richly deserved the honor at the hands of his constituents, in the Thirty-third District. In personal appearance, he is large in stature and circumference. He is genial and pleasant in association, and kind, considerate and generous in disposition. He is one of the wise men of the House, upon whom the people rely for protection against fraud and experimental Legislation.

HON. CALVIN M. ROGERS.

The subject of this sketch was born on a farm in Monroe County, Missouri, February 15th, 1835, and is, therefore, forty-eight years of age. His father, Aleri, was one of the pioneers of his native State, and Mr. Rogers' earlier history is but a repetition of the experience of the innumerable army of farmers' boys, which has fought its way to fortune and fame, by its own noble efforts and unflinching determination. His mother, whose maiden name was Mary Davidson, was one of those noble, and warm hearted women, who train their sons in the way they should go, with full confidence that, when older, they will not depart from it. In 1836, the family removed from Missouri, to Warren County, Illinois, where their children were reared upon free soil, and amid surroundings well calculated to convert the youth to the faith of those, who were Loyal Democrats. Mr. Rogers received a good common school education and afterward attended Knox College, at Galesburg, Illinois, for two terms. He turned his attention to farming, upon attaining his majority, and is still engaged in that most necessary and honored avocation. He became a Republican, with the commencement of his political career, and has never abandoned his party, which, in recognition of his services, elevated him to a place in the Board of Supervisors of his County, and retained him in that position for six consecutive years, as the representative of Hale Township. In 1882, he was chosen as one of the Representatives of the Twenty-seventh District of the Lower House of the General Assembly of the State, a position, which he is filling with honor to himself and satisfaction to his constituency. He possesses a power of penetration, which enables him to form opinions quickly and correctly. He is shrewd and enthusiastic in conversation, and always endeavors to turn things to good account. In person, he is tall and compactly built; wears a full beard, and is rather more dark than light in complexion. He is a man whose very presence inspires confidence—one whom all regard as honorable and honest. He is very obliging and generous in disposition.

HON. JESSE J. ROOK.

Mr. Rook was born in Chicago, January 2d, 1850, his father at that time being a tanner. Mr. Rook has always resided in Chicago, although he has traveled extensively, for the purpose of increasing his fund of knowledge, by greater and more extended opportunities for observation. His literary education was obtained in the public schools of Chicago, where he won a scholarship in the Bryant & Stratton Business College, by his good record in a competitive examination at the close of his course. He made a good use of it, and, as a result, has a very fine practical, business education. After leaving the latter institution, he accepted a position in the Chicago Postoffice, in 1871. That was his first public position. He is a member of the Roman Catholic Church; but does not affiliate with any of the secret orders. He is a Republican in politics, having never been anything else, and not feeling that there is any just necessity for breaking his political faith or changing his relations to the party. He was elected to the House of Representatives in 1882, by a majority of two thousand two hundred votes over both of his Democratic competitors, in a Democratic District—the Eleventh, of Cook County. Mr. Rook is a young man of excellent talents, and bids fair to avoid the indiscretions, which are often perpetrated by men of his age, in public positions, steer clear of the rocks of over-confidence, and attain an enviable position on the scroll of fame. He is rather below the average stature and is dark in complexion. He is neat and tidy in dress, and very social, generous and kind in his intercourse with his constituents. He is a man of rare independence and determination.

HON. JAMES M. ROUNTREE.

This gentleman was born in Washington County, Illinois, in the year 1833. His parents were Greenville and Lydia Young Rountree. His father was a farmer, and miller, in Washington County, where he yet resides, and is one of the representative citizens of that locality. Mr. Rountree is a resident of Nashville, and represents the Forty-second District in the Lower House. His education was obtained from the family library, at home. When yet a boy, Mr. Rountree began learning the blacksmith's trade. After graduating as a "smithy," he learned the carpenter's trade, and then began the study of law in his own private library, which he had been collecting, and which he has kept adding to, until to-day it is the best law library in Washington County. Mr. Rountree was Master in Chancery from 1866 to 1870, and held the office of State's Attorney for his County, from 1876 to 1880, and in 1882 was elected to his present office, defeating his opponent on the Republican ticket, Mr. Defreese, by 1930 votes, and this, too, in a Republican District. Mr. Rountree has always been a Democrat, but he refused to vote for Greeley when he ran for the office of President. Mr. Rountree is a member of the Order of Odd Fellows. He owns four hundred acres of land in this State, and is comfortably fixed in life. In appearance, Mr. Rountree is rather portly, and is a pleasant, sociable gentleman and shrewd Legislator.

HON. ELBERT ROWLAND.

Mr. Rowland was born in New York City, April 28th, 1832. His father was a merchant tailor, who removed to Illinois in 1840, locating at Olney, Richland County. He obtained his literary education in the common schools of Illinois, but, being ambitious to follow in the footsteps of Æsculapius, he entered the New York Medical College, where he was graduated in the Department of Chemistry, in 1858, and in the Medical Department, one year later. He began the practice of his profession in New York City, where he remained until 1861, when he entered the Army as Assistant Surgeon, of the Twenty-seventh Regiment of New York Volunteers. He retained his place in the service of the United States, until 1863, when he returned to Olney, where he has resided and enjoyed a lucrative business ever since. He is now Surgeon of Post No. 92, Grand Army of the Republic, at his home. He is not a member of any church, but is a Royal Arch Degree Mason, and a Comrade in the Grand Army of the Republic, as above stated. He is a confirmed Democrat, and, although prominently identified with the local interests of his party, has hitherto refused all nominations, with the exception of that upon which he became a candidate for Representative in the Thirty-third General Assembly. In the convention, which placed him in nomination, he received the entire vote upon the first ballot. This is one of the remarkable things of political history. There are few political conventions, which are unanimous in sentiment. In person, Mr. Rowland is of average stature, and dark complexion. He wears a magnificent black beard of great length. He is deliberate, yet fluent in conversation, and genial and kind in disposition. He stands high in his profession and the estimation of his associates, political and otherwise. He is very precise and clear in delivery, and a forcible debater in most respects. He has been Chairman of the Local Democratic Central Committee, for seventeen years; is also a member of the Board of Censors of the College of Physicians and Surgeons, at Evansville, Indiana, and was one of the Committee to examine candidates for the West Point Cadetship, in his district, in 1880.

HON. JAMES M. SCURLOCK.

Mr. Scurlock first looked upon the faces of men and women, in Williamson County, Illinois, September 24th, 1844. His father was a farmer, and James probably owes much of his success in life to the fact that the obstacles which lay in the way of successful and profitable agriculture in that day, were very numerous, and could be overcome only by the greatest and most perseverent effort. He undoubtedly had his share of hard experiences, which, if we had space to relate them, would cause the farmer boys of this day of machinery and convenient markets, to open their eyes in amazement, that people then lived at all. His education was solely derived from the public schools of the country, and individual effort. In 1863, he removed to Carbondale, Jackson County, where he how resdes. He is, by occupation, a dealer in produce and agricultural implements. He belongs to no church; but is a Free Mason of the degree of Knight Templar. He has always been a Republican in politics, and has served two years as Alderman, and eight years, as Treasurer of the city of Carbondale. He was elected to the House of Representatives in 1882, polling a very large vote. In person, he is large and well proportioned, dark in complexion, and a very handsome man in appearance. He is polite and gentlemanly in his intercourse with the people, and is a fluent conversationalist, influential debater and generous gentleman, who does honor to the office which he holds.

HON. AUSTIN O. SEXTON.

Mr. Sexton was born in Chicago, in the year 1852, his father being at that time a contractor and builder. His education was acquired in the Chicago public schools, he being a graduate of the High School, of the class of 1872. After two years of arduous study in the office of a practicing attorney, Mr. Sexton was admitted to the Bar in 1876, on the fourth day of July. He does not belong to any church; but is a member of the Ancient Order of United Workmen and Independent Order of Forresters. In politics he is unquestionably Democratic to the very core, and, being so from conviction, his opponents will find it a difficult matter to convert him to their faith, although they fully realize that he is a valuable acquisition to any party. He was first elected to the House of Representatives in 1876, and was re-elected in 1878, 1880 and 1882 by increased majorities. He is a popular man, not alone in his District, but, also, in the honorable body of which he is a member, having received the full vote of his party for Speaker at the present session, and being defeated, only because his party was in a hopeless minority. In personal appearance, he is tall, well proportioned and decidedly good looking. He has a splendid voice, and is never afraid or ashamed to let it be heard upon proper occasions. He is well informed, affable and generous in disposition, and dignified, yet not over-bearing in demeanor. He is one of the Democratic leaders in the House, and is undoubtedly a good man in his proper sphere.

HON. JOHN C. SEYSTER.

This gentleman was born at Oregon, Ogle County, Illinois, May 12th, 1854. He has never resided outside of the State in which he was born, and received an academic education at Rock River Seminary, located at Mt. Morris. He entered the Union School of Law, at Chicago, in the fall of 1876, remaining one term, when he completed his course of study in the office of the Honorable William Barge, of Dixon. His preceptor is regarded as one of the leading members of the Bar, of Northern Illinois. He was examined in the Appellate Court and admitted to the Bar in 1878, since which time he has been engaged in practicing his profession at Oregon, his native city. He is a promising young lawyer, and has already secured a place in the hearts of his neighbors and clients, which many far older lawyers might justly regard with envy. He is not a member of any church, nor does he affiliate with more than one secret society. He is an enthusiastic member of the Independent Order of Odd Fellows, and is as proud of the principles of that fraternity as his lodge is well satisfied with his practice of them. He is a Democrat, and has been nothing else since attaining his majority. He was elected to represent his district in the Lower House of the Thirty-third General Assembly, in 1882, running far ahead of his ticket. In personal appearance, Mr. Seyster is below the medium height; wears no beard; has blue eyes, and is well proportioned. He dresses very neatly and tastefully, and is a smooth but incisive talker. He is positive in opinion, and possesses excellent judgment and a calm temper. He is an unusually successful advocate in jury cases.

HON. REDMOND SHERIDAN.

We now have the pleasure of presenting to our readers the
"legislative baby." Mr. Sheridan, though youthful in appearance, as well as in fact, is neither a babe in stature or intellect.
The above epithet expresses the idea that he is the most youthful
member of the Thirty-third General Assembly. He was born
in Chicago, December 12th, 1859. His parents were Redmond
and Agnes Sheridan, who claim relationship with the poet of the
same name. Mr. Sheridan's father was a prominent dealer in
boots and shoes, at the time of his child's birth, and is still engaged in the same trade. He provided facilities for a good
education, and his boy became a graduate of Dyrenfurth College, Chicago. At the time of his election to the Legislature,
he was engaged as a clerk in the wholesale liquor house of H.
H. Schufeldt & Co. He has read law for the purpose of increasing the range of his education, and is a shrewd reasoner and
sensible talker. He is a member of Company "K," Second Regiment Illinois National Guards, at present. He has once offered
his resignation, but the boys desire so greatly to keep him in
the ranks, that they refuse to accept it. Mr. Sheridan is a member of the Catholic Church, and also belongs to the Independent
Order of Forresters. He was elected on the Democratic ticket,
running one thousand two hundred votes ahead of his associate
Democratic majority candidate. He represents the Fourth District of Cook County, and resides in Chicago. In person, Mr.
Sheridan is smooth-faced, slender and boyish; but, notwithstanding his youthful appearance, he is acute in observation, and
fearless in discussion. He will rise, with the first important occasion, into public notice, for he realizes that he was sent to the
House of Representatives to advocate the interests of his constituents, and he is sure to endeavor to fully perform his mission.

HON. LOUIS CHARLES STARKEL.

This gentleman was born at Prange, Bohemic Austria, September 1st, 1839. His father, true to the instincts of the race of which he was a representative, was a skilled architect. The family came to the United States in 1850, locating in Ohio, whence the subject of this sketch emigrated to Carlisle, Illinois, in 1859, where he began practicing his profession as a physician and surgeon. His education was acquired in the common schools of Ohio, and professional knowledge added to it by a course of study in the Cincinnati Medical College. Mr. Starkel is now engaged in the practice of medicine, however, having temporarily, at least, retired. He is a Free Mason of the Thirty-second Degree, and a Knight Templar. He is now the Grand Warden of a Grand Commandery of that order. He is, and has always been, a staunch boat on the sea of government, guided by the pilot which he deems safest—Democracy. The party has honored him with the office of County Clerk, which he has held since 1873, until he was elected to the House of Representatives from the Forty-Seventh, or Belleville District, in 1882. Mr. Starkel is a quite prominent factor, not only in the affairs of the General Assembly, but in the Democratic councils of the commonwealth, and, judging from the success of his townsman at the last election, may yet leave the hungry opposition to mourn over another success in the Sucker State. In person, Mr. Starkel is tall and robust—a nicely proportioned man, in fact—ambitious, yet cool and collected in thought, in times of excitement. He is as generous and kind as one could wish, and hardly ever jokes. He was the Democratic nominee for State Auditor in 1880, but was defeated.

HON. GEORGE M. STEVENS.

Mr. Stevens was born near Waterloo, Shefford County, Canada East, April 4th, 1846. His father was a seaman in early life, but, at the time of George's birth, was engaged in farming. In 1865, Mr. Stevens removed to Vermont, but did not remain there long, coming to Springfield, Illinois, in 1867, and locating at Nokomis, Montgomery County, in 1872. His education was acquired in the common schools of Canada, the Springfield High School and the Ann Arbor, Michigan, Law School, where he was graduated in 1872, and since that date, he has been practicing his profession at his Montgomery County home. He has the reputation of being a very shrewd and successful lawyer. He does not commune with any of the religious denominations, but is a Royal Arch Mason. He is a Democrat, politically, believing that the Constitutional methods and conservative theories of that party are best calculated to develope and perpetuate Republican institutions. He has occupied the position of City Attorney of Nokomis since 1876, until his election to the House of Representatives in 1882, from the Fortieth District, by a majority of two thousand votes. In person, Mr. Stevens is slightly above medium stature; wears a full beard, and is kind, affable and polite to all with whom he comes in contact. He is a careful debater and a generous and capable man, who is no more honored by his election than is the office, which he fills. Mr. Stevens is a self-made man, having left his father's home at the age of seventeen, since which time he has been thrown entirely upon his own resources, and, what he is now, is entirely the result of his own exertions.

HON. JOHN D. STEVENS.

Mr. Stevens was born at Carrollton, Greene County, Illinois, February 8th, 1826 His father was then engaged in the business of a hatter and furrier, driving a flourishing trade with the Indians at Louisiana, Missouri, who infested that part of the State in great numbers, in that early day. In 1828, his parents emigrated to Hazel Green, Wisconsin; but, in the fall of the same year, returned to Illinois, sailing down the river in an old-fashioned keel-boat. In 1829, the family engaged in the fur trade, in Louisiana, Pike County, Missouri; but, in 1833, settled in Hancock County, Illinois, where Mr. Stevens now resides. The old gentleman can relate many entertaining stories of early Illinois history, and delights in dwelling upon the scenes of danger and tragic, or amusing incidents of the olden time. The education of Mr. Stevens was acquired in the country schools of Hancock County. He is the proprietor of the Stevens House, a large hotel at Carthage, in his county; but does not conduct it himself, although he has acted as "mine host" during six years of his eventful life. He has spent the greater portion of his life in farming and mining. He is a Democrat, and has served as Sheriff of his county, two terms. In 1882, he was elected to the House of Representatives, running over five thousand votes ahead of his ticket. He is one of those substantial men, who are too honest to indulge in trickery, and can be trusted for the integrity of motives, which is often required to bridge over a political crisis. He is one of those kind and considerate old gentlemen, whom everybody loves; is large and portly in physique, and as gentle and sympathetic as a woman in his disposition. He is generally respected and beloved for his noble qualities of heart and mind.

HON. THEODORE STIMMING.

He is a German by birth. He was born near Berlin, Prussia,
April 2d, 1830. His father followed the avocation of a hatter
and furrier, for a livelihood. Mr. Stimming came to the United
States in 1849, and located at Cincinnati. He moved to Iowa in
1854, and located in Chicago in 1872. He was educated in the
Gymnasium, in Berlin, and was graduated for the purpose of
serving in the Army, one year, the laws in relation to military
service being less rigorous at that time than now. After coming
West, he worked upon the Lake Shore and Southern Railway,
purchasing an interest in a riding school in Cincinnati, a short
time afterward. He afterward kept a hotel, and, soon after that
became the representative of Kohler & Frohling, of San Fran-
cisco, traveling and selling to wholesale dealers, in car-load lots.
He was Superintendent of the North Division Postoffice, of Chicago, when elected to the House of Representatives in 1882. He
was a Volunteer in the First Iowa Regiment, in April, 1861, and
participated in the battle at Wilson Creek, Missouri. He re-
enlisted in the Thirty-first Iowa, on the first three hundred thousand call, and was a participant in the battle at Arkansas Post,
where he was promoted from the First Lieutenancy to a Major-
ship, for meritorious services on the battle-field. He was at
Vicksburg, Lookout Mountain and Atlanta, where the gallant
McPherson fell. He was made a Lieutenant Colonel before
Atlanta, marched with Sherman to the sea, and was mustered
out in August, 1865. He is not a church member, but is an Odd
Fellow, member of the Encampment and Uniform Degree, and
Knight of Honor. He is a staunch Republican, and was elected
from the Sixth Chicago District. He is very genial and kind in
disposition, good natured in debate, and has a smile for every-
body. In speech, he is pleasant and agreeable, and has a slight
German accent, which lends to his conversation a somewhat remarkable charm.

HON. GEORGE G. STRUCKMAN.

This gentleman first gazed upon the beauties of nature, in the northern part of Germany, in 1835. His father was overseer in a coal-mine. In 1850, his parents, with their family, emigrated to the United States, locating in the town of Hanover, in Cook County, Illinois. He was educated in the district school of his village, and afterward enjoyed some advantages in good, private schools in the City of Chicago. In September of 1861, Mr. Struckman enlisted in Company "H," of the Fourth Regiment of Missouri Cavalry and was chosen First Sergeant. He served until promoted after the Battle of Pea Ridge, to Second Lieutenant, November 1, 1864, when he was mustered out of the army in the latter capacity. Mr. Struckman is one of the proud sons of toil, of the grandest agricultural State in the Union, owning a farm of one hundred and sixty acres near Hanover, in Cook County, his post-office address, however, being Elgin, Kane County. He is one of those German sons of Industry, who came to the land of the free, poor, and have amassed fortunes. In politics, he is a Republican, having supported that ticket with his first ballot as well as the last. He has been a Justice of the Peace for twelve years, Assessor for ten years and served one term as Township Supervisor. He is not a church member; but is a Free Mason. He is physically large and portly; sandy in complexion; wears a full beard and is a shrewd politician, and jolly conversationalist, and is genial and affable in his intercourse with the people, and his associates in the House of Representatives.

HON. HENRY STUDER.

Mr. Studer was born to Peter and Elizabeth Studer, the maiden name of the latter being Ruby, in Switzerland, March 1st, 1823. His father was a farmer, and Henry's early days were fraught with the valuable experiences of farm-life, to be derived from labor on Swiss lands. Mr. Studer came to the United States in 1850, locating at Olney, Richland County, Illinois, where he now resides. His education in youth was such as the common schools of his native country afforded; but he has learned to speak the English language very fluently, and close observation has enabled him to master some of the most difficult business problems. For some years after locating in Olney, Mr. Studer followed the business of a wholesale grocer, but having accumulated a neat little fortune, he has now retired from that business. He has held many minor offices of honor and trust in the county and city governments, and was a Deputy in the office of the Provost Marshal, after the War. He became a member of Fremont's Body Guard, in 1862. He is a member of the German Reformed Church, and a Free Mason of the degree of Knight Templar. He became a Republican in 1856, during the campaign of John C. Fremont, and has adhered to the tenets of that party ever since. He was elected by a larger vote than any of his colleagues, to a place in the House of Representatives of the Thirty-third General Assembly, and, is also a director of the Olney National Bank, which has a capital of $60,000. In person, Mr. Studer is large, portly and stamped with the physical characteristics of his fatherland. He is fair in complexion; polite, talkative and agreeable, and has a slight foreign accent in speech, which gives a charming interest to his conversation. He is a careful man, and does not fear the opposition, or anybody else. He takes a great interest in all financial affairs pertaining to the State Government.

HON. DAVID SULLIVAN.

He was born in Ireland, April 3d, 1856, and came to this country with his parents, when quite young. His family had lived in this country several years prior to his birth, his father being an American Citizen at that time, although residing in his native country. Upon his second arrival in this country, the father of Mr. Sullivan went, with his family, to the town of Yonkers, New York, where he resided for a few years, eventually removing to Marquette County, Michigan, where he and his wife now reside. Having acquired a limited knowledge of the "art preservative," he left home at the early age of fifteen years, and went to Chicago, where he immediately secured employment as a compositor on the *Chicago Times*. He afterward read law in the office of Olney & Crocker, but completed his course of study under the tutorship of Hon. T. A. Moran, one of the Circuit Judges of Cook County. His education was acquired in the common schools of his various places of residence, and the composing room. In religion, he is a Catholic; in politics, an uncompromising Democrat He was a Representative in the Thirty-second General Assembly, having been elected from the First Chicago District, and was reëlected from the same district as a minority candidate in 1882. In person, he is very tall and well proportioned, has dark hair and a light moustache. He is frank and positive in character, and cannot endure any sugar-coating or soft-soaping. He is incisive in speech, and says precisely what he thinks, irrespective of results.

HON. MICHAEL A. SULLIVAN.

This gentleman was born in St. Louis, October 19, 1858, and is now twenty-four years old. His parents reside in St. Clair County, at present. His father was a contractor and grocer, who frequently figured in politics as a logical and forcible stump-orator. He was the author of the first side-walk ordinance ever adopted by the government of East St. Louis, then a small town. The subject of this sketch received an academic education, graduating from the St. Clair County High School, with high honors, in 1876. He immediately re-entered the same school in the capacity of an instructor, and remained until last fall, when the voice of his constituents invited him to the Legislative halls of his State. He was elected as a Democrat, running ahead of his ticket. He is a pronounced friend of the laboring classes, and though young, his voice will be heard in their defense upon all proper occasions. He is remarkable for his energy, which was no less a prominent characteristic of the boy at play, than the young man, poring over his books in the school room. He always stood high in his classes, and was foremost in the sports incident to the career of a school boy. He is a talented young man, whose career in State affairs has but commenced; but, if his people should see fit to continue him in office, we have no doubt that he will soon occupy a prominent place among our law-makers. His energetic and studious habits will win him friends and fame, if pursued with the same perseverance in the future as in the past. His constituents must have recognized rare merit in him, to elect him to such a responsible position at this early period of his life. He is engaged in reading law and will complete his course in June, 1883.

HON. EDWARD B. SUMNER.

This rising young statesman was born in Winnebago County, Illinois, November 14th, 1850, and is, therefore, but thirty-two years of age. His parents were Ephriam Sumner and Betsy, his wife, *nee* Blake, who resided upon a farm, and the early training of their son, who is now such a prominent figure in local politics, was of that simple and substantial type, which has produced most of the ablest professional men of our country. Mr. Sumner is now a resident of Rockford, in the county of his birth. He is a graduate of the Rockford High School, of the class of 1866, of the University of Michigan, class of 1871, in the literary department, and of the law department of the same school, of the class of 1873. Mr. Sumner chose the law as his profession, and has enjoyed a profitable and extensive practice in Rockford, his home. Although quite young, and a new acquisition to the Bar, he was made City Attorney of Rockford, in 1878. He was elected to the Thirty-second General Assembly as a majority candidate, and re-elected to the Thirty-third Assembly in the same manner. He is a sound Republican in politics, and is one of the most faithful members of the House. His reputation for fidelity to his official trusts is as great in the body, of which he is a member, as among his constituents. He is forcible and eloquent in speech, firm in disposition, and affable and courteous in his intercourse with the people. In person, he is a little above the medium height, manly and dignified in bearing, and of light complexion. It is a significant fact, that he has held many elective offices in his county, and has never yet occupied the rather unpleasant position of a defeated candidate. He is Chairman of the Committee on Judicial Department, at the present session, and was a member of the Judiciary Committee at the session of 1880.

HON. PETER A. SUNDELIUS.

Mr. Sundelius was born in Sweden, and is a graduate of the Royal College at Gottenburg, having pursued a classical course of study of no less than ten years duration. He has been a tutor in college, editor of a Swedish newspaper, and is now a clerk in the Recorder's office in Chicago, being granted a leave of absence to attend to his duties as one of the law-makers of his State. Mr. Sundelius was a member of the Tenth Regiment of Connecticut Volunteers, during the Rebellion, and was severely wounded at Petersburg, Virginia, April 2d, 1865. He belongs to no church, but is a member of the Grand Army of the Republic, Post No. 28, in Chicago. He is a very determined and conscientious Republican in politics, and was elected to the House of Representatives of the Thirty-third General Assembly, by a plurality of 1,897½ votes, from the Thirteenth District. Mr. Sundelius is, perhaps, one of the best educated men in either branch of the Legislature. His knowledge of the classics is probably unequalled in any branch of the State government, and he is an able writer and speaker, and an excellent penman. He is a very retiring gentleman in disposition, and seemed very much averse to going before the public in the form of a hero, when approached for information, upon which to base a sketch of his life. In person he is tall and slender, and bears the stamp of excessive mental labor. He is polite and dignified in manner, and shrewd and powerful in argument.

HON. JOHN S. SYMONDS.

This gentleman is of average stature, inclined to portliness, and genial and social in disposition. His hair is quite gray, and he is plain and unassuming, in both dress and speech. He was born in Cayuga County, New York, January 18th, 1833. His father was a farmer. April 23d, 1857, he came to Xenia, Clay County, Illinois, and having acquired a good common-school education in his native State, at once became a farmer and dealer in grain. He has been remarkably successful in business, and has amassed a very handsome fortune. His landed estates aggregate about a thousand acres, and he has hay-presses, warehouses, etc., of very great value. He is yet engaged in buying and shipping hay and grain, and enjoys the best possible reputation for honesty, business sagacity and strict integrity. Although so wealthy, he is not parsimonious, the generous impulses of his nature controlling him in his intercourse with the world. He is a Baptist in religious belief, and is a Free Mason in good standing. Politically, he is a Democrat, although he was a Republican during the War. He became a Democrat by force of the excesses and extravagancies of the administrations succeeding the Rebellion, and does not feel that the party has ever sufficiently recovered from those conditions to justify him in supporting it. He is an acute reasoner, and an enemy to all sorts of reckless expenditure in governmental affairs, State or National. He has held various local offices, and was chosen to represent his district in the Lower House of the Legislature, in 1882, by a very handsome plurality.

HON. DANIEL TAYLOR.

Mr. Taylor was born in Argyle, New York, in July, 1832. In 1855, he came to Illinois, locating in the City of Kankakee, where he has since resided. His education was obtained in the common schools of his native State, and, although he is too modest to say so, there is no doubt in the mind of the writer, that he has been a very close observer and careful reader, throughout his life. He is not a member of any church organization, but is a Free Mason. By occupation, he is a dealer in stone, and manufacturer of tile, brick and lime, although himself a "brick," to employ slang phraseology, but not a very "hard bat." He says he would prefer to have nothing said concerning his business, but the historian must be faithful to his subject, even if the latter is subjected to strange importunings and covered with Legislative anathema. Seriously, however, Mr. Taylor is one of those pointed and witty gentlemen, who are always on good terms with the world, enjoy life, and are the center of a large circle of admiring friends. He is a Democrat in politics; has held numerous local offices of honor and trust; was a member of the Thirtieth General Assembly, representing the minority party in the Sixteenth District, and was reëlected in 1882. He is not above average in stature, light in complexion, and rather reticent upon the subject of self, but a very excellent speaker upon ordinary topics, or proposed Legislative measures. He is polite, affable and generous in his intercourse with the public.

HON. JAMES A. TAYLOR.

Mr. Taylor was born in Chicago in 1858, and is now twenty-five years of age. His father was a metropolitan contractor and builder, at the time of his birth, conducting a heavy business. He was one of the earliest settlers of Chicago, being one of its trustees when it was but a village. He is a veteran of the War of 1812, and was a prominent politician in the earlier history of the city, where he now resides, at the advanced age of eighty-seven years. Mr. Taylor is a graduate of Notre Dame University, and has chosen the real estate business as his occupation. He was one of the prime movers in the organization of the First Regiment of the State Militia, and took an active part not only in its formation, but its duties, also. He is a gentleman of enthusiastic mind and fine tastes, and delights in seeing everything in apple-pie order. In politics, he is a Democrat, and has a firm hold upon the suffrages of the people of his political faith in the district, from which he was elected to the House of Representatives, in 1882. In this connection, it may not be deemed inappropriate to state that his father is the oldest Democrat in Chicago. In person, Mr. Taylor is a small man, who dresses neatly, and is polite and genteel in his bearing and conduct, as the most fastidious could reasonably desire, He is a quick and incisive speaker and, when engaged in discussion, causes one to wonder that so much power can be stored in so small a body.

HON. RICHARD H. TEMPLEMAN.

Mr. Templeman was born near Fredricksburg, Tauquier County, Virginia, April 20th, 1833. James Templeman, his father, was a typical Virginia farmer, and Richard endured all of the hardships and privations incident to an agricultural life, during the early period of his existence. He was educated in the public schools of his native States, Ohio and Maryland. Mr. Templeman came to Illinois in 1852, locating in Logan County, and has never since that time changed his place of residence. He does not hold membership in any church or secret society, and is strong minded, liberal and firm in his convictions in regard to sectarianism and its concomitants, though not aggressive or overbearing in his opinions. He has been for many years, and now is engaged in farming and breeding fine stock. He has a magnificent herd of Short-horn cattle, and takes great pride in its superior merits. His farm consists of two hundred and sixty acres of number one Logan County lands, in an excellent state of cultivation. He was born a Democrat, and has no desire to be disinthralled from his hereditary political preferences. He has held many minor offices in his township and county, among which may be enumerated those of Township Supervisor, Clerk, Treasurer and School Treasurer. He was elected to the House of Representatives in 1882, as a minority candidate, polling a very heavy vote. In person, he is tall and portly. When quite young, he had the misfortune to lose an eye, by accident. He is jovial in disposition, kind and generous—a man capable of warm friendship, and no less worthy than capable. He is a good, solid Legislator, honest, willing and competent.

HON. JOHN W. THOMAS.

Mr. Thomas says he was born in Montgomery, Alabama, thirty-eight years ago. His father was a steward on a steamboat, when John was born. Mr. Thomas came to Illinois in 1868, locating in Chicago, where he now resides. He had received a liberal education and followed school teaching for a livelihood for some time after coming to this State, afterward abandoning that and establishing himself as a grocer. He soon determined to become a lawyer, however, and entered the office of Hawes and Lawrence, the former of whom is now Judge of the Superior Court in Chicago, where he pursued the usual course of study, and was, in due time admitted to the Bar. He is a member of the Baptist Church, and also of the order known as Knights of Wise Men. Politically, he is a full blooded Republican. He was a member of the Thirtieth General Assembly of Illinois, and was afterward a clerk in the Treasury Department at Washington, resigning the latter office, when elected to the Thirty-third General Assembly of his State, in 1882. He is a Representative in the Lower House, elected by a larger vote than that polled by any other candidate in the Third Chicago District. He is the only colored man in either house of the Assembly, is intelligent, well read, polite and affable. He is a good speaker, and is far superior in power of intellect to a large proportion of the paler faced members of this Assembly. He is kind and generous in disposition and does not show any of that vanity which characterizes the conduct of many men, who have risen from an humble station in life to a prominent and responsible position in the government of his State. He has been a member of the order known as Brothers of the Union, for years, and was President of the same for five years.

HON. HARRY C. THOMPSON.

This gentleman was born at Virginia, Cass County, Illinois, on August 6th, 1849. His father was a merchant for forty-five years, and was the first County Clerk Cass County ever had. Young Thompson received his education at the Asbury University, in 1860-2-3, and removed to St. Louis in 1865. While in St. Louis, he was engaged in the commission business. He removed to Greene County, in 1875, remaining one year, engaged in farming and civil engineering. He then returned to Cass County, and engaged in farming his lands near Philadelphia Station. He soon afterward married Miss Lilah Hall, of Virginia, and is now devoting his attention to his farm and breeding fine horses. He is not a member of any church, nor does he affiliate with any of the secret societies. He is a well informed man, having read law for his own satisfaction and in order to enable him to successfully manage the affairs of his already extensive and constantly increasing business. He is a Democrat from the crown of his hat to the soles of his shoes, and was elected to the House of Representatives on that ticket in 1882, over his opponent, by a very handsome majority. In person, Mr. Thompson is rather above the average stature, dark complexion, a man of great physical strength. He is quiet in demeanor, and genial and polite to all, enjoys a joke as well as anyone, a shrewd financier and generous hearted gentleman, of whom his constituents are justly proud.

HON. SAMUEL H. THOMPSON.

Mr. Thompson was born in Pickaway County, Ohio, November 12th, 1829. His educational advantages were very poor, his only opportunity for acquiring knowledge having been attendance upon night schools, and his own senses, of observation and apprehension. He removed to Illinois in 1860, and located in Pekin; but, in 1863, went to Peoria, where he engaged in merchandising. He succeeded well in business from the very first, and has now retired with a comfortable fortune and is enjoying the fruits of his labors, in his more youthful days. In religious belief he is a Universalist. He is also a member of one of the secret orders. Politically, he is a consistent and reasoning Republican, as old as the party itself, and as faithful to its principles as any of its devotees could reasonably desire him to be. He was Post Master of Darbyville, Spink County, Ohio, prior to coming to this State, for four years. Since he came to Illinois, he has been a Deputy United States Revenue Collector at Pekin. He was elected to the House of Representatives in 1882, by a majority of seventeen hundred votes over his colleague on the same ticket. In person, Mr. Thompson is large and corpulent, wearing a full beard and looks just what he is, a merchant, who is resting after thirty years of fatiguing business. He is genial, social and kind in his intercourse with the public, and generous, though justly careful in his dealings with his fellow men.

HON. JAMES T. THORNTON.

This gentleman was born in Kentucky, in 1823, and is, therefore, now sixty years of age. His father was the Sheriff of Green County, Kentucky, at the time of the birth of this son, and died, when the latter was but three years of age. His mother, formerly Miss Ann Barret, was a typical Kentucky matron, and spared no pains to impress upon the mind of her son a proper appreciation of his ability, duty and destiny. How many prominent men of our country owe so much of what they are to the careful training, which they received at the knee of the noblest, truest and best friend man ever possessed—a mother! How grand and exalted does the man of eminence appear to us, when he, in the meridian of his glory, remembers this, and does honor to her memory! In 1833, Mr. Thornton came to Illinois, locating in Sangamon County. He followed merchandising for five years, first at Magnolia, Putnam County, then became a farmer, and, in 1845, removed to Iowa. He again became a resident of Putnam County, Illinois, three years later, and has resided there ever since, following the occupation upon which all others are equally dependent—that of a farmer. He was educated in the district schools of Illinois, and what he knows in excess of that instruction—and it is much—was acquired by individual effort. He is no member of any church or society, and his religion is to do right. Politically, he is a Republican, as old as the party itself, and no less vigorous. He was a Representative in the Twenty-ninth and Thirty-second General Assemblies, and occupies his accustomed place in the Thirty-third. On the issue of temperance, he is a pronounced Prohibitionist. His farm consists of three hundred and seventy acres of land, and is very valuable. He has very fine herds of Shorthorn and Durham cattle, of which he is justly very proud. He is not above the average in stature, just and generous in natural impulse, and careful and conscientious in all he says and does.

HON. CHARLES H. TRYON.

Bela H. Tryon and Harriet, his wife, formerly a Billings, were the parents of a happy family on a Massachusetts farm, June 22d, 1827, in Franklin County, in the Bay State. Mr. Tryon and his parents emigrated to New York State in 1830 and remained there until 1837, when they came to Illinois, locating in McHenry County. His education was acquired in the district schools of the various localities in which his boyhood was passed. Mr. Tryon chose the avocation of his father and is now engaged in farming in the county where he resides. He is one of the prominent agriculturalists of his part of the State. He was a Captain in the Ninety-fifth Illinois Infantry, in 1862–63, serving but one year. He is not a member of any church; but is a Free Mason. He is a staunch Republican, never having severed his allegiance to that party since he bestowed the favor of his suffrage upon its candidates in 1856. He is quite a political favorite in his county and district, and has been a Justice of the Peace and Township Supervisor for several years. He is serving his first term, as a Representative, in the Thirty-third General Assembly, having been elected to that position of honor in 1882. He is a careful and rather shrewd reasoner, inclined to investigate the merits of every measure upon which he is expected to vote, and ever on the *qui vive* for anything that bears semblance to a job or fat place, at the expense of the people, without rendering adequate returns. He is the avowed enemy of all sorts of swindlers, games and experimental legislation, being ardently devoted to the material necessities and practical interests of his constituents. He is tall and well proportioned, somewhat effected by age and a life of necessant toil, his hair a little sprinkled with the silvery fringe of time, and his manner rendered rather sedate and caustic with the varied experiences in life. He is very gentlemanly and sensible in speech and is kind and generous in natural impulse. He is a very safe man for the position which he holds.

HON. WILLIAM UPDYKE.

This gentleman was born in Trenton, Monmouth County, New Jersey, August 18th, 1831, to Josiah Updyke, a farmer, and Mary, his wife. When he was but seven years of age, his parents emigrated to Ohio, from which State they came to Illinois, in 1858, locating on a farm of one hundred and ninety-five acres, near Robinson, in Crawford County. The only schooling he obtained was during the residence of his parents in Ohio, when he was permitted to attend the district schools about two months out of each year. The schooling which qualified him for his present honorable office, was obtained by his own determined and perseverent efforts. The experiences of his early life gave him a keen relish for knowledge, and his thirst never yet has been quenched. He has served as County Treasurer of Crawford County, for three consecutive terms, commencing in 1873. He is a Master Mason and member of the Methodist Episcopal Church. Mr. Updyke has a farm of two hundred and sixty-five acres in the vicinity of Robinson, and is largely engaged in breeding and dealing in fine Short-horn cattle. He is an uncompromising Democrat, and was never anything else, politically speaking. He was elected as a Representative to the Thirty-third General Assembly, in 1882, over G. W. Lewis, by a majority of four thousand five hundred votes. Mr. Updyke is a typical modern farmer, in appearance. He is plain but tidy in dress, solidly and compactly built, gruff, yet genial and affectionate in manner, methodical and cool in argument, and, generally speaking, a man, who knows what is right and means to do it at all hazzards. He is a Legislator upon whose strict integrity and firm convictions his constituency can confidently rely.

HON. ROBERT D. UTIGER.

Mr. Utiger was born at his present home in Madison County, Illinois, October 11th, 1841. His father was a farmer, and Robert follows in his footsteps, preferring to help feed the multitude, rather than consume the fruits of the honest labor of others. His farm consists of two hundred acres of the excellent farming lands of his county, and Mr. Utiger cultivates it in a very systematic and business like manner. He is one of those farmers, who take an honest and justifiable pride in the manner in which their lands are managed and everything is conducted in a systematic and intelligent way, which does honor to the governing mind. The education of this gentleman was acquired in the district schools of his county. He is, and has always been a Democrat in politics, and has held various positions of honor and trust, among which may be mentioned Supervisor, for five years, Justice of the Peace, for six years, and Post Master of Alhambra, for twelve years. He was elected to the House of Representatives in 1882, from the Forty-first District, which is Republican, by a small majority. In person, Mr. Utiger is not above medium height, wears a full beard, is dark in complexion, a shrewd politician, and a plain man in dress and speech. He is one of the members, whose very appearance would belie charges of dishonesty and corruption to the satisfaction of all, and he is noble and generous to a fault. Would that there were more of his kind in both branches of the Assembly.

HON. GEORGE H. VARNELL.

Mr. Varnell was born at Georgetown, District of Columbia, February 2d, 1833. His father was a brick-layer by trade, and descended from English ancestors. Mr. Varnell came to Illinois in 1861, locating at Mt. Vernon, Jefferson County, where he read law in the office of Farmer & Casey. He was admitted to the Bar in 1864. His education was acquired in a Catholic School in Georgetown, D. C. He began business as a house, sign and ornamental painter, after a three years apprenticeship in Washington, D. C., having passed a portion of his boyhood on the Chesapeake and Ohio Canal. When he established himself in business, he had cash capital amounting to twenty-five dollars, and, in 1861, before coming West, was worth sixty thousand dollars. He owned a large and valuable plantation near the place where the Battle of Bull Run was fought, but it was so pillaged and devastated by the armies as to become almost worthless. Although reared a Catholic, he now holds no membership in any church. He is an Odd Fellow, Knight of Honor, and member of the Order of Knights and Ladies of Honor. He has always been a Democrat, and has held many public positions of responsibility. He has been Mayor of his city for eight years. He has been Chairman of the County Central Committee of his party, and a member of the State Committee. A child of poverty, working on a canal boat at four dollars per month, clad in a suit which cost one dollar and twenty-five cents, he has risen, by his untiring exertions, to affluence and honor. James C. Clark, of the Illinois Central Railway, was Captain of the "Hugh Smith," the canal boat, whose mules little George Varnell urged along the tow-path on the Chesapeake and Ohio. Both are now men of mark. Mr. Varnell is short and stout in person, and affable, hearty and kind in disposition. He is a man, who first makes sure his position, then goes in to win. He never does anything hastily or rashly. He is largely interested in the hard lumber trade and saw mills. His constituents have the utmost faith in him, irrespective of party.

HON. ALEXANDER · VAUGHEY.

"For he himself hath said it,
And it's greatly to his credit,
That he is an Irishman!"

He was born on the boggy soil of Ireland, June 15th, 1836, to John and Ellen Vaughey, who were engaged in farming and stock-raising. His grandfather, in honor of whose memory the subject of this sketch was christened Alexander, was made a prisoner in the Tara Hill Rebellion, of 1798. Mr. Vaughey came to the free shores of America, in 1855, and located in New York; but came West the next year, and cast his fortunes among the hospitable people of Grundy County, Illinois. He was not fully satisfied with his location, and moved to LaSalle County, in 1857. He acquired friends in a very short time, and soon became an important factor in local politics. He has held offices of honor, emolument and trust in his town and county, to such an extent that we cannot even mention them within the limited space allotted to this sketch. He is a sterling Democrat, and is considered one of the sachems of the party in the district from which he was elected. He is a member of the County, Congressional and Senatorial Committees of his party. He has been a member of every State Democratic Convention, which has been held in Illinois, since 1863. His education is collegiate, and he has never lost many opportunities for learning by observation and experiment. He is a Catholic, and holds membership in the Ancient Order of Hibernians. He was elected to the Thirty-second and Thirty-third General Assemblies, by rousing majorities. He is a very popular man in the Twenty-third District, and the probabilities are that we will find him a member of the Thirty-fourth Assembly. He is short and heavy in person, jovial and witty in conversation. His eyebrows have a lowering appearance, which is in marked contrast to the merry twinkle which they overshadow. He is as generous as one could reasonably desire, and, being a fine scholar and forcible speaker, he is one of the strong men of the House.

HON. HENRY F. WALKER.

Born in Claremont, New Hampshire, on the 17th of July, 1817, the subject of this sketch is now sixty-five years old. His parents, Solomon and Charity, resided upon a farm at the time of his birth, although his father also pursued his avocation as an architect and builder. In 1825 he came west, locating in Michigan, where he remained until 1855, when he moved to Amboy, Lee County, Illinois. Mr. Walker was connected with the Illinois Central Railway until 1865, when he removed to Chicago, when, after a residence of five years in that city, he removed to Hinsdale, Du Page County, Illinois, where he began practicing the art of healing the sick. His education was received in the common schools and academies at the various abiding places of his parents. He is a member of the Methodist Episcopal Church, but does not affiliate with any secret society. He is a Republican in politics, but was elected as a Representative to the Thirty-third General Assembly as an independent candidate, exceeding the vote of the regular nominee by about eleven hundred majority. He is one of the strong men of the House, and, although abrupt in speech, is polite and dignified in his relations with the people. He possesses all of the shrewd and acute qualities of a born and bred Yankee, and is positive and invulnerable, when he has thoroughly made up his mind to advocate any given position. In person, Mr. Walker is below the average stature, his hair and beard are immaculate in whiteness, and he has an air of patriarchal dignity, which wins for him the respect and good offices of all who are associated with him in society, politics or religion.

HON. DAVID W. WALSH.

Mr. Walsh was born at Chicago, Illinois, March 1st, 1850, and has resided in his native city ever since. His father is one of the Cook County Justices of the Peace. Mr. Walsh was educated in the public schools of Chicago, and has served as a clerk in his father's court, and read law at times, as an occupation, since he has attained his majority. He is a very popular man, and has a large circle of friends in the district from which he was elected to the General Assembly, and other portions of the city. In religious belief, he is a Catholic, but does not hold membership in any of the secret orders. He is a Democrat in political faith and works, and has never been anything else. He was one of the majority candidates for membership in the Lower House of the General Assembly in 1882, and was elected by a very handsome plurality, from the Fifth Senatorial District, of Cook County. He is a married man, and has a family consisting of six children. In person, he is a little above the ordinary stature of man, fair in complexion, inclined to corpulency, and conveying an idea of more than usual strength and positivism, by his physical appearance and dignified bearing. He is a man of varied talents, and is kind and genteel in his intercourse with the public.

HON. ANDREW WELCH.

This gentleman was born in Canada West, July 9th, 1844, his father being a teacher by profession, at that time. In 1864, Mr. Welch came to Illinois, locating at Yorkville, Kendall County, where he now resides. He was educated in the common schools of Canada, under many disadvantages; but, thanks to an ambitious spirit and energetic disposition, he is now a very well educated and broad-minded man. He is engaged in dealing in agricultural implements—an occupation as essential to the welfare of the world, in this enlightened day of labor-saving machinery, as the honored occupation of farming. In 1865, although not yet a citizen of the United States, Mr. Welch enlisted in the One Hundred and Forty-seventh Regiment of Illinois Volunteer Infantry, serving until the close of the Rebellion. He is a Free Mason, but holds no communion with any church organization. In politics, Mr. Welch is a Democrat of long standing and undoubted fidelity to the cause of his party. He has been Collector of his township, and was elected to the House of Representatives in 1882, from the Seventeenth District, without opposition. He is connected in business with the Union Corn Planter Company, of Peoria, Illinois. In person, he is large and portly, of dark complexion, and a sun-shine disposition. He is a man of much force of character, and such amiable qualities as endear him to all with whom he associates. The meetings of the House would be deprived of much of their rich humor and sunny spirit, if he should be stricken down.

HON. JOHN H. WELSH.

This gentleman is a Canadian by birth, having been born at Bellevue, in the Upper Dominion, June 11th, 1834. Morris Welsh, his father, was a shoe-maker by trade, and moved with his family, to New York State, in 1840. The education of Mr. Welsh was acquired in the common schools of the Empire State. After attaining a sufficient age, he was apprenticed to a miller, serving a term of two years, and afterward followed the business thus learned. He came to Illinois in 1852, locating at Tiskilwa, Bureau County. The military record of this gentleman is very brief. He was drafted, and preferring to be a live miller rather than a dead hero, he employed a substitute. He is a man, who believes in Christianity, but is not a member of any church. He is a Royal Arch Mason. Mr. Welsh is a Democrat, and feels that his political preference is based upon sound reason and good judgment. He has been Supervisor of his township, ten years, Township Clerk, six years, and a member of the School Board, fourteen years. He was elected from the Nineteenth Dis. trict as a minority Representative, in 1880, and re-elected in 1882. He is a man of firm convictions, cool judgment and sterling integrity. He is as honest and frank as anyone could wish, and is free from that vanity, which sometimes prompts men to prevaricate, for the purpose of courting popular favor. In person, he is tall and strong, kind, generous and considerate. He possesses none of that false idea of dignity, which sometimes prompts men to look down upon their inferiors, and there is no such thing as haughtiness in his nature.

HON. AUGUST WENDELL.

This gentleman was born in Prussian Germany, November 11th, 1838, his father being a wagon maker by trade. In 1856, the subject of our sketch came to Illinois, locating in Chicago, where he has continued to reside since that time. His education was acquired in the common schools of his native country, but he has become quite proficient in the use of the English language, as a result of his thoughtful and observant habits. He learned his trade under the direction and instruction of his father, and is now proprietor of one of the largest and best appointed wagon factories in the West. It is located in Chicago, and known as August Wendell's Wagon Manufactory. In religious faith, he is a Lutheran, and belongs to the Mutual Aid Association, of Illinois, and a German Order known as D—— O—— H——. In political conviction, he has ever been a faithful and persistent Republican, and has found no good cause for changing his political associations, or forsaking the staunch old ship, to which he is indebted for his safe and successful voyage to the House of Representatives of the Thirty-third General Assembly. He represents the Ninth District of Cook County. In person, he is large and portly, dark in complexion and pleasant, genial and obliging in his intercourse with the people. Mr. Wendell is truly an honest Representative, who cannot be induced to support any measure, which seems tainted with fraud or jobbery. He stands by his party upon party measures, but when called upon to speak his convictions through his vote, he stands upon no platform save that of pure manhood and strict integrity.

S.H. West.

HON. SIMEON H. WEST.

Mr. West was born in Kentucky. The names of his parents are Henry and Mary West. He is another of the farmer's boys, who have risen from the plow, to stand in the forums of their State Government. He received a common school education in the State of his birth, and came to Illinois in 1851, when he began farming. He has pursued this honorable calling assiduously from the date of his birth, employing the first two years of his experience, as an apprentice to his mother, in the milking department of the farm government. In 1873, he was elected as a member of the Board of Supervisors of McLean County, and was re-elected each year until 1881. He is not a member of any church, although he is a moral and upright man in his daily walk and conversation. He bluntly states his case as "not admitting of any middle-man between himself and his God." He was born and raised an "Old Line Whig," but, in 1858, became a Democrat, under the banner of Douglas, because he "had no place else to go," the Whig party having been swallowed up in the slavery issue, between the Democrats and Republicans, and he feeling that Democracy covered the demands of right and justice, better than Republicanism. He was elected to the House of Representatives from the Twenty-eighth District, as a minority candidate, in 1882. Mr. West possesses all of the sterling qualities of mind and heart, which are calculated to endear one to his associates. Though blunt in expression, he "has a heart as large as an ox," and, upon acquaintance, he is admired and respected. He is a hearty joker, and an assiduous laborer for the good of his constituency. He scrutinizes every measure carefully, before he votes, and is as firm as the unshaken rocks, in his opinions and positions. He gives this characteristically blunt history of himself: "Born in a log-cabin, and rocked in a sugar-trough, in Bourbon County, Kentucky, and learned to paddle his own canoe at a very early age." He never followed beaten paths further than they lead in a proper direction, and, when they seem to go wrong, he does not hesitate to blaze his own pathway, regardless of fear or favor.

HON. SAMUEL C. WILEY.

He is a "Down East Yankee," having first seen the light of day in the State of Maine, November 11th, 1833. Charles, his father, and Sarah, his mother, were tilling the fertile soil for a livelihood, when God sent little Sam, to sweeten their joys and soften their sorrows. He may have possessed all of the proclivities, which are ascribed to the inventor of "wooden nut-megs," but we are not in possession of exact information upon this point, and will not risk the chances of wandering from the truth, into which the subject might beguile us. However his youth may have passed, in the very budding time of his manhood, he was made a resident of La Salle County, Illinois. This was in 1844, and in the common school of the Sucker State, he found the only educational advantages, which he ever enjoyed. He is engaged in farming and as a lumber merchant, at Earlville. He has served his county as one of its Board of Supervisors for about seven years, and has held other and numerous positions of honor and trust in his county and district. He is an ardent Democrat, and has been one since the days of his youth. Upon its principles his political history is founded, and he does not seem to think that his faith has been, or ever will be unworthily bestowed. He was elected to the House by a plurality of some 2,000 votes, in 1882, and is earnestly endeavoring to cast his vote and raise his voice in behalf of the constituency, which has been honored in proportion to the honor bestowed upon him by his election. In personal appearance, Mr. Wiley is tall and well built, fair in complexion, and alert in his movements and conduct. He is sympathetic, kind and generous in disposition, and is shrewd and sensible in debate and conversation. While he may not be familiar with the wire pulling proclivities of the professional politician, he is, nevertheless, a strong man, whose friendship is valuable and enmity dangerous. He is trustworthy and fearless, and if he ever inadvertantly votes awry, we venture the assertion that no one can charge evil motives as the cause of his mistake.

HON. FREDERICK A. WILLOUGHBY.

Mr. Willoughby was born in New Haven, Connecticut, where he resided until he attained the years of manhood. His father was a carriage manufacturer, and left nothing that would develop his son's native talents, undone. Frederick was placed in the best academies, being graduated from Russell's Farmers' Military School, and attending the Yale preparatory course at Hopkins Grammar School. Our subject was an untiring student, and completed his professional studies within the classic walls of Yale College. He was early imbued with the principles and doctrines of Democracy, and was a somewhat noted sumporator before attaining his majority. He has adhered to the party with undiminished fidelity ever since. At the commencement of his professional career, Mr. Willoughby coupled journalism with his legal labors, and was, from time to time, connected with the Daily Press of his native city. Had he seen fit to pursue that profession, he would have probably become one of its most distinguished devotees. In 1869, he came to Illinois, where he now resides, and has since been engaged in the practice of the law. He is one of the leading members of the Knox County Bar. He has been City Attorney of Galesburg, and a member of its Board of Education. He is a master of several languages, writing and speaking German with fluency. In personal appearance, he is a man of commanding presence, about forty years of age; kind and generous in disposition, polite and courteous in business intercourse. In debate, his resources are almost unlimited, and he is a polished and fluent speaker. He is one of the most scholarly and well informed members of the House of Representatives, and it is quite evident to one, who has observed his demeanor and public efforts, that his constituency committed no error in electing him to the honorable position which he so ably fills. He is the minority Representative from the Twenty-second District, having been elected, although there was another Democratic candidate in the field.

HON. ERWIN E. WOOD.

He is a native Illinoisan, born at Plainfield, Will County, February 6th, 1848. His father is a large farmer, and both he and his wife came from the Eastern States. Mr. Wood was educated at the Northwestern College (German), in Plainfield, and subsequently attended, for four years, the Northwestern University, at Evanston, being in the same class with Speaker Collins. He acquired valuable experience from connection with a Republican newspaper in Nebraska, of which he was editor for two years. When but sixteen years of age, he enlisted in the One Hundred and Thirty-second Regiment of Illinois Volunteers, serving the last year of the war. He came to Chicago from Nebraska, and became assistant editor of the *Evening Journal*, a position which he filled for six years. His original anecdotes were widely copied, and the New York *Graphic* published his portrait as one of America's noted writers. He temporarily abandoned journalism, and pursued the study of chemistry and assaying, for three years, when he boxed his apparatus and went to the mountains and plains of the West, where he invested in railway and mining interests, and the shipment of dressed beef, by which efforts he has already secured a comfortable fortune. He possesses a very fine collection of minerals and geological specimens, as the result of his eight trips across the continent, within the past three years. He has an excellent eye for art, and his clay models of "Palmy Days," and "Against the Grain," have been widely copied in plaster, and sold as novel designs in statuary. His family is identified with the Methodist Episcopal Church, but he holds no membership in any religious or secret society. Mr. Wood is married, and his beautifully furnished residence in Springfield, is a favorite resort for the local *elite* and a large circle of friends. He is a Republican, and has been one of the West Park Commissioners, of Chicago, bearing a good official reputation at the close of his term. He was elected to the House of Representatives in 1882, in a largely Democratic district (the Fifth of Cook County), by a very handsome plurality.

HON. HENRY WOOD.

Mr. Wood was born at Randolph, Orange County, Vermont, November 10th, 1824, his father then being engaged in earning his living, by plying the honorable and indispensable avocation of a farmer. The family removed to Tunbridge, in the same county and State, soon afterward, and, in 1836, came to Illinois, locating at Sycamore, DeKalb County, where the subject of this sketch now resides. His education was obtained in the common schools of the Green Mountain State, and those of Illinois. Mr. Wood followed the example of his father, in choosing his occupation, and is now extensively engaged in farming. He owns three hundred acres of excellent lands in Illinois, and one hundred and sixty acres in Iowa, and devotes a great deal of attention to breeding Short-horn cattle, and Poland-China hogs. Mr. Wood is a Congregationalist, and has always been a leader, and has faith in a living God; but, belongs to no secret society. He is a very pronounced, yet consistent Republican, who had a hand in the first organization of that party, and has been one of its faithful adherents and effective advocates, throughout its career. He has served two terms as Supervisor of his township, and was a member of the House of Representatives in the Thirty-second General Assembly, being unanimously re-nominated and triumphantly re-elected in 1882. In personal appearance, he is of medium height, plain and honest in features, and equally plain, but neat nevertheless, in dress. He is kind, obliging and generous in disposition, and is regarded as a straightforward and conscientious Legislator.

HON. THOMAS WORTHINGTON, Jr.

He is a Tennessean by birth, having first beheld the beauties of this world at Spencer, in that State, June 8th, 1852, while his parents were visiting there. His father was a physician, and his mother, a daughter of Col. Kennedy Long, of Baltimore, Maryland. His father was a member of the State Senate of Illinois, in the Thirteenth and Fourteenth General Assemblies. Mr. Worthington came to Illinois in infancy. He is a graduate of Cornell University, New York, of the class of 1873, and of the Chicago Law School, class of 1877. In pursuing his search for legal knowledge, he also read law with Senator Archer, of Pittsfield, Pike County, and Hoyne, Horton & Hoyne, of Chicago. He is now engaged in practicing his profession in Pittsfield, where he has already made an enviable reputation for himself, as an able and assiduous young lawyer. He is a Mason, of the Degree of Knight Templar. Politically, he is a Republican, of life-long duration and well dignified ideas. He received ninety-seven votes out of the one hundred and twenty-two, constituting the Senatorial Convention of his party, and was elected to the House of Representatives in 1882, by a handsome plurality. He is a very astute law-maker, and an equally acute observer of what is going on about him. He will win his way to fame, if retained in office. In person, he is above medium stature, fair in complexion, amiable in manners, and kind and generous in disposition. He will not risk voting, until he has closely scrutinized the measure under consideration, and then, woe be unto it, if he discovers a flaw or taint of fraud.

HON. ARCHELAUS N. YANCEY.

Mr. Yancey was born in Montpelier, Orange County, Virginia, March 24th, 1844. At the date of this gentleman's birth, his father was a farmer and planter. Mr. Yancey's early experiences do not materially differ from those of many other men, who have begun careers of usefulness and honor, by the incidents and duties of farm life. In 1867, his parents came to Illinois, locating at Bunker Hill, Macoupin County. The education of this Representative was academic and collegiate. He passed through a preparatory course in Hilton Academy, Virginia, afterward entering and graduating from Dartmouth College, New Hampshire. His professional education was acquired in the Michigan University, from which he is a regular graduate of the Law Department, of the class of 1867. Mr. Yancey is a lawyer of great prominence and acknowledged ability. He practices his profession at Bunker Hill, where he resides. In politics, he is a Democrat, by descent, education, and premeditated determination, to employ an idiomatic expression, "He is born, bred, and dyed in the wool." He was elected to the House of Representatives in 1880, and re-elected in 1882, being appointed a member of the Judiciary Committee at each session. In religious faith, he is an Episcopalian, and is a member of the Masonic fraternity—a Master Mason. In person, Mr. Yancey is rather above the average stature, large and corpulent. He has a fine intellect, the cultivation of which has not been neglected, in any perceptible particular. He is one of the most successful debaters on the floor of the House of Representatives, nearly always securing the passage of his bills—in fact, we believe he has never yet failed in convincing the assembled Representatives that the measures introduced by him are wise ones, and securing their passage.

THE RAILWAY COMMISSION.

HON. WILLIAM M. SMITH,

CHAIRMAN OF THE RAILROAD AND WAREHOUSE COMMISSION.

"Billy Smith," as he is known throughout the length and breadth of Illinois, was born in Franklin County, Kentucky, May 23d, 1827. He removed to St. Louis County, Missouri, in 1840, and, in 1846, to the northern part of McLean County, Illinois, where he has since resided. His education was such as the common schools of the time afforded When nineteen years of age, he began working on a farm, by the month, at ten dollars per month. This continued for four years, and the last year his wages were raised to twelve dollars and a half per month. From these wages he had saved one hundred dollars, and, in 1849, he entered eighty acres of land, at one dollar and twenty-five cents per acre, which he improved and still owns. He lived on the farm until 1857, when he moved to Lexington, Illinois, and entered the mercantile business. He was elected on the Republican ticket, from McLean County, to the Twenty-fifth, Twenty-sixth and Twenty-seventh General Assemblies of Illinois, and was made Speaker of the House of Representatives of the Twenty-seventh Assembly, in 1871. The history of the Republican party in Illinois, could not be written without reference to the labors of Mr. Smith. He was present at that party's birth, and has followed its fortunes with singular fidelity. He is thoroughly identified with the progress of the State, and much of the legislation of the last twenty years bears the impress of

his genius. He early viewed, with apprehension, the encroach-
ment of corporate bodies upon the rights of the people. He was
appointed Railroad and Warehouse Commissioner by Governor
Cullom, in January, 1877, and was chairman of that board for
six years. Time has proved the wisdom of his selection. As
the advanced position now occupied by the Railroad Commission
of Illinois, is largely due to his untiring zeal in the execution of
the law, which he was instrumental in creating. He was a member of the State Board of Agriculture for many years, until failing health compelled him to resign. He is a member of the
Methodist Church, and of the Masonic Fraternity.

HON. WILLIAM H. ROBINSON,

MEMBER OF BOARD OF RAILROAD AND WAREHOUSE COMMISSIONERS.

Mr. Robinson was born in Lawrence County, Illinois, January
31st, 1837, his father being a farmer. When yet a mere boy, his
family removed to Indiana, the education of our subject being
acquired in the public schools of that and his native State. In
1857, William removed to Fairfield, Illinois, where he studied
law After his admission to the Bar, in 1860, he began the
practice of his profession, in the same place, where he is now regarded as an eminent lawyer. He was a delegate to the National
Republican Convention, which met at Baltimore, in 1864, also,
to the conventions of 1868 and 1876, at Chicago and Cincinnati,
respectively. He was Presidential elector from his Congressional
District in 1872. He enlisted in Company "G," Eighteenth
Illinois Infantry, in 1861, and was elected and commissioned
Lieutenant. He was detailed as Adjutant of the Regiment,
Colonel—afterward General U. S. Grant, acting as mustering
officer at Camp Anna, Union County, Illinois, until November of
the same year, when he was discharged on account of disability.
He was appointed Railroad and Warehouse Commissioner by
Governor Cullom, January 20th, 1881, as the legal member of the
Board. During the two years he has held this office, Mr. Rob-
inson has rendered valuable services to the shipping and producing interests of the State, and his cause has met the universal
approval of the people.

HON. GEORGE M. BOGUE,

MEMBER OF THE RAILROAD AND WAREHOUSE COMMISSION.

This prominent gentleman was born at Norfolk, St. Lawrence County, New York, January 21st, 1842. His father and mother were named Warren S. and Sally, respectively. His education is chiefly such as he could secure in the common schools of the Empire State, although he afterward pursued a partial course of study in Cayuga Lake Academy, at Aurora, Cayuga County, New York. Mr. Bogue came to Chicago in 1856. His first position was that of a clerk in a railway freight office, where he continued for about three years. In 1864, he was employed in the Land Department of the Illinois Central Railway Company, remaining three years, when he engaged in general real estate business in the city of Chicago—a calling which he has continued to pursue since that time, and in which he is now engaged. In 1864, he was elected Town Clerk of the Town of Hyde Park, Cook County, but resigned in 1866. Three years later, he was elected Town Treasurer of Hyde Park, and reëlected to the same office three times in succession. He resigned the office early in 1873. He was elected a member of the Board of County Commissioners of Cook County, in 1872, on the general ticket, serving one term. In 1874, he was elected to the Lower House of the General Assembly, serving one term, as a Republican Representative from the Second Senatorial District. He was appointed Railroad and Warehouse Commissioner, in 1877, by Governor Shelby M. Cullom, and has served six years. In recognition of his great merits as a railway business man, Mr. Bogue was unanimously elected Arbitrator for the three Western Pools, known as the Southwestern Railway Association; Iowa Trunk Line Association, and Colorado Trafic Association. He is a Republican in politics, and a Presbyterian in religion. Mr. Bogue is one of the best business men connected with the Railway interests of the Northwest.

HON. JOHN MOSES,

SECRETARY OF THE RAILROAD AND WAREHOUSE COMMISSION.

This gentleman was born at Niagara Falls, New York, and came to Illinois when a small boy, forty-five years ago, residing at Winchester, Scott County, until his accession to his present office. Mr. Moses possesses a very excellent education, and has held numerous positions of honor and trust in his county, district and State. In political belief and practice, he is a firm, yet consistent Republican. He was Circuit Clerk of Scott County four years, and County Judge, four years. He was also a member of the Lower House of the General Assembly, in 1875. He was Private Secretary to Governor Richard Yates, from 1862 to 1864, when he materially assisted in forming the Seventieth Illinois Regiment. He was appointed by Lincoln, as Internal Revenue Assessor, for the Tenth District. He held that office for three years. He was appointed Secretary of the Railway and Warehouse Commission in 1880, and has discharged the duties of that office faithfully and ably ever since. As a politician, he is prominent and influential, having very materially aided his party by his writings for numerous newspapers, and by his unremitted energy in the work of conventions. His office is a model of neatness and orderly arrangement, and he is thoroughly conversant with its duties and requirements. Judge Moses is certainly not out of place in the honorable position which he now occupies. He is a strong personal friend of Senator S. M. Cullom.

J. OTIS HUMPHREY,

LEGAL SECRETARY, RAILROAD AND WAREHOUSE COMMISSION.

The subject of this sketch was born on a farm near Jacksonville, Morgan County, Illinois, December 30th, 1850. His parents—both natives of Ohio—were married in 1844, and five years later, removed to Illinois. The boyhood and youth of Mr. Humphrey were passed upon the farm, near Auburn, Sangamon County, where his father has resided since 1855. His mother died in 1864. His education, begun at the country school near his home, was supplemented by a classical course at Shurtliff College, Alton, where he was graduated with class honors in 1876. During his course, he devoted considerable attention to the subject of oratory, in which he developed much ability, and was chosen by the faculty of his college, as her representative at the Inter-collegiate contest of Illinois, held at Jacksonville, in 1875, in which he won the second honors. He also received the Mills prize medal, awarded for excellence in oratory, on the day

of his graduation, in a class of fourteen. He studied law with
the firm of Robinson, Knapp & Shutt, in Springfield, and was
admitted to the Bar in 1880, during which year he was Chief
Clerk in the office of the Census Supervisor of the Capital District.   In the autumn of that year, he was employed by the
Railroad and Warehouse Commission, since which time he has
served the Board as its Legal Secretary. He has recently formed
a law partnership with Hon. H. S. Green and F. W. Burnett,
Esq. The firm will rank among the strongest in the State.
There are few men in Illinois, whose fortune seems so full of
promise as that of Mr. Humphrey.   He is popular with the
masses. His good qualities, added to his character, ability and
zeal, leads us to predict for him a career of great success and
extended usefulness. He is a prominent Odd Fellow.

THE NEW RAILROAD AND WAREHOUSE COMMIS-
SION.

HON. WILLIAM NEWELL BRAINARD,

PRESIDENT OF THE RAILROAD AND WAREHOUSE COMMISSION.

This gentleman was born in Madison County, New York,
January 7th, 1823. He is a lineal descendent of the Brainards,
of the collonial history of Connecticut.   His grandmother was
one of the few, who escaped the fearful Indian massacre at
Wyoming. By occupation, his father was originally a hatter,
but afterward became a farmer.   Our subject was educated at
the De Ruyter Institute, in his native village. He afterward
taught school and read law for some time, but, in 1845, removed
to Rome, New York, where he engaged in business connected
with transportation and warehouse business, on the Erie Canal.
He went to California in 1850, and engaged in business as a
grain and produce dealer, in Sacramento, where he ran for
County Treasurer, as a Democrat, and was completely over-
whelmed by know-nothing votes. He was elected City Clerk of
Sacramento in 1856, and served one year, when he concluded to
locate in Chicago, which he did in 1857. He has resided in that

city and vicinity ever since. He has been a member of the Chicago Board of Trade for twenty-five years, has served as one of its directors three terms, and, as Vice President, three terms. He was one of the founders of the so-called "Call Board." Governor Beveridge appointed him as one of the Board of Canal Commissioners in 1873, and served four years in that capacity. He has been a Republican for the last twenty-five years. He is a noble looking and kind hearted gentleman.

HON. CHARLES T. STRATTAN,

MEMBER OF THE RAILROAD AND WAREHOUSE COMMISSION.

Mr. Strattan was born at Wellington, Ohio, May 7th, 1853, his father then being proprietor of a general store, and a miller. The family came to Illinois in 1855, locating in Mercer County, but removed from there to Mount Vernon, Jefferson County, where Charles and his father now reside, in 1857. The father of our subject in now engaged in general merchandise and manufacturing. Charles was a careful student and persevering young man, generally. He longed for a good education, and his father afforded him ample opportunity to acquire it. He pursued his studies in the common schools with unusual diligence, and succeeded in leaving them with a far better than merely rudimentary education. After having made good use of his common school privileges, he entered McKendree College, at Lebanon, Illinois, and, after an incomplete course, continued his researches at Washington University, St. Louis, Missouri, and the Wesleyan University, of Ohio. His career, since attaining his majority, has been essentially that of a teacher. In 1872, he began teaching in the public schools of Mount Vernon, continuing until called to Nashville, Edwardsville and Smith Academy, the latter being a St. Louis institution of learning. He has always been a Republican, was elected to the House of Representatives in 1880, and received the nomination of his party for the office of State Superintendent of Public Instruction in 1882, but was defeated at the polls. He was appointed to his present office by Governor Hamilton, in February, 1883.

HON. EDWARD C. LEWIS.

MEMBER OF THE RAILROAD AND WAREHOUSE COMMISSION.

This gentleman was born in LaSalle County, Illinois, October 5th, 1844. His parents were Samuel R. Lewis and Ann E. (Harley) Lewis, his father being identified with the pioneer movements of the Abolitionists, of Pennsylvania. After coming to Illinois, his father continued pursuing the avocation of a farmer, was afterward, in 1857, made County Treasurer of LaSalle County, serving four years, and was State Senator from 1878 to 1882. Edward's education was acquired in the common schools of his county, Lake Forrest Seminary, Chicago University, and Wheaton College. He then read law in the office of Glover, Cook & Camp, at Ottawa, Illinois, and was admitted to the Bar. After seven years of successful practice, he became a farmer, in 1873, and has continued to exercise that most honorable calling since that date. He has been an avowed Republican, ever since he can first remember, and was a member of the Board of Supervisors of his county, seven years. He was Chairman of the Board from 1880 to 1881. This is a large and populous county, and its Board numbers forty-five members. He is a member of the Congregational Church, and a Free Mason, of the Knight Templar degree. His present residence is Deer Park, La Salle County, Illinois, He was appointed one of the Railroad and Warehouse Commissioners in February, 1883, by Governor John M. Hamilton. He is well qualified for the responsible position, and in every way worthy of the honor thus conferred upon him.

HON. NOBLE D. MUNSON,

SECRETARY OF THE RAILROAD AND WAREHOUSE COMMISSION.

Mr. Munson was born at Bristol, Vermont, September 21st, 1829. The father of our subject was a merchant and iron manufacturer, and the son learned the same trade and profession, during his boyhood. The education of Mr. Munson was acquired in the common schools and academies of his native State. Mr. Munson came to Chicago in 1852, and entered business in the employment of the Michigan Southern Railroad. He gradually worked his way until he became Division Superintendent of the Chicago, Burlington & Quincy, remaining in that position until in July, 1878, when he resigned on account of ill health. Since 1881, he has been engaged in the hard lumber trade in Southeast Missouri and Arkansas, until appointed Secretary of the Railroad and Warehouse Commission, in March, 1883. Mr. Munson is an Odd Fellow of the rank of Past Grand, but is not a member of church. In politics, he is a Republican, his father having been a Whig prior to the Rebellion, and Noble espousing the cause of the Republican party when it came into being. His residence, prior to his appointment, was at Quincy, Illinois, but he has now located at the State Capital. In person, Mr. Munson is rather portly, kind, polite and affable. He is a man of wide experience in railroad affairs, and is thoroughly qualified for his honorable position.

STATE BOARD OF AGRICULTURE.

HON. STEPHEN D. FISHER,

SECRETARY OF THE STATE BOARD OF AGRICULTURE.

Mr. Fisher was born in Charlotte, Vermont, March 7th, 1822. When but one year of age, he removed with his parents to Essex, New York, where he attended the common schools. He also gained a portion of his education by a course of study at West Point Academy. He came to Rochester, Illinois, in 1844, and taught one term of three months in the Baker District, Sangamon County. He afterward had charge of the schools at Rochester, in the same county, for one year, when he returned to his New York home, and pursued the same avocation there. He again came to Illinois in 1850, and taught the Rochester school two winters, when he married Miss Marion J. St. Clair, who died in 1867. After his marriage, Mr. Fisher located at Waynesville, Illinois, where he became book-keeper in a general store. The firm for which he worked, removed to Atlanta, Illinois, two years later, and regarding his services as indispensable, took him along. He remained with this house until 1875, when he came to Springfield and was appointed Secretary of the State Board of Agriculture, a position, which he has filled with marked energy and ability ever since. Previous to acquiring his present office, he had been a member of the Board of which he is now Secretary, for four years, and member of the State Board of Equalization for three years. He married Miss Elzina M. Benton, his present wife, October 20th, 1868. Mr. Fisher is a staunch Republican in politics, and thoroughly understands the affairs of his office. His official reports are methodically prepared, and yet so simple as to enable the most obtuse farmer to understand them, if he can read at all. He is evidently the right man in the right place.

COL. CHARLES FRANCIS MILLS,

ASSISTANT SECRETARY AND CHIEF CLERK STATE BOARD OF AGRICULTURE.

Mr. Mills was born at Montrose, Pennsylvania, May 29th, 1844, his father being a lawyer and journalist. The family came to Illinois in 1855, locating at Upper Alton. He has been actively engaged in farming and stock breeding, near Springfield, since the war. The Elmwood farm, of which he is proprietor, has a national reputation among breeders and dealers in fine stock. He served during the war as a private in Company "C." One Hundred and Twenty-fourth Illinois, and Hospital Steward in the regular army. He is also a very active member of the State Militia, being Adjutant of the Second Brigade. He is a member of the following orders: Masons, Odd Fellows and Grand Army of the Republic. He has been Secretary of the Sangamon County Fair Association for years, and is connected in a more or less prominent manner with all of the leading Agricultural and Stock Breeders' Associations of the country. He has held the presidency of some of these national associations, and is one of the most prominent breeders of fine stock in the country. He is now serving his tenth year as Assistant Secretary and Chief Clerk of the State Board of Agriculture. He is pre-eminently in place in this office.

JOHN W. WHIPP,

ASSISTANT SECRETARY OF THE STATE BOARD OF CHARITIES.

Mr. Whipp was born in England in 1824, and came to Illinois at the age of fourteen, locating at Beardstown. His education was acquired in England, and he worked on a farm for seven years, after coming to this country. From the time of attaining his majority until thirty years old, he was a clerk at Beardstown. He afterward read law. He then came to Springfield, and was a clerk in Bunn's Bank, for about eight years. In 1857, or 1858, he does not exactly remember which, he was called as an expert, in the celebrated Matteson Scrip Case, being the principal witness, and succeeding in bringing to light the frauds which had been perpetrated against the State. He was assistant State Treasurer under Butler, for three years, after which, he removed to Bloomington, where he was a partner in the banking house of Holder & Company. Six years ago, he was appointed to the position which he now holds. He is a staunch Republican, of course.

CHARLES WESLEY DAY,

SECRETARY STATE BOARD OF PHARMACY.

Mr. Day was born at Wilmington, Delaware, May 3d, 1849. He came to Illinois in 1873, and has since resided in Champaign and Wabash Counties. He received a good, practical education in his native city, and afterward, served an apprenticeship to a druggist, and attended lectures at the Philadelphia, Pennsylvania, School of Pharmacy. At the early age of sixteen years, he enlisted in the Union Army, serving two years. He is a Free Mason of the Rank of Knight Templar. In politics, he has always been an uncompromising Republican, of the Stalwart persuasion. In 1881, during the month of July, he was appointed one of the members of the then newly created State Board of Pharmacy, and was chosen to fill the vacancy caused by the resignation of the Secretaryship by Frank Fleury. He is well qualified for his position, and is diligent and accurate in the performance of his duties.

FRANCIS A. FREER,

(Omitted in list of Senate Officers.)

CLERK OF GROUP NO. 2, SENATE COMMITTEES

Mr. Freer was born at Butler, Pennsylvania, April 6th, 1843, his father being a carpenter and joiner by trade. His paternal

ancestors were French Hueguenots, and were prominently identified with the struggle for American Independence. In 1859
the family came to Illinois, where Francis acquired his education in the public schools and Hedding College, from which he
graduated in 1871. He earned means for attending college by
hewing timber, and laboring in the harvest-field, during vaca-
tions. He is a Republican, and has been a Justice of the Peace
in Knox County, for three years, resigning in 1879, when he removed from Henderson to Galesburg, where he now resides.
He was a private soldier during the war. He is clerk of the
Senate Group, No. 2, consisting of the Committees on Penal and
Reformatory Institutions, Education and Educational Institutions, and County and Township Organization.

DR. JOHN H. RAUCH,

SECRETARY OF THE BOARD OF HEALTH.

John H. Rauch was born at Lebanon, Pennsylvania, September 4th, 1828. He was graduated from the Medical Department
of the University of Pennsylvania, in the spring of 1849. In
1850, he located at Burlington, Iowa, where he entered upon the
practice of his profession. His attention was directed to the relation of ozone to disease, in 1850. During the prevalence of
cholera, he called the attention of Congress to the necessity of
providing medical aid for those engaged in marine pursuits on
Western waters, and succeeded in his effort, being made one of
the committee to select sites for marine hospitals. He was also
successful in having the cemetery used as a burial place for victims of cholera abandoned, on account of the increase of cases
following the interment of victims, near his home. In 1855-56,
he assisted Professor Agassiz in collecting material for his work,
"The Natural History of the Northwest," securing a valuable
collection of piscatorial specimens. He afterward visited South
America, to investigate the sanitary condition of the ruins of
Venezuela, during which he made a valuable collection for the
Chicago Academy of Natural Sciences. He is a prominent
member of numerous medical societies, having been President
of the American Medical Association, in 1858. He is a member

of most of the well known scientific associations of the United
States.   He is the author of many scientific and medical trea-
ties, principal among which are "The Medical and Economical
Botany of Iowa," and "Intramural Interments and their Influences
on Health."   In 1857, he was elected to the chair of *Ma-
teria Medica*, in Rush Medical College, Chicago, a position
which he retained three years.   He served as Surgeon and Medical Director during the entire war, being brevetted Lieutenant
Colonel.   He was instrumental in organizing the Chicago Board
of Health, of which he was an efficient and valuable member.
In 1870, he wrote a "Sanitary History of Chicago."   He has
been Secretary of the State Board of Health since its organization, and is one of the best informed scientists in the country.
He is almost master of the sciences, and is a valuable acquisition
to the State Government.

HON. EGBERT B. BROWN.
MEMBER STATE BOARD OF EQUALIZATION.

This gentleman was born in Jefferson County, New York,
October 24th, 1816.   His ancestors had come to this country with
William Penn.   Although Quakers, the ancestors of Mr. Brown
were active participants in the War of 1812, on the Michigan
frontier.   Our subject had but few educational advantages ; but
he made the most of his sopportunities, and now is a thoroughly
informed gentleman.   In 1833, he removed to Chicago, where he
was a clerk in the house of Hubbard & Co., for two years.   In
1838, he sailed on board a whaler, as a man before the mast, on
a voyage in the South Pacific Ocean, being made a harpooner in
two years, and was successful in the performance of the duties of
his hazzardous occupation.   Returning to the States in 1842, he
engaged in mercantile pursuits in Toledo, Ohio, where he built
the first large grain elevator west of Buffalo.   During his residence in that city, he was Mayor one term.   Being engaged in
railroad business, he naturally followed the course of construction,
and, in 1856, was engaged to open the trade for the Wabash
Railroad in St. Louis, being so employed when the War of the
Rebellion called him to the field.   He assisted in recruiting and
organizing the Seventh Regiment of Missouri Volunteer Infantry
and became its Lieutenant Colonel.   In May, 1862, he was commissioned Brigadier General of Militia, and, in November of the

same year, President Lincoln commissioned him a Brigadier General of Volunteers, for meritorious and commendable services. He served from the first part of the war until Nov. 10th, 1865, when, his term being ended, he resigned. He was wounded three times, once in the shoulder, once in his hip and once in another portion of his body. His wounds have been quite painful during late years. The State Legislature of Missouri tendered a vote of thanks to his command for its services in repelling an attack led by Gen. John Marmaduke. Gen. Brown received a wound that confined him to his bed for nearly a year, in this engagement. He is a member of the Episcopal Church, a Mason and Odd Fellow. In politics, he is and has always been a Democrat. He was unanimously nominated to his present office, having no opponent in the convention or at the polls. He resides at Hastings Landing, Calhoun County, and is a well informed, enegetic and noble old gentleman.

HON. HENRY C. FELTMAN,

MEMBER OF STATE BOARD OF EQUALIZATION.

Mr. Feltman was born in St. Louis, Missouri, December 15th, 1849. His father, Charles Feltman, was a grocer and baker at that time. The family removed to Salem, Illinois, where Henry now resides, September 2d, 1852, and the subject of our sketch received a good substantial education in the public schools of that city. Henry was a lively, mischievous lad, who took great pleasure in the sports and amusements incident to his time of life, and was ever ready to turn an honest penny. Ex-Governor Henry Warmouth, the Carpet-bag governor of Louisiana, was a boy in Salem, and Henry Feltman was frequently associated with him in sport or business. It is said that Young Warmouth at one time took a contract to black a number of stoves at fifteen cents each, and hired Feltman and other boys to do the work for five cents each, while he bossed the job. The truth of this Tom Sawyer like story is vouched for by Mr. Feltman and numerous old residents of Salem. Mr. Feltman was somewhat ambitious, and read law with Hon. John B. Kagy, was admitted to the bar in September, 1872, and is now a partner of his preceptor. The firm of Kagy & Feltman enjoys a lucrative and constantly increasing practice. He married Miss Emma C. Kagy, daughter

H. C. Feltman.

of his partner in business in 1875 and they now have three children—two boys and one girl. Mr. Feltman is not a member of
any church, but is an Odd Fellow and Knight of Honor. In the
former order, he has been Grand Marshal of the Grand Lodge.
In politics he is an uncompromising Democrat, and has held
numerous local offices of honor and trust in his city and township. He has been Mayor of Salem, two terms. He was elected
to his present office by a large majority, from the old Sixteenth
Congressional District—the Nineteenth under the apportionment
of 1882. Mr. Feltman is a man of noble impulses and generous
disposition and has many friends and few enemies.

SENATE COMMITTEES.

JUDICIARY.

Hunt, Chairman; Condee, Torrance, Fifer, Adams, Morris, Campbell, Mason, Clark, Sunderland, Whiting, Shaw, Archer, Walker, Rinehart, Merritt, Edwards, Duncan, Lemma.

JUDICIAL DEPARTMENT.

Clark, Chairman; Fifer, Torrance, Mason, Campbell, Condee, Morris, Tanner, Laning, Bell, Vandeveer, Hamilton, Rinehart, Kelly, Walker.

RAILROADS.

Tanner, Chairman; Condee, Mamer, Adams, Fifer, Rogers, Hogan, Evans, White, Whiting, Walker, Merritt, Lemma, Rinehart, Kelly, Shumway, Cloonan.

CORPORATIONS.

Condee, Chairman; Mason, Hogan, Mamer, Kirk, Evans, White, Fifer, Ainsworth, Torrance, Kelly, Laning, Bridges, Gillham, Cloonan.

APPROPRIATIONS.

Secrest, Chairman; Sunderland, Fifer, Kirk, Ihorn, White, Campbell, Clough, Needles, Lemma, Rinehart, Hamilton, Bell, Seiter, Hereley.

REVENUE.

Needles, Chairman; Morris, Ainsworth, Rice, Sunderland, Whiting, White, Clough, Torrance, Lemma, Laning, Merritt, Duncan, Hereley, Bridges.

WAREHOUSES.

Mason, Chairman; Hogan, Condee, Fifer, Mamer, Ihorn, Wright, Bell, Seiter, Bridges, McNary.

MUNICIPALITIES.

White, Chairman; Adams, Condee, Fifer, Secrest, Evans, Ruger, Tanner, Mamer, Laning, Shaw, Cloonan, Hereley, Walker, Rinehart.

FINANCE.

Sunderland, Chairman; Hogan, Berggren, Tubbs, Ray, Kelly, Seiter, McNary, Hereley.

EXPENSES OF GENERAL ASSEMBLY.

Ainsworth, Chairman; Whiting, Secrest, Mamer, Edwards, Kelly, Bridges.

INSURANCE.

Evans, Chairman; Sunderland, Campbell, Mason, Tanner, Needles, Berggren, Laning, Vandeveer, Merritt, Shumway, Hamilton, Edwards.

BANKS AND BANKING.

Rice, Chairman: Rogers, Tubbs, Wright, Vandeveer, Seiter, Shaw.

STATE CHARITABLE INSTITUTIONS.

Fifer, Chairman; Fletcher, Kirk, Rice, Sunderland, Adams, Clough, Tubbs, Torrance, Bell, Gillham, Bridges, Hereley, McNary, Laning.

PENAL AND REFORMATORY INSTITUTIONS.

Berggren, Chairman; Tanner, Hunt, Secrest, Fletcher, Ruger, Snyder, Needles, Ray, Kelly, Merritt, Walker, Vandeveer, Shumway, Hereley.

PUBLIC BUILDINGS AND GROUNDS.

Kirk, Chairman; Ainsworth, Tanner, Torrance, Clough, Hamilton, Bridges, Archer, Duncan.

EDUCATION AND EDUCATIONAL INSTITUTIONS.

Torrance, Chairman; Tubbs, Whiting, Rice, Wright, Ruger, Ray, Kirk, Lemma, Walker, Edwards, Duncan, Shumway.

CANALS AND RIVERS.

Ray, Chairman; Whiting, Rice, Adams, Ainsworth, Clough, Condee, Campbell, Hunt, Bell, Duncan, Shaw, Archer, Seiter, Shumway.

AGRICULTURE AND DRAINAGE.

Rogers, Chairman; Snyder, Wright, Sunderland, Hunt, Ihorn, Evans, White, Clark, Archer, Kelly, Shaw, Gillham, Cloonan, McNary.

HORTICULTURE.

Tubbs, Chairman; Fletcher, Ihorn, Rogers, Gillham, Vandeveer, Seiter.

MINES AND MINING.

Ihorn, Chairman; Morris, Clark, Ainsworth, Hunt, Evans, Lemma, Duncan, Seiter, Laning, Cloonan.

LABOR AND MANUFACTURES.

Ruger, Chairman; Rice, Rogers, Whiting, Gillham, Hereley, McNary.

COUNTY AND TOWNSHIP ORGANIZATION.

Morris, Chairman; Fletcher, Wright, Snyder, Ainsworth, Tanner, Ray, Secrest, Rogers, Ihorn, Gillham, Archer, Shumway, Edwards, Bridges.

FEES AND SALARIES.

Hogan, Chairman; Fletcher, Berggren, Snyder, Tubbs, Hamilton, Rinehart, Laning, Bell.

PRINTING.

Campbell, Chairman; Adams, Wright, Rice, Rogers, Secrest, Merritt, Cloonan, Vandeveer.

MILITARY AFFAIRS.

Clough, Chairman; Ruger, Condee, Evans, Mason, Needles, Secrest, Tanner, Vandeveer, Gillham, Lemma, Hereley, Merritt.

ROADS, HIGHWAYS AND BRIDGES.

Fletcher, Chairman; Secrest, Kirk, Sunderland, Hogan, Clark, Snyder, Whiting, Ray, Archer, Bell, Kelly, Bridges, Hamilton, Gillham.

FEDERAL RELATIONS.

. Adams, Chairman; Torrance, Secrest, Kirk, Hunt, Needles, Rinehart, Seiter, Duncan.

ELECTIONS.

Wright, Chairman; Needles, Morris, Berggren, Ihorn, Mamer, Archer, Shaw, McNary.

STATE LIBRARY.

Snyder, Chairman; Fletcher, Clark, Hunt, Ray, Morris, Hamilton, Vandeveer, Edwards.

ENROLLED AND ENGROSSED BILLS.

Morris, Mamer, Edwards, Shaw.

GEOLOGY AND SCIENCE.

Snyder, Chairman; Clark, Hunt, Berggren, Kirk, Ruger, Walker, Shumway, Duncan.

MISCELLANY.

Mamer, Chairman; Hogan, Evans, Ruger, Mason, Clark, White, Rice, Bell, Shumway, Edwards, McNary, Cloonan.

COMMITTEES ON VISITATION.

Penal and Reformatory Institutions—Torrance, Bell.
State Charitable Institutions—Kirk, McNary.
Educational Institutions—Tubbs, Gillham.

HOUSE COMMITTEES.

JUDICIARY.

Chairman, Morrison; Littler, Fuller, Calhoun of Vermilion, Cowperthwait, Manahan, Bethea, Worthington, Hoffman, Cooke, Gregg, Yancey, Linegar, Quinn, Kimbrough, Sullivan of Cook, Willoughby.

JUDICIAL DEPARTMENT.

Sumner, Crews, Boyer, Messick, Johnson, Parish, McCartney, Erwin, McFie, Littler, Billings, O'Mara, Day, Baker, Grear, Kinman, Purnell.

CORPORATIONS.

Parish, Pearson of McDonough, Hawker, Worthington, Adams, Parker, Curtis, Walker, McFie, Cooke, Cronkrite, Billings, Murray of Sangamon, Gregg, Baker, Purnell, Sullivan of Cook.

RAILROADS.

Mitchell, Manahan, Thompson of Peoria, Littler, Hiatt, Crews, Calhoun of Vermilion, Harper, Emerson, Lawrence, Herrington, Cronkrite, Yancey, Welch of Kendall, Carlin, Sexton, Day.

WAREHOUSES.

Harper, Thompson of Peoria, Rogers, Thomas, Ray, Mitchell, Pearson of Madison, Fuller, Curtis, Jones, Cronkrite, Billings, Sheridan, Carlin, Henry, Gallup, Clinton.

APPROPRIATIONS.

Pearson of Madison, Black, Funk, Lawrence, Collier, Coats, Foster, Scurlock, Hiatt, Hawker, Cronkrite, Crandall, Baker, Kimbrough, Kinman, Taylor of Kankakee, Welch of Kendall.

EDUCATION.

Erwin, Hester, Stimming, Emerson, Worthington, Jones, Wood of Cook, Calhoun of Vermilion, Fairbanks, Bethea, Sullivan of St. Clair, Willoughby, Kimbrough, Brink, Lodge, Rountree, Canniff.

STATE INSTITUTIONS.

McFie, Hoskinson, Jones, Thomas, McCartney, Lawrence, Hiatt, Tryon, Wood of Cook, Walker, Richardson, McNally, Canniff, Updyke, Purnell, Starkel, Herrington.

REVENUE.

Littler, Fuller, Cowperthwait, Boyer, Crews, Crocker, Calhoun of Vermilion, Mathews, Parish, Haines, Herrington, Linegar, Starkel, Day, Klupp, Willoughby, Taylor of Kankakee.

AGRICULTURE, HORTICULTURE AND DAIRYING.

Thornton, Tryon, Roane, Hawker, Ansley, Cowperthwait, Hammond, Boardman, Brown, Funk, Templeman, Utiger, Jennings, Wiley, West, Downing, Cleary.

CANAL AND RIVER IMPROVEMENT.

Adams, Fairbanks, Mathews, Wood of DeKalb, Lackie, Owen, Cleaveland, Hoffman, Wood of Cook, Hawker, Duffy, Quinn, Crandall, Vaughey, Gallup, Jennings, Klupp.

INSURANCE.

Fuller, Cleaveland, Johnson, Lawrence, Parker, Hiatt, Black, Pedersen, Kennedy, Nichols, Taylor of Kankakee, Day, Murray of Sangamon, Sexton, Vaughey, Herrington, Kinman.

DRAINAGE.

McCartney, Worthington, Tryon, Studer, Roane, Owen, Foster, Calhoun of DeWitt, Boardman, DeBord, Cleary, West, Pratt, Updyke, Stevens of Hancock, Templeman, Jennings.

FINANCE.

Crews, Scurlock, Studer, Jones, Walker, Pearson of McDonough, Calhoun of DeWitt, Goodspeed, Kennedy, Ricks, Caldwell, Newton, Klupp, Pratt, Varnell.

PENITENTIARY.

Collier, Calhoun of Vermilion, Hester, Black, Studer, Wendell, Walker, McFie, Pearson of Madison, Henry, Sheridan, O'Connell, Varnell, Ricks, Fellows.

MUNICIPAL AFFAIRS.

Manahan, Pedersen, Thompson of Peoria, Wendell, Littler, Rook, Sundelius, Harper, Stimming, Gregg, Linegar, Crafts, Clinton, Hay, Scyster.

PUBLIC BUILDINGS AND GROUNDS.

Thomas, Hawks, Owen, Coats, Fairbanks, Harper, Thornton, Scurlock, Duffy, Varnell, Rowland, Mette, Clark, Cox, Thompson of Cass.

COUNTIES AND TOWNSHIP ORGANIZATION.

Brown, Rogers, Thornton, Pedersen, Ewing, Hawks, Nowers, Haines, Gregg, Welch of Kendall, Brink, Taylor of Cook, Utiger, Thompson of Cass, Rountree.

LABOR AND MANUFACTURES.

Black, Wendell, Pederson, Rook, Emerson, Manahan, Honey, Hoskinson, Thomas, O'Mara, Higgins, Sullivan of St. Clair, Moore, Newton, O'Connell.

ELECTIONS.

Cooke, McFie, Calhoun of DeWitt, Black, Thompson of Peoria, Morrison, Bethea, Coats, Haines, Linegar, O'Mara, Grear, Kimbrough, Crafts, Quinn.

STATE AND MUNICIPAL INDEBTEDNESS.

Cleaveland, Rankin, Rogers, Nichols, Wood of DeKalb, Foster, Goodspeed, Struckman, Canniff, Murray of Scott, Seyster, Dugan, Stevens of Hancock, Utiger, Hay.

MILITIA.

Calhoun of Vermilion, Erwin, Nowers, Lackie, Nichols, DeBord, Collier, Mitchell, Stimming, O'Mara, Templeman, Rountree, Bez, Greathouse, Taylor of Cook.

RETRENCHMENT.

Rankin, Foster, Hammond, Hawks, Thornton, Sumner, Wendell, Wood of DeKalb, Goodspeed, Dugan, Moore, Abrahams, Downing, Stevens of Hancock, Pratt.

PRINTING.

Kennedy, Coats, Fairbanks, Emerson, Hammond, Pederson, Lackie, Wood of DeKalb, Sundelius, O'Shea, Clark, Clinton, Updyke, O'Connell, Walsh.

ROADS, HIGHWAYS AND BRIDGES.

Goodspeed, Thornton, Funk, Boardman, Hammond, Ray, Hester, Brown, Haines, Welsh of Bureau, Felker, Caldwell, West, Wiley, Crafts.

FISH AND GAME.

Hiatt, DeBord, Hoffman, Honey, Mathews, Kennedy, Parker. Pearson of Madison, Hay, Symonds, Ricks, Cox, Clark, Sullivan of St. Clair, Henry.

COMMERCE.

Johnson, Ewing, Coats, Lackie, Honey, Adams, Curtis, Richardson, Downing, Dugan, Abrahams, Symonds, Ricks.

MINES AND MINING.

Messick, Emerson, Hoskinson, Owen, Hammond, Adams, Ray, Gallup, O'Shea, Billings, Wiley, Bez, Higgins.

FEES AND SALARIES.

Pearson of McDonough, Sumner, Boyer, McCartney, Manahan, Mathews, Collier, Sundelius, Yancey, Welsh of Bureau, Greathouse, Walsh, Cleary.

PUBLIC CHARITIES.

Wood of DeKalb, Nowers, Foster, Hawker, Rogers, Scurlock, Wendell, Ewing, Yancey, Grear, Rowland, Seyster, Greathouse.

BANKS AND BANKING.

Funk, Roane, Crocker, Johnson, Cooke, Pearson of McDonough, Fairbanks, Rankin, Vaughey, Caldwell, Welsh of Bureau, Carlin, Brink.

LICENSE.

Parker, Stimming, Boardman, Crocker, Struckman, Messick, Bez, Mette, Sheridan, Quinn, McNally.

FEDERAL RELATIONS.

Stimming, Boyer, Sumner, Crews, Ewing, Adams, Symonds, Thompson of Cass, Cox.

CLAIMS.

Ewing, Crocker, Cleaveland, Ansley, Nowers, Fellows, Higgins Murray of Sangamon, Crandall.

EXECUTIVE DEPARTMENT.

Cowperthwait, Studer, Curtis, DeBord, Parish, Cooke, Stevens of Montgomery, Felker, McNally.

CONTINGENT EXPENSES.

Struckman, Thompson of Peoria, Black, Mitchell, Rankin, Crandall, Stevens of Montgomery, Taylor of Cook, Starkel.

LIBRARIES.

Wood of Cook, Curtis, Ansley, Erwin, DeBord, Lodge, Rowland, Fellows, O'Shea.

GEOLOGY AND SCIENCE.

Curtis, Parker, Ansley, Wood of Cook, Lodge, Duffy, Moore.

RULES.

The Speaker, Morrison, Mitchell, Pearson of Madison, Sexton, Herrington, Cronkrite.

MISCELLANEOUS SUBJECTS.

Rook, Ansley, Brown, Cleaveland, Abrahams, Felker, Murray of Scott.

ENROLLED AND ENGROSSED BILLS.

Sundelius, Thomas, Mathews, Rook, Murray of Scott, Mette, Walsh.

TO VISIT REFORMATORY INSTITUTIONS.

Nichols, Messick, Hawks, Sullivan of Cook, Purnell.

TO VISIT EDUCATIONAL INSTITUTIONS.

Calhoun of DeWitt, Honey, Lackie, Richardson, Stevens of Montgomery.

TO VISIT CHARITABLE INSTITUTIONS.

Walker, Ray, Roane, Welsh of Bureau, Newton.

INDEX.

*.—Subordinate or employe.   †. The county of Senators is given.

www.ingramcontent.com/pod-product-compliance
Lightning Source LLC
Chambersburg PA
CBHW021040030726
47496CB00006B/1620